CATFISH CAFÉ

The Thomas Black Novels

The Mac Fontana Novels

CATFISH CAFÉ

EARL EMERSON

THE BALLANTINE PUBLISHING GROUP
NEW YORK

A Ballantine Book
The Ballantine Publishing Group

Copyright © 1998 by Earl Emerson, Inc.

All rights reserved under International and Pan-American Copyright Conventions. Published in the United States by The Ballantine Publishing Group, a division of Random House, Inc., New York, and simultaneously in Canada by Random House of Canada Limited, Toronto.

http://www.randomhouse.com

Library of Congress Cataloging-in-Publication Data
Emerson, Earl W.
   Catfish cafe / Earl Emerson. — 1st ed.
      p.   cm.
   Sequel to: Deception pass.
   ISBN 0-345-42202-3 (alk. paper)
   1. Black, Thomas (Fictitious character)—Fiction.   2. Private investigators—Washington (State)—Seattle—Fiction.   3. Seattle (Wash.)—Fiction.   I. Title.
PS3555.M39C3   1998
813'.54—dc21   98-5478
                                                                            CIP

Text design by Jie Yang

Manufactured in the United States of America

First Edition: August 1998

10   9   8   7   6   5   4   3   2   1

CHAPTER 1

Luther Little drove dead bodies around Seattle the way some people drove pizzas, his primary mission, at least in his own mind, to make delivery before the goods got cold. Luther loved dead folks the way other people loved cats or guns or Elvis collectibles.

For Luther there was nothing as soothing as bagging inert bodies and hauling them to the mortuary; nothing as satisfying as dressing up in his high boots and black uniform to haul polished boxes to the cemetery in front of a queue of headlighted cars. Luther had been a Seattle cop, a cab driver, a sheet-metal worker, a coffee vendor, a janitor, a burglar, a chicken rancher, and a few things he was probably ashamed of; but as far as he was concerned, this was the best job he'd ever held. Every day Luther woke up hoping somebody had died. Luther passed out his card, expecting customers to ask for him by name.

Luther's passion was all-encompassing. He loved the way the motorcycle cops buzzed ahead of the processions and stopped traffic at the intersections. Luther loved the stillness of his passengers—the fact that they would never move again.

Luther even loved watching the bereaved relatives as they grieved. It wasn't that he was hardhearted or that he gloried in their tears; he just loved everything about the dead.

Luther found the labor of the departed reassuring in a way that no other toil had ever been, and he basked in the primordial and fundamental confidence that people were dying and he wasn't one of them—at least not today.

To Luther death was a profession, an amusement, a calling, all rolled into one. Sometimes it was also a very sly joke, as it was that sun-splashed Friday morning when he picked me up under the maples in the loading zone in front of our building and failed to tell me the copper-trimmed box behind us contained Mrs. Scott.

He parked in front of our building on First Avenue in Pioneer Square, and when he got out of the hearse to shake my hand, his black uniform with jodhpurs was impeccable, the bill of his visored cap pulled so tight on his brow that the veins at the side of his head fibrillated in the light. I could see the curb reflected in his polished leather boots. The overall cut and style of his clothes were reminiscent of a 1930s movie.

A small, wiry African American with thick features and short hair flecked with gray along the temples—thinning on top so that the May sunshine glinted off his scalp—Luther Little was, according to my calculations, fifty-four. He could have passed for thirty-four. His teeth were bright and slightly bucked in a wide, even curve that pushed at his lips. You would be hard pressed to say he was handsome or even that he looked arresting, and nobody would have pegged him as a particularly phenomenal conversationalist, but Luther had more women chasing him than anybody I knew.

After we fastened our seat belts, he fired up the huge, quiet engine, pulled the hearse smoothly out into traffic, and when we hit the stoplight, he squinted across the velour seat back at me.

"How's the private-eye business?" he asked.

"Busy. What about the mortuary business? People still kicking off at a dependable rate?"

"They all got to die. You're looking good, man. You still riding that bicycle?"

"And lifting weights a little."

"I go down to Seattle U and run the track four times a week. I do fifty push-ups every morning, and most times I do a hundred sit-ups at night. But you look good. You look real good, Thomas."

"You look like a kid."

Luther Little smiled quietly. The light changed and we moved forward. "Aren't you and me a couple of rag-ass liars?" he said.

I laughed.

He hit a pothole of exposed red brick. "Let me tell you why I need to talk, Thomas, and then you can help me or go your own way, whichever. You remember my oldest, don't you? Balinda? My oldest that I had with Laronda?"

"Played point guard on the girls' basketball team at Garfield? Sure. I went to some of her games."

Luther edged the hearse up close behind a cab at the stoplight at Main. "I won't lie to you. She been in trouble the last couple years, but she got herself wrapped up in a real dinger this time."

"When I last saw her, she must have been around sixteen."

"She's twenty-four now. A growed woman. She's even got her own little baby."

"You never told me this."

Luther grinned but did not take his eyes off the road. "Name is Toylee. I'm a grampa. She's five years old and just like her mother, quick as a spark out of a light socket. I'm a sure-enough grampa. You can't know how it feels, Thomas, to know your line is going on. You hear what I'm saying? I'm nothin', but I'm somethin'."

"I don't have any kids, but I think I know what you mean."

"If you follow baseball you probably know the father. Guy's name is Dion Williams. He played for Garfield. A couple years ahead of Balinda. Went to college and then into the minors."

"I don't follow baseball much." I didn't bother to ask if his daughter had married. Luther would have mentioned it if she had. In his mind marriage was as big a step as death.

He made an illegal left off First Avenue and headed up South Jackson. He'd been a Seattle cop long enough that he still thought he was impervious to traffic regulations.

It was early May, and Seattle was going through one of its freaky hot streaks. The city was wilting like a rose, the afternoons topping out in the low nineties, the humidity suffocating.

My office was in Pioneer Square, the heart of old Seattle, replete with tourists, pigeons, and going-somewhere young execs, as well as going-nowhere panhandlers and homeless men in too many clothes—no Hawaiian shirts or Bermuda shorts for these folks, their bodies traveling clothes racks.

Years earlier, as a Seattle police officer, Luther had been my mentor and first partner. Now, for reasons both similar and dissimilar—I shot someone/Luther was shot by someone—he and I had retired from the department and moved on to more seductive ventures.

I was a private investigator.

Luther drove dead people around town.

Riding around in the air-conditioned hearse with its blacked-out windows was a little like leading a parade after the rest of the procession had turned off to follow a different route, yet I had to admit I kind of liked it. I felt like we were a couple of scary characters out of a Stephen King novel.

Two young men with ponytails eyeballed us as they carried a rolled-up carpet across the street, and Luther said, "Driving this thing, it's like you're the devil's own whip hand. People look at me like I'm in here making the selections myself. Sometimes I wish I was."

"What kind of trouble is Balinda in?"

"She went missing Monday night. So that's what . . . four, five days? She didn't say goodbye to nobody. Left her daughter. Left her purse. Left all that shit."

"You said she had problems before."

"Drugs."

"I'm sorry to hear that."

"Yeah . . ." Luther stopped at a red light and turned to me. Despite bending a traffic statute now and then, he was a good driver, a man who, unless he was at a light with his foot on the brake, rarely looked away from the road to make eye contact with his passenger. Now that he'd divulged the purpose of our tête-à-tête, it occurred to me that his motive for wanting to talk in the car was to eliminate having to look me in the eye. Luther took considerable pride in his children and endured great agony when one of them jumped the tracks. It must have been difficult to let an old friend like me see his daughter's dirty laundry.

"It's like this," he said. "Balinda's been off the stuff, but I'm afraid she's gonna get back on."

"Crack cocaine?"

"The first two times. Then it was smack. See, Thomas, Balinda loves that little girl like life itself, and when Toylee was born she was determined not to screw up again. She did once about three years ago, but me and Laronda put her in a place over in Bellevue and they did a real fine job with her. Now Balinda's missing and Laronda won't even talk to me."

"You know if you need help, I'm all yours, Luther. I've got a couple of projects, but I'll put them on hold."

"You mean that?"

"You and me are buddies, Luther." Surprisingly, when I looked at him, Luther had tears in his eyes. I wanted to tell him why I was so eager to do him a favor, but putting it into words, besides making me look bad, would have made it trite. It was hard to know if Luther ever thought about it, but I owed him. My unspoken debt had been a burden on my conscience for years, and this was a chance for reimbursement. "Tell me what's going on."

"That's just it. I don't know. Balinda's missing. Laronda and Pookie aren't talking. I don't know what's going on."

Laronda was Balinda's mother, Pookie her grandmother. As far as I knew, they still lived in a house up over Lake Washington across the street from Leschi Elementary School. Luther lived by himself a couple of miles away in a two-story house near Gai's Bakery. At last count he had five children with three different mothers all residing within fives miles of him. It was hard not to be aghast at Luther's domestic entanglements. He had more girlfriends than he could keep track of, and every time I ran into him, he buttonholed me for advice on some amorous imbroglio.

Luther and his children lived in the Central District in Seattle, an area of town positioned on the hump of land between downtown proper and Lake Washington. The area was populated by a diversity of African Americans, Latinos, Asians, and whites—many of them poor, many of them newcomers, having immigrated in the last few years from east Africa, Central America, Cambodia, Thailand, California.

Though he made good money to supplement his pension, most of Luther's cash went to his children. Luther thought often of his kids and worried about them the way only an absent, or semi-absent father could.

Although she had not married Luther or even lived with him, Laronda Sands had given birth to three of his children, and somewhere in the middle of their relationship had found the time and resentment to bear a fourth child by another man. It wasn't that Laronda was promiscuous, because as far as I knew, she'd only had the two sexual involvements in her life. It was just the way things were.

Ten years earlier, the oldest of Luther and Laronda's children, Lyle, had died of leukemia. At twenty-four, Balinda was now the oldest. Their youngest daughter would be around seven or eight by now.

"See, Thomas, she could be anywhere. When she was doping, she was in Nevada, Colorado, all over the country lookin' for ways to score. Only reason we ever knew where she was— I'd have friends run her name through the computer to see where she got arrested. It's hard when people know your daughter's a dopehead." Luther's husky voice dropped to a whisper. "Thomas, she done things you don't even want to think about your daughter doin'."

"What are you going to do if she's back in the drug life?"

"Last time, we got her into a group facility over in Bellevue. Cost a fuckin' fortune. She ran away, hopped over the fence, and about got herself killed on the freeway, off to be with some no-good dopehead Cuban boyfriend who was tryin' to pimp her out, but—and this is a story in its ownself—we found her and took her back. Lately, she been living with her mother and working and everything. Until Monday night when she took off."

"What happened Monday night?"

CHAPTER 2

"Toylee's father, Dion, was givin' Balinda a hard time. They both worked down at Catfish Café. She wasn't gonna get rich there, but she was going to school and bringing home a check and doing something for the world. She quit 'cause Dion was bugging her. After that, she got mixed up with some white guy. You gotta know, Thomas, Balinda's been trained by Laronda and Pookie—all the women in that house think whites are the devil's disciples—so this was the first time I ever knew her to be doin' anything with a white guy. Anything legal. He came by the house 'bout a month back. They all seen him. Everybody in the family 'cept me. I didn't know nothin' about it."

"What happened?"

"Her grandmother . . . Pookie—You remember Pookie . . . ?"

"I remember you talking about her."

". . . Monday night, musta been two in the mornin', Pookie calls and tells me Balinda's wrecked her car and she's missing and the police are there. Balinda left her purse in the car. Her keys too. There was blood all over the seats. And the white guy she been seeing? He was in the car too. I got his name

8

from the paper. My own daughter in this kind of jam and I'm getting information from the paper."

"To make the paper it must have been a pretty bad accident."

"I ain't told you the worst. The white dude? Somebody lit his ass up."

"Shot him?"

"Killed his ass."

"I read about that. I didn't realize your daughter was involved."

"You know Homicide would like nothing better than to put that shooting on a black girl with no money and no resources. It was her car. Her purse was on the floor by the driver's door. But you ask me, there was somebody else in the car, 'cause the white dude was found shot in the backseat but there was blood in the front passenger seat too. You ask me, a second passenger turned around and capped him. That's what I think. And when the shots went off in that little car, Balinda panicked and crashed. Ran it right down an embankment offa where Thirty-first goes down the hill at Jackson. Only about five, six blocks from the house."

"What's SPD saying?"

" 'Where's your daughter? The pimps and the drug pushers and the porno freaks done lost her, so we'll take her. Turn her over.' You *know* they want to pin this crap on her. But listen to me, Thomas. The white guy was shot four times. In the backseat. How could Balinda do that and still be driving? It don't make no sense."

"No, it doesn't. She'd crash." Luther gave me a look. "Sorry. I didn't know Balinda that well, but from what I knew of her, you're right. She couldn't have killed anyone."

Luther's face relaxed a little as he turned back to the street. "Near as I can tell, her mother thinks she fired him up and is hiding somewheres. Maybe because I was a cop, she thinks I'll be on the police side of all this. Hell, Thomas. I just want my little girl home and out of trouble."

The Balinda Sands I remembered, despite being a star shooting guard on the Garfield High basketball team, was a slight and timid young woman of light complexion, even though her father, Luther, was medium to dark-complected. Laronda, her mother, and Pookie, her grandmother, were both light-skinned too, a condition that Luther claimed made Laronda feel superior to him. Practically speaking, Balinda had been too small for her high school basketball team, where most of the players were close to six feet or taller, but she'd made up for size with spirit, tenacity, and quickness. It surprised me to learn she'd been on drugs, and I told Luther as much.

"It's that cocaine, man. Her goddamned Cuban dopehead boyfriend talked her into trying it 'just once,' and the next thing she knew, she was stealing from me and peddling her ass out on Yesler."

"Scary."

"Ain't it, though?"

Balinda was an attractive young woman whose hazel eyes penetrated into whomever she was looking at in a way that made young men's hearts flutter. She'd made good grades and had been a star singer in the choir at school as well as in church. The last time I saw her, she wanted to be an astronaut.

CHAPTER 3

Luther was wheeling the hearse around Chinatown in what appeared to be an aimless pattern, scanning the sidewalks as we spoke.

"You check the hospitals?" I asked.

"That and her friends. The bank. She don't have no credit cards. It's like she up and disappeared."

"What does Laronda say about all this?"

"To me? Nothin'."

"How were you getting on before this happened?"

"You know Laronda. I can't remember the last time she gave up any pussy."

"I mean about her daughter being missing. Isn't she concerned?"

"I think she figures Balinda shot that white guy, and she don't want Balinda to be found. I'm even thinking she knows where Balinda is. She sure don't seem worried about her bein' hurt or in danger—except from the police. Maybe you and I can drive over around suppertime and talk to her."

"You think I can wheedle information out of Laronda you can't?"

"Yes, I do. Pookie'll be there. D'Witt. Shawn. The kids. You wanta meet outside the Douglass-Truth Library and we can drive over together?"

Kathy and I had plans to dine out with another couple, but I accepted Luther's invitation and said, "Tell me what you know about the shooting."

"White guy's name was Benjamin Aldrich. A elementary school teacher. Got hisself shot three times in the torso from the right side and once in the throat from the left."

"Two different shooters?"

"Probably not. All the bullets were from a .32 automatic." Luther glanced at me.

"The kind of gun a woman might carry."

"Balinda didn't have no guns. I'm pretty sure of that. It was around midnight. Some couple from Iran driving by the scene spotted headlights down in the woods. They found Balinda's car on the embankment all wrapped around a tree. When the man went down, he discovered the body in the back. I talked to him. He don't know nothing. The police found Balinda's purse in the car. Damn. I'm still makin' payments on that car. Twenty-four years old and she ain't even got her life together so's she can buy her own car. Damn, Thomas! I talked to her friends. I even looked up her old boyfriends. One of 'em's a cop, works out of the South Precinct. Then I bumped up against Dion so hard I felt sorry for the boy."

"Dion?"

"Dion Williams, I told you about. Balinda had Toylee with him. Works over at Catfish Café."

We'd been cruising for almost ten minutes now, and the casket in the back was becoming an undeniable presence in my thoughts. "Luther," I said. "Is that a stiff in back? In the casket?"

"It's Mrs. Scott. We call that one a Blue Finch Copper. It's a nice box. Got a light blue velvet liner you gotta run your hand over to really appreciate. Real comfy."

"Is that why you didn't want to park the car? Because you didn't want to leave Mrs. Scott?"

"People steal caskets. They dump the body and sell the box."

"Isn't she supposed to be somewhere else?"

"If I'd known you were squeamish, I woulda dropped her off at Lake View Cemetery before I came over."

"Is she belted in?"

Luther gave me a tiny smile. "They say she used to be a madam in Arizona somewhere, but that's prob'ly a rumor. I know you think I'm dissing her, but as long as I don't drink while she's in the car, I feel in my heart I'm okay." Luther lowered his voice conspiratorially. "Amelia wanted to climb in back a few times and gimme some on top of the box, but that's the sort of activity you don't want to do, not unless you're really in a bad spot and can't get pussy no other way."

Amelia was one of his longtime girlfriends back when we were in the police department. "You did it in the back with Amelia?"

"Only until she got religion. Now she won't hardly do it nowhere. I don't want you to get the wrong idea. We never actually did it on top of the box. Always over to the side there."

"You still see Amelia?"

"Once in a while. I guess it tells you something to know I been loving a junkie for ten years. She's off the stuff now. Been off for a long time. She got religion so bad it makes my corns ache. And she's eatin' cough syrup. Got a job too, but that doesn't keep her from tryin' to sponge off me. She called me up the other night and wanted me to run her over forty dollars. She run outta cough syrup."

I could tell from the sudden change in his expression he'd been talking about Amelia only to get his mind off his daughter. He said, "The car was full of birth certificates."

Luther pronounced it *birf* certificates.

"The car . . . ?"

"Balinda's car. Birth certificates. Nine of 'em."

"Who for?"

"Homicide wouldn't say, except they were all for around the same date thirty years ago. All I can figure is he was into drugs too and they were passing bad paper. Balinda's been into all them rackets. She used to run this scam where she went to apartment houses, read the names on the mailboxes, and then rang a bell at random and told whoever answered that so and so down the hall—some name she'd read off a box— was her grandmother or her boyfriend's mother or whatever, and that she'd been sent down to get change for a fifty-dollar bill. If they were sap enough to give her the cash, she'd tell 'em she would be right back with the bill. See, Thomas, no one wants to tell a black girl to her face they think she might be stealin', so they almost always let her walk off with the money."

"You're thinking she was running a scam with this Benjamin Aldrich?"

"Or running a scam *on* him. Either way, if she's back on the soup, she could be anywhere."

"Maybe it was a drive-by. Maybe some gang-bangers were going through their initiation. Maybe they pulled up alongside and shot him through the window."

"If that's what happened, where's Balinda?"

"Hiding out? Maybe she knew one of them."

"Now that's a possibility I honestly never thought of, Thomas. I was so fixated on her being back on dope. I gotta tell you, though, I was thinking at first she was maybe kidnapped, but why would anyone kidnap a poor black girl? Right? It's not like we're sittin' on a pile of money."

If he hadn't already thought of it himself, I didn't want to be the one to remind him that there were other motives for kidnapping a young woman. "Listen, Luther. Has she got an attorney?"

"Balinda? She don't have a dentist unless I send her to

mine. You think there's a chance your wife would handle it? I've heard good things about her."

"I was going to suggest that. I'll talk to Kathy about it."

"Thanks, man."

I'd seen Luther upset, but I'd never seen him any more upset than he was now. I had the feeling Balinda's recovery from drugs was the last dam on the river for Luther. I had the feeling he couldn't let any water over this one or it would wash away everything he'd ever hoped for in life.

After we firmed up the arrangements for that evening, Luther chauffeured me back to my office at First and Yesler, dropped me off, and drove away with Mrs. Scott.

CHAPTER 4

The morning heat was beginning to seep out of the sidewalks and the brick buildings downtown, the air spiced with the brew of creosote from the piers and coffee from the Starbucks shop across the street. A Japanese freighter was being pulled into Elliott Bay by tugs. Like a series of puffy, white asterisks, a row of clouds hung over the Olympic Mountains on the western horizon.

Most people never saw past the colorful kites in the windows of Magic Mouse Toys on the corner, but our building was the next one in on First Avenue. Across the street was Pioneer Square itself. Actually triangular in shape, it was a small, cobblestoned park with a totem pole, an ornate glass-topped pergola, half a dozen wrought-iron benches, and about half as many homeless people holding them down. Last winter two men had frozen to death in a nearby doorway, so I was glad to see the weather warm up.

I got off the elevator on our floor and breezed past the reception island where Beulah was flirting with a bicycle messenger. Lately, she'd taken it upon herself to romance the bike messengers and UPS delivery guys with her Technicolor blue eyes and a whole raft of risqué jokes. Beulah was a pistol.

The office formed a backward L, with the main doors at the joint, my room at the end of the short leg. My office could have passed for a large closet, but managed to house a sink and countertop at the back of the room, a desk centered in front of the window, and another desk dominated by a computer terminal against the wall. For guests I had two mismatched chairs, a red one and a blue one. My windows looked out over First Avenue, but in the spring and summer, unless I angled right up against the window, I couldn't see much more than the tops of the maples across the street.

Kathy Birchfield was sitting behind my desk, with her shoeless feet up on the corner, reading a draft of an interview we'd conducted the day before with a diamond salesman from Atlanta. He'd accused a hotel in town of negligence after $185,000 worth of gems were stolen from his room while he was downstairs having dinner with a woman he'd just met in the hotel bar. Clearly, he'd been scammed. I sat in on the interview as a witness. Most lawyers found it tough putting themselves on the stand and taking depositions from themselves, so they hired some dummy to witness their interviews and take notes. In this office, I was that dummy.

"Hey, Sister. You look comfy."

Setting the report down on my desktop, she got up, stepped into a pair of clogs, and walked up to me in a light yellow summer dress. Kathy was a brunette, her hair long and thick and almost black. Today she wore it in a single braid. She had a pale, milky complexion, and I liked to think she was the most beautiful woman in the city, but then, I was biased.

"What's cookin'?" she asked, kissing me on the chin.

"Think I've got a client for you. Remember my old friend, Luther Little? His oldest daughter, Balinda, turned up missing Monday night. They found her car wrapped around a tree.

There was a dead man in it. From gunshots, not from the accident. Luther's been looking for her all week. He seems convinced she's okay but hiding out somewhere. He wants to know if you'll represent Balinda when we find her."

"What's she like?"

"She was a sweet kid in high school, but I think she's slipped a few notches since."

"Sure. I'll talk to her when you find her."

"Good. About tonight. I've got good news and bad news."

"You're not going to make me cancel on the Reids again? This will be the second time in a month. They're going to think we don't like them."

"I don't. She's a nag and he's a pompous ass."

"He probably thinks the same about us."

"No. He thinks I'm an irresponsible, lower-class moron with a fitness addiction and a lucky streak."

"A lucky streak?"

"He can't figure out how I got you."

"How *did* you get me?"

"The raffle, remember?"

"Oh, yeah. So is that the bad news? You can't make it tonight?"

"Right. Luther and I've made plans."

"What's the good news?"

"When you get home tonight, the Big Kahuna's going to be waiting in bed for you."

"The Big Kahuna?" Looking disappointed, she opened the door and walked out. "Whatever you say, but I was hoping to sleep with *you*."

I sat down and thought about Luther Little. For two years we worked out of the same car, and later we both worked first watch out of the South Precinct. Together we'd handled residential burglaries, drunks, domestic disputes, car wrecks, prowlers, drug dealers, suicides. We'd shared untold confidences, and at one time were as close as brothers.

Luther's epiphany came late one wintry night after he was

cruising the parks along the lake, checking for abandoned cars and beer parties. He encountered a suspicious vehicle in the parking lot outside the Leschi Yacht Basin. He'd seen the car earlier in the evening at another parking area several miles south near Seward Park, and at that time the red, two-door Honda Accord had been occupied by a pair of Asian males. Now it held the same two males, plus another male and a female in the backseat. Cops who've been on the streets a few years learn to go with their instincts, and Luther had a feeling there was something wrong with the picture.

He swung around behind the car and let his headlights wash over the Accord. All four people in the car sat bolt upright, immobile and rigid. Not one of them turned around to see who he was or what he was doing. That in itself was suspicious.

Luther punched up the vehicle on his computer and discovered it was registered to a man in Ballard named Ian Inggersohl. It was not on the hot sheet, but then nobody in the car looked as if he might be named Ian Inggersohl either.

Shining his spotlight on the Accord, Luther got out and stood behind the driver's door, his flashlight in his left hand, his right hand free to reach his weapon if need be—basic police procedure. The man behind the wheel either spoke English poorly or pretended to. He handed Luther a driver's license. Luther asked him to get out, but he either didn't understand what Luther was saying or he feigned ignorance. Luther caught only a glimpse of a small Asian woman with a blanket over her lap in the backseat on the other side of the car. He saw no evidence of alcohol or drug paraphernalia, though he thought he detected alcohol on the driver's breath.

Finally, after much urging by Luther and some discussion in another language between the car's occupants, the driver climbed out. Luther put him in the position and frisked him.

As he was doing this, the front seat passenger climbed over the gear shift console and crawled out the driver's door on his hands and knees, even though Luther warned him to stay inside. When the driver turned to help his friend, Luther pushed him face first against the car.

As all this was happening, there was a sudden movement in the backseat and Luther spotted a six-pack of empty beer bottles under the blanket across the woman's lap.

Before he could get control of the two men outside, he heard a pop and found himself staggering backward.

What he later learned was that the third man, the man who was still in the backseat, had pulled a gun and reached around through the open driver's door and shot him. With his vest on, it felt like a punch in the stomach. Now he had two men outside the car and a third with a gun in his hand coming out.

To confuse matters, he heard a baby crying.

"Drop your weapon!" he shouted, pulling his own pistol. The shooter was standing in front of the car now but behind one of the other men. Luther didn't dare take his eyes off them. The sounds of a baby crying in the back of the car grew more insistent.

"Ma'am?" Luther said. "Are you all right? Ma'am?"

The three men were talking at high speed in a foreign language. Still partially hidden behind his two friends, the man with the gun leveled it at Luther and said, "Drop your gun!"

"You drop it, motherfucker!" Luther said.

"No. You drop your gun!"

"It ain't gonna happen." Luther had been shot over a routine stop. And furthermore, he realized if he fired at the man with the gun, he might hit one of the unarmed men or the woman or the baby.

"Ma'am?" he repeated. "Are you all right back there?"

No answer.

"Drop your goddamn gun!" the man said. "Now, cop! I'm not going to tell you again. I'm going to count to three, and if your gun isn't on the ground, I'm going to shoot."

They were standing less than fifteen feet apart, each pointing his weapon at the other. Luther had a nine-millimeter

Glock. The other man had a large caliber automatic. Three men were facing him, and he'd only frisked one of them. The driver, who appeared to be weaponless, walked toward him, slipping on the ice and holding his empty hands out in a give-me-the-weapon posture.

The man with the gun said, "One . . ."

Before he could say "Two," Luther fired a pair of carefully spaced shots past the two unarmed men and into the chest of the man with the gun. He crumpled. The second man, the one who'd originally climbed over the driver's seat and onto the ground on his belly, raised a weapon Luther hadn't seen until that instant and proceeded to empty it at him.

It all happened so quickly, and Luther had been so concerned with the baby in the car, the woman, and the unarmed man approaching him that, for a moment or two, he didn't know he'd been hit again.

He found himself on the ground, his face on the pavement. He tried to roll over, but his right arm wouldn't move. He could barely breathe, probably because one of the men from the car was standing over him, kicking his ribs. Most of the blows were absorbed by his bulletproof vest. It wasn't until one of his assailants started kicking him in the head that Luther rolled over, felt his own weapon under his hip and grabbed it in his left hand.

There were more gunshots from the car, six or seven of them. Luther heard slugs ricocheting off the pavement near his face, bits of ice and macadam and lead stinging his cheek.

He fired four shots at the man above him and then began crawling toward his car. Behind him, he could hear the man with the gun dry-firing. He'd run out of bullets but was still pulling the trigger.

Luther glanced behind and saw the Accord, both doors still open, moving slowly toward him.

It was at this point that he managed to get hold of his portable radio and call for help.

I was the closest unit.

What I saw when I got to the parking lot was Luther in front of his patrol car, with two broken legs and a finger on his right hand shot off. There were tire tracks across his trousers. He had a slug in his neck and another in his hip. If he hadn't been wearing the vest, they would have killed him, for later there were six more slugs found in the Kevlar.

The Accord was idling thirty feet away. A body lay forty feet in front of the Accord and ten feet from Luther. As I skidded into the lot and placed my vehicle between Luther and his assailants, the remaining two males, using their car as a shield, began firing at me. Later, forty-seven shell casings from two different weapons were found in the lot. Most of those bullets had been directed at Luther. A few had whistled past my ears.

I bailed out my passenger door with my shotgun and crouched behind a front wheel only feet from Luther.

"Don't shoot into the car," Luther said. "There's a woman and a baby in there."

I shot the first man in the leg under his car. The second man, who had been wounded earlier by Luther, saw what I was doing and crawled behind a wheel. When reinforcements arrived a minute later, he quickly stood with his hands on his head and cried, "Police brutality! Police brutality!"

The two men Luther shot lived. The man I shot lived.

There *was* no baby. The woman in the backseat had been hiding booze, guns, and a cat under the blanket in her lap. The squalling Luther heard had come from the cat. The car had been stolen but had not gotten onto the hot sheet yet.

Although they all had criminal records, the shooting had been done on a whim.

In court they said they ran over Luther by accident. One man, the original driver, claimed he'd been an innocent party in the affair and didn't know anything about any of it. He said Luther brutally shot him for no reason and that Luther's unprovoked assault touched off the incident.

Luther couldn't get the prosecutors to agree that the crime

had been attempted murder. Instead they charged two of the men with assault. They never charged the woman who'd been handing weapons out of the car. The man who did most of the shooting received a sentence of four and a half years. Nobody ever knew who was driving when the Accord ran over Luther, so there were no charges on that. Luther fell into such a funk over the light jail terms that he retired from the police department.

Luther had always been sullen, but after the shooting he became convinced he was living on borrowed time, and strangely, perked up somewhat.

After I'd known him awhile, I realized his depression was occasioned by a life that had been wobbling toward the gutter since he was seven. Whenever Luther spoke about why he was feeling good or bad on a particular day, without fail he attributed his mood to either getting or not getting pussy. The way Luther figured life, the sun rose and set in the next vagina. It was a good day if he got some, a bad day if he didn't, a downright evil day if he hadn't had any in a while. Despite having more girlfriends than the Pope had rings, the bad days outnumbered the good by a fair margin.

When I finished reminiscing, I called a contact at the telephone company and asked her to give me copies of phone bills from the Sands household for the past three months. I called a researcher named Hilda, who worked out of southern Oregon, and asked her to get me everything she could on Benjamin Aldrich and Balinda Sands. I telephoned Homicide downtown and learned that Arnold Haldeman was handling the case.

He wasn't in, so I left a message, made a few calls for some other clients, had a light lunch downstairs at Mitchelli's with Beulah, and went for a bike ride to West Seattle in the afternoon heat.

CHAPTER 5

When I got back to the office at quarter till five, people were leaving the Mutual Life Building early, their undisciplined departures a testament to the spring fever that had infected the city.

I'd purchased an olive-and-mushroom pizza two blocks south at À La Française and was eating it on the steps of the Mutual Life Building as I watched streams of blue-clad pedestrians make their way toward the Kingdome for a game between the Mariners and the Brewers. Fans liked to save dollars and hassle by parking uptown and walking through Pioneer Square.

When I went upstairs, the office was empty and quiet. After a few minutes a phone rang down the hallway behind a locked door. Two minutes later it rang again. From the high windows of my office I could see the wind combing the sunny maples across the street.

Kathy'd left a note with a large red kiss on it atop my desk, saying she was going to have dinner with Fred and Randi and she hoped all went well with Luther tonight. She reminded me to bring the Big Kahuna home, as she was looking forward to meeting him.

Arnold Haldeman from Homicide had called back, which was as unexpected as it was curious, because he had perfected a careless and offhand manner of snubbing me which he indulged almost without exception.

When I got him on the line, we pretended to like each other for a few moments, and then he said, "Black, why are you sniffing around the Aldrich shooting?"

"Remember Luther Little? Retired a few years back?"

"A wiry black guy? Always dotted his i's and crossed his t's. I even know when he went out. Right before you did. He's the one got shot all to pieces down the lake by some Orientals. Woulda died if some asshole hadn't stepped in and saved him."

"They were Asians. Orientals are usually rugs. And the guy who saved him wasn't that much of an asshole. The car you found Aldrich in the other day belonged to Luther's daughter."

"Balinda Sands is Little's daughter?"

"Right."

"So Luther's trying to keep her out from under a murder rap, huh?"

"Are you charging her with murder?"

"It remains to be seen, but I wouldn't discount it for a hot New York minute. You don't know where she is?"

"I'm trying to find her for Luther. Kathy's going to represent her if that becomes necessary. I was sort of hoping it wouldn't."

"What you're saying is I can hold back whatever I want, but you're going to get it all on discovery. Right? So I might as well fill you in so you can use my information to find her, and then you'll turn her over to me and we'll all be in four-leaf clover. You'll have earned your fee. Luther will have found his daughter. And I'll close this file."

"Something like that."

"You really working with Little, or is this another load of your horseshit?"

"Damn straight. We have a meeting in a couple of hours."

"I want us both to be clear on this, Black. I give you a few tidbits, and you let us know as soon as you locate her."

"Deal."

"I really don't think you're smart enough to button your own pants, Black, but you might just stumble onto this girl."

"Even idiots get lucky."

"So what we got is this, basically. Some Joe Blow Citizen just moved here from the Mideast found her car Tuesday morning a little past midnight. When our citizen goes down to see if anybody is hurt, he finds a blue Escort about eighty feet down a hillside, a man's body in the backseat. He starts to pull the body out of the vehicle and discovers (a) he's dead, (b) he's been shot. He calls it in on his car phone. Guy's been in this country four months and he's packing around a cell phone.

"One of the officers on the scene pulls a purse from under the driver's side dash. Belongs to Balinda Sands. That was four days ago. We figure her for the driver. The car was registered to her. The dead guy's a teacher from Tacoma. White guy. Turned out he was an Eagle Scout. A jogger. It was all in the paper. That's what we've got."

"It's not much."

"We'll have more when you bring in the girl."

"You have any idea who shot him?"

"Your little Miss Sands shot him."

"How could she if she was driving and he was in back? She had to keep control of the car and reach around to shoot him both at the same time?"

"But she didn't keep control of the car, did she?"

It was the same point I'd made with Luther, but it annoyed me that Haldeman used it against me. "You don't even know for sure she was in the car."

"We got her prints off the wheel."

"She owned the car. Her prints would naturally be on the wheel."

"The prints had blood on them. I think we can convince a jury she was driving. I think we can even convince a jury she killed him. Do I sound sure of myself?"

"You always do. How many times was he shot?"

"Three to the torso. One in the neck."

"What about the third party?"

"What third party?"

"People don't drive around in small cars like that with one passenger in the backseat unless there are two people in front."

"Don't get too smart for yourself, Black. There was some evidence of a third party, but we haven't confirmed it."

"What evidence?"

"Blood."

"You've typed the blood?"

"If there's a report back, I haven't seen it."

I had a feeling he was lying. "What makes you think the blood wasn't Balinda's? Maybe she was shot too, or injured in the accident. She may have been kidnapped by whoever did this."

"Black, a minute ago you weren't even willing to admit she was in the car."

"You find any blood around the driver's seat?"

"Yep. On the windshield. The passenger seat and the back. You're really interested in this, aren't you?"

"I'm just trying to figure out what happened."

"Don't strain yourself. I told you what happened. When you've been at it as long as I have, you get a feeling in your bones, Black. That's what I've got right now. A feeling in my bones."

"Any witnesses?"

"None that we know of."

"Explain to me why you think the other passenger wasn't the shooter."

Haldeman's voice grew weary. "First off, we don't know there was another passenger. Plus, Aldrich was shot three times in the right side. How're you going to do that to somebody sitting directly behind you?"

"How are you going to do that to somebody sitting behind and to the right?"

"Easy. He was sitting sidesaddle on the seat, maybe looking out the back window."

"Doesn't it make more sense that somebody outside the vehicle shot him? Maybe through a window after the crash? What about gangs? The neighborhood's rife with them."

"Rife? Been studying our vocabulary-builder calendar, have we? We know it wasn't gang-bangers because there weren't any bullet holes in the car body. They all went right into the victim. True, the right rear window was busted out, but that was shattered in the collision."

"So why couldn't they have shot through the empty space where the window had been?"

"Trust me."

"Was it an automatic?"

"Yep. But we only found one empty casing. Outside under the frame of the car."

"So they crashed, and then he was shot."

"No, she shot him from inside, then tried to clean up the scene and dropped one of the empty shell casings where she couldn't see it in the dark."

"Pretty extraordinary girl. Shoots a guy in the backseat while driving a car, then remembers to pick up the shell casings but forgets her purse."

"Look, Black. I'll be honest with you. I see three possibilities here. They were driving along, got into it, and she reached back and shot him, after which they crashed. Or they were driving along, got into it, and then crashed, after which she reached around and shot him. The third possibility is she shot him through the neck while they were driving, because that bullet went from left to right. Then they crashed, she got out and went around the car and let him have it through the broken window, three shots to his right flank."

"He was shot from the left and the right?"

"You heard me." I didn't know why Arnold Haldeman was so eager to give me this skimpy information, but then, he probably figured we were going to hear it from spies in the department anyway. Then too, considering it was Haldeman, there was a good chance I'd somehow been snookered.

CHAPTER 6

At six-forty when Luther pulled up in the wine-colored hearse, I was standing in front of the Douglass-Truth Library watching a squad of bicyclists doing track-stands at the stoplight in their colorful jerseys and flashy helmets. I wished I was with them. Mrs. Scott's Blue Finch Copper casket had been replaced by a somewhat less sumptuous model with a heavily shellacked outer shell. As I walked over to the vehicle, Luther rolled down the passenger-side window.

"Who's in the box?" I said.

"Nobody."

"Maybe I should follow in my car."

"I told you, it's nobody."

"What'd you do with Mrs. Scott?"

"Let her off up at Lake View."

"And this one's empty?"

"Man, you *are* squeamish," Luther said as I leaned against the windowsill. "It's for Jordan Richards, but they ain't got him ready down at the home yet. Remember Richards? Played for the Colts? Died Wednesday. Forty-eight years old. He used to show up down at Celebrity's all crippled up from his playin' days. Always had him a fine-ass babe on his arm. Sometimes two."

It was a warm evening, and Luther had the air-conditioning cranked up so high I felt a chill as soon as I got in. I was beginning to get the feeling Luther drove the hearse far more often than necessary, that he was addicted to the dread a shiny new hearse evoked.

"That's what I need me," Luther said. "A couple of fine-ass babes."

"I thought you had plenty of women."

"I need me somethin' regular. A girl I can count on."

"The only way to get somebody you can count on is to *be* somebody you can count on, Luther. Women resent it when they find out you're fooling around."

"Now you've put your finger on the basic problem with all women. That there resentment."

Luther wore neatly pressed dark green slacks and a stiff-looking plaid shirt, looking as he always did in civilian clothing, small and insecure, which was probably why he'd worn a uniform so much of his adult life.

Driving at a snail's pace, he tried to fill me in on the family, supplying names, ages, and abbreviated biographies.

Pookie Sands owned the house and by all rights should have been Luther's mother-in-law. Laronda, the mother of three of Luther's progeny including Balinda, was the primary breadwinner for the household. By anybody's calculations, she should have been Luther's wife.

The children in the house were difficult to keep straight. Shawn Brown was Luther's teenage son by another woman, but he was living in the Sands household because he couldn't get along with his own mother and her new boyfriend. Shereffe, at nine, and Toylee, at six, were inseparable. Toylee was Balinda's daughter, and Shereffe was Luther and Laronda's youngest daughter, making them niece and aunt respectively.

D'Witt Sands, Laronda's son by another man, had recently turned twenty and was in a wheelchair from a shooting five years earlier in the Rainier Valley.

We drove east on Yesler, down the hill to Thirty-first at the corner of Leschi Elementary School, then two blocks north. In the heat of the evening, kids dallied on sidewalks, families sat on stoops, neighbors conversed over lawn sprinklers, and a company of men sat on a Pontiac on the corner of Twenty-eighth and Yesler and passed around a bottle in a paper sack. Front doors and windows were propped wide in many of the houses we passed, curtains flapping like tongues at the street.

We parked directly in front of the Sands home in a pleasant neighborhood half a block north of the grade school. The house had two stories with an attic space, and, because of remodels over the years, the dormers on the second story made it look like a top-heavy dowager. It was the most run-down house in the area. It faced west on a north-south street and sheltered a lineup of abandoned cars along the north wall, most with their hoods up, as if they'd been forsaken in the midst of repair. The outer north wall of the house had been scraped and prepped but remained unpainted. From the number of old tarps, car parts, and toys lying up against the house, completion of the project wasn't slated for any time soon.

Luther said, "All them cars belong to Raymond, Laronda's brother. He's the one I told you about years ago was in Joliet."

"I remember you mentioning an ex-con in the family, but I don't remember the details."

"He don't even live here anymore. He's not anybody."

In the evening shade up the street, some boys were throwing a sponge-rubber football. A recorded melody from an ice cream wagon drifted over from the next street.

Two little girls dashed out of the house, leaped off the porch, and catapulted themselves into Luther's arms, first his granddaughter, Toylee, and then his nine-year-old daughter,

Shereffe, who almost knocked him over. Shereffe was cute, but Toylee made you want to bust out smiling. She looked like her missing mother, Balinda, whose features had been fuzzy in my memory until that moment. Both girls wore their hair in multiple braids held together with small, colored beads. They wore shorts, sandals, and sleeveless blouses and were giggling nonstop.

When Luther introduced us, Shereffe, the older one, so-bered up and shook my hand, while Toylee rushed over and hugged my leg in a death grip.

"Toylee. Come on now," Luther said. "You know better than that. Leave Thomas his leg." He peeled her off, and we all went up the walkway toward the house, the girls pestering Luther for money, which he produced from his pockets with elaborately feigned reluctance.

"Come and see my tunnels," Shereffe said.

"Shereffe doin' tunnels," Toylee said.

It wasn't until we'd stepped onto the porch that I saw D'Witt inside the front door in his wheelchair. He was as bro-ken as his name was. Toylee raced ahead, took his clenched fist in her hands, pried open his fingers, and dropped a quar-ter she'd pirated from her grandfather into it, then meticu-lously closed his fist around the coin as if wrapping a present.

D'Witt was light-skinned, with broad, well-developed shoulders and upper arms and a set of atrophied legs that protruded awkwardly to one side from hips as thin as a fold-ing chair. He wore jeans, a sleeveless shirt that showed off his shoulder muscles, and a ragged pair of fingerless cycling gloves, the same brand I favored.

D'Witt pretended to be a stoic, but the attention he got from the two girls was more than recognition; it was adora-tion, and he clearly took great pleasure in it.

There was a long story behind his birth, and it involved Laronda bearing a child with another man as revenge against Luther for some sexual indiscretion. He'd had a somewhat tragic birth and now was living a somewhat tragic life. D'Witt's father lived in California and had served time for embezzlement.

D'Witt shook my hand with a pipe-wrench grip while Luther introduced me as somebody who'd worked with him in the "old days" when he was with the police.

"You eat yet?" Luther asked no one in particular.

"Chicken," Toylee said excitedly. "I got the wishbone."

"And mashed potatoes," Shereffe added. "With snap peas and okra. Gramma Pookie made a coconut cake too."

I looked down at Toylee and said, "What'd you wish for?"

"Don't you know anything? You gotta dry the bone on the windowsill first."

"That's right. I forgot how to do it."

Luther gave me a sideways look and whispered, "She knows I'm allergic to coconut."

Pookie had made a dessert he couldn't eat, and he took it as a personal insult. It was hard to figure, since he hadn't eaten dinner with them and, as far as I could tell, hadn't been planning on it.

Despite the pizza I'd surrounded earlier, I was beginning to develop a yearning for fried chicken, my head awash in the smells of hot butter and mashed potatoes.

Luther said, "The women in this house are always doin' me."

"I ain't doin' you," Toylee said, hanging off her grandfather's arm until he staggered like a drunk.

"That's right," Luther said lovingly. "You and Shereffe always been good to me. You been good too, D'Witt." He glanced at the young man in the wheelchair, who had turned from us and was watching the street.

"Ain't no way I can be anything *but* good," D'Witt mumbled.

The girls went back to a low coffee table with papers and open books on it, while Luther and I headed toward the kitchen. Before we'd gone ten feet, D'Witt said, "I'm the one asked for coconut."

His statement was more a defense of Pookie than a recitation of events, and I wondered if he naturally adopted the peacemaker role in family disputes or just this one. While we forged into the bowels of the house, D'Witt remained by the door, where a bar of sunshine from the setting sun warmed his legs. I wondered if he could feel it.

The rooms were large and furnished sparsely, a loving concession, I thought, to D'Witt's wheelchair. The wallpaper was faded and stained behind a large felt portrait of a sorrowful Jesus with a halo over his head. Several of the walls in the living room were devoted to religious artifacts: crosses, sconces, and paintings. Another wall was devoted to Martin Luther King and included framed and yellowed newspaper clippings from the day after his assassination. I wanted to stop and read them, but Luther wasn't in a stopping mood. The carpets were threadbare, the hardwood floors laced with nicks and scars from decades of kids. All in all, the house was tattered but as neat as a new car on the showroom floor.

In the living room a boy in his mid-teens was slumped in front of the finest piece of furniture in the house, a television, his torso horizontal across the sofa cushions, head cricked at an awkward angle against the seat back.

Luther stopped and called out. "Shawn?"

The television wasn't so loud that he couldn't hear Luther, but Shawn didn't look up.

D'Witt rolled into the room behind us and said, "Shawn! Your father's speaking to you."

While D'Witt was light enough to almost pass for white, Shawn was as dark as Luther and, of all Luther's offspring I'd met to date, favored him the most—his features, carriage, and, from what I knew of the boy, his mood swings. Shawn wore overlarge jeans pulled halfway down his buttocks, a pair of colorful boxer shorts beneath. The look he gave his father was sullen, bored, and a tad resentful. I didn't know him well enough to label it an act, although I figured it was.

"How you doin', Shawn?" Luther said. "I want to introduce you to my friend. Remember that time I was on crutches when you was little? Thomas here is the man who saved my life."

Only after I extended my hand did Shawn reach up to shake with me, and then it was without getting off the sofa. Compared to D'Witt's, his grip was weak and dispirited. He turned back to the television and let us leave the room unmolested either by conversation or consideration.

Under the mouthwatering scent of dinner, the house smelled like my grandmother's when I was a kid, an almost ineffable meld of floor wax, furniture polish, mothballs, and toast.

The women were in the kitchen.

Pookie Sands was a thin, stern, stately woman who could have passed for fifty, though I knew her to be at least eighty. Aside from worry lines on her forehead, she had almost no wrinkles, her skin tight and firm-looking. Pookie's hair was tied back in a scarf, her dark eyes centered behind thick, heavy-looking glasses that didn't want to stay on her nose. She wore a long, burgundy dress and clunky black shoes and managed to look both servile and forbidding. It was easy to believe Luther's claim that she had buried her head in a Bible twenty years earlier and forgotten to take it out. Luther told me she was his children's primary caregiver when he wasn't with them, a role that, because of her sternness, griped him no end.

Laronda sat at the table in a business suit. Both these women looked as if they'd gone to high schools where they were expected to fight once a week. I didn't know where Pookie's hardships had sprung from, but I knew a lot of Laronda's wouldn't have happened if she'd never met Luther.

Two heavyset women Luther later introduced as neighbors backed out of the conversation as soon as we entered the room. Laronda was finishing up a plate of chicken, hers the only place at the table. She resembled her mother, the same slim-waisted, small-breasted frame, the same long limbs and long, oval face, the same nose and lips, the same poor eyes, although her glasses were modern and didn't make her look anywhere near as forbidding as Pookie.

Because I entered the room in front of Luther, I had a feeling for a split second that Pookie imagined I was an intruder who had somehow slipped past the phalanx of children out front. When she spotted Luther, she turned back to the sink.

"Hey, Pookie," Luther said, failing to sound casual. "Hey, Laronda."

Before broaching the subject of Balinda, Luther said to Laronda in a tone that told everybody in the room it had been said before, "Has Shawn done any homework all week?"

"Now don't be jumping on *my* back," Laronda said, without looking up from her supper. The pitch and volume of her voice drove both the neighbors out the back door. Pookie, who was cleaning plates at the sink, watched the exchange out of the corner of her eye. "He ain't even my boy, and you bring him here and want me to raise him?"

"You know why he can't stay over at his mother's. You agreed. I appreciate you giving him a roof and all, but these kids require time on your part—"

"Time? I'm out there working sixty hours a week to put bread and butter on the table. And you—fooling around with all those cadavers. How long could that take?"

Pookie and I looked at each other without expression.

It was a large kitchen with an old-fashioned spigot over two porcelain-clad iron basins and high, white cabinets that looked as if they'd been installed at the turn of the century. The counters were Formica, the edges wrapped with metal. The linoleum was speckled and wavy in spots.

I knew the house belonged to Pookie, but had no idea how long it had been in the family or how she'd acquired it. Pookie Sands had worked outside the home until Laronda and

Luther's youngest daughter, Shereffe, came on the scene nine years earlier, which meant Pookie had been working until her late seventies. Judging from what I was seeing in the kitchen, she continued to cook and clean and watch over her brood like a mother hen.

Their voices were growing louder, and now Laronda was fixing Luther with eyes that would have burned all the hair off my chest. Luther gave back a look that was almost as caustic. I'd seen him cranky, but I'd never seen it come on so quickly.

I said, "Luther, we didn't come here for this."

"You don't even go to Shereffe's school functions!" he said.

It was his last salvo, and his words echoed up and down the canyons of the kitchen battlefield like distant cannon fire. Except for the sound of running water in the sink, the room grew deathly quiet. Pookie scraped chicken bones off a plate into an old-fashioned yellow waste can with a lid she raised with a foot lever. The fork she was using as a scraper made odd music against the plate.

"Laronda," I said. "We've come to do something about finding Balinda."

In the silence that ensued, Laronda stood slowly, carried her dishes to the sink, then cleared and rinsed them.

"Who *are* you?" she asked, looking at me for the first time.

"I'm a private investigator. My name is Thomas Black."

"We gotta do everything to find Balinda," Luther said. "Our baby could be hurt somewhere or in the hands of killers. And if that ain't the case, you know as well as I do we need to get her before she gets back on the stuff."

Laronda leveled a look at Luther, who was now standing across the table. "Balinda's not hurt, and she's not going back on dope."

"How do you know?"

"I suppose you told *him* all about her." She gestured at me.

"Tell us what you know about the white boy," Luther said.

Laronda turned to look at Pookie, who'd ceased work at the sink. Whatever passed between the two women took only a split second, then Laronda took off her suit jacket, draped it over her arm and said, "You leave Balinda alone. She knows what she's doing."

"You know where she is, don't you?" Luther said.

Laronda didn't reply.

I said, "We understand the dead man in her car had visited here. Did you know him?"

"Just some salesman," Laronda said quickly.

"What was he selling?"

"Pony rides, for all I know. I don't even remember. It was a month or more ago."

"What was Balinda doing with him that night?" Luther asked.

Laronda glowered at Luther and said, "Don't you dare find her. She's gone for a reason."

"Damn, Laronda," Luther said. "You think she killed that white boy, don't you? That's why you don't want her found. You think she killed him and ran."

"I think no such thing."

"Then we gotta find her before she starts back on it."

"Balinda's done using stuff. I know that and you know that."

"She was done before. Nobody's ever done."

CHAPTER 7

In the residual heat from dinner, the kitchen seemed like the warmest place in the city.

"How did a salesman who dropped by the house at random come to be with Balinda a month later?" I asked.

Nobody answered.

Luther put his knuckles on the table and leaned on it. "What was he sellin'?"

"It wasn't *drugs*, if that's what you mean," Laronda said. "I'm not even convinced the man who visited a month ago *was* the man in the car. The police have been wrong before."

"The police aren't wrong," Pookie said, her voice flat. "They gave me his driver's license. I told them. Benjamin Aldrich. He came here to see you, and then he came back. . . ."

Laronda gave her mother a scathing look which Pookie bore with an equanimity most people could not have sustained. "He did *not* come back."

"Oh, he did. A couple times a week. Balinda would go out and set in his pickup truck with him, and they would talk."

"That's not true, Mother, and you know it. He came one time, and Raymond ran him off."

"He come back. And he was smart as a whip. Solved three of my conundrums standin' out there on the front porch. I don't know what they talked about out there so long, but they got along like a couple of hens in a roost."

"Except one of them wasn't a hen," Laronda said bitterly.

"The question is," Luther said, "did you know him?"

"Don't use that tone of voice on me, Luther."

Luther had the look of a man in a foxhole, shells screaming across the sky. "You gotta help us out here, Laronda. We don't find her . . . you know what's going to happen."

The report of Aldrich coming to the house a couple of times a week and sitting outside in the car with Balinda—typical drug behavior—had rekindled his forebodings. It wasn't helping any that Aldrich had been white. Nobody in the kitchen was saying it, but you could see by the way they avoided my eyes that there was a black/white thing going on. I wondered if Laronda thought I wasn't going to notice that she didn't look me directly in the eye. I wondered how many white people had done the same to her.

"Get your suspicious mind out of the gutter," Laronda said. "He wasn't selling drugs. Why would somebody come to me selling drugs? It was vacuum cleaners or time share condominiums. I forget. I hardly got to see his face, when Raymond came through that back door and took him by the collar and on out the front."

"That's Raymond," Pookie said, nodding. "That's what Raymond did."

I was beginning to remember some of Luther's stories about Raymond now. He was Laronda's older brother, the ex-con. Years ago when we were riding around in a patrol car together, Luther spoke of Raymond, calling him "my jailbird buddy." The fondness Luther had once professed for him seemed to have vanished over the years.

"Mother, how could you let him sneak around after Raymond threw him out? How could you do that to this family?"

Pookie chewed the inside of her cheek and gave her daughter a blank look. She was standing so still she could have been a mannequin.

"Tell us about Balinda and Aldrich," I said, looking at Pookie.

"They was runnin' together," Pookie said, breaking off eye contact with her daughter and addressing Luther. "It wasn't just here at the house. They went off together two, three times."

"Mother! Stay out of this. This is *my* daughter!" Laronda said.

Pookie turned savagely back to Laronda. "And my granddaughter. You in *my* house, girl. When I'm dead and gone, you can have it, but before then you don't talk to me like a child. And don't turn your back on me, young lady."

Laronda, who had started for the far door, heeled back around and squared off with her mother. In movement she was as gawky as Pookie, both of them tall, thin, forbidding women with nearly identical worry lines stamped on their brows like radiator grilles on a similar make of car.

Luther glanced at me and we exited by the door we'd come in, leaving the two women alone.

In the living room, Shereffe and Toylee showed us a school project Shereffe had been working on. Shereffe had gathered pictures of railroad tunnels in the western United States, including the Milwaukee Road tunnel at Snoqualmie Pass, now a part of the 130-mile Iron Horse Trail, a recreational trail created from the abandoned railway and available for hikers and bicyclists. When I told Shereffe I had been in that tunnel, that it was open to foot and bicycle traffic in the spring and summer months, Toylee asked if I could take them there.

"Now, leave old Thomas alone, Toylee," Luther said. "Thomas has got his own life."

"He can take us, Grandpa," Toylee said excitedly. "I know he can."

"I can take you there my ownself," Luther said.

"But you won't," Toylee said.

"I'll take you," I promised. "And Luther too. We'll all go." Turning to Luther, I said, "I think she knows where Balinda is."

"Laronda? Laronda don't know *anything*," Luther said disgustedly. "She always wants to mess me up. Whatever I want, she don't want. That's her way. Believe me. She doesn't know nothin'."

"Are you talking about Mommy? Do you know where she is?" Toylee asked, leaping up. "You know where she is?"

"No," Luther said, giving me a lugubrious look as he picked Toylee up and set her against his hip. "We're looking for her. That's why I brought Thomas along. He's good at finding people."

"Can I come?" Toylee asked.

"No," Luther said. "You're too small."

"Can I?" Shereffe asked. "I'm bigger."

"Sorry," Luther said. "Not this time."

"Which time?" Shereffe asked. Clearly these two had been ignored in all the hoopla surrounding Balinda's disappearance, and just as clearly, both had been deeply affected by it.

Leaving me to my own devices, Luther took the girls upstairs. Shawn hadn't looked away from the television since our return to the living room, and now that the others were gone, I couldn't tell if he even realized I was in the room. He and I were both aliens in this house, his mother living across town with a boyfriend he couldn't get along with; my wife across town having dinner with a couple I couldn't stand.

A few minutes later Pookie came in and snapped, "Move your feet this minute, young man!" Her voice was so sharp, her tone so insistent, that I looked down to see what I was standing on, but she was talking to Shawn Brown. Without glancing away from the tube, he dropped his feet to the floor.

Pookie looked me over carefully and said, "Luther don't have many white friends."

"We've been friends for a long time. What did the police ask when they were here?"

"Been twice. First it was the uniformed officers. Then on Wednesday it was a little bald-headed man with a mouthful of big words."

"Arnold Haldeman?"

"That's him. He said they were after Balinda for murder."

"Do you think she killed him?"

"Lord, no. Balinda liked Aldrich. That was plain."

"Where do you think Balinda is?"

"You askin' this old woman?" She stared at me with her clear, hazel eyes. "Off hidin' with friends."

"Luther checked all her friends."

"*Luther* don't even *know* all her friends. She got friends from when she was away, friends Luther never heard of. She got friends *I* never heard of."

"What happened Monday night?"

"Balinda went out late and never came back. And no, I didn't see Aldrich or anybody else with her."

"Did she say anything before she left?"

"Not that I recall. She was watchin' the *Tee*-V when I went up to bed. So was the girls. Laronda was working late. I don't know where the boys were. D'Witt don't sleep much, so he's always wheelin' around in the dark. Next thing I know, the *po-leece* are at the front door."

"Did Balinda say anything to you about Aldrich?"

"I try to mind my own business where my granddaughter's love life is concerned, Mr. Black. If you want to know, Balinda's always had a lot of men hanging around. No one special lately."

"Except Aldrich?"

"Right. And she was doing something else she never done before. Asking about the family. About when she was born.

When her brother, Lyle, was born, God rest that poor boy's soul."

As we spoke, Laronda and Luther entered the room looking like a couple of football players running through a play. Laronda strode briskly, clasping a small, leather-bound book in her hands. Luther was close on her heels, hands outstretched toward the book, even though it was clear Laronda wasn't going to give it up. When she saw Pookie and I were talking together, Laronda gave her elderly mother a look.

Pookie turned away, and I knew we'd spoken our last tonight.

Laronda said, "I *should* really call the police on you, Luther. This is Balinda's."

"The girls handed it to me."

"Balinda's address book? Like you didn't put them up to it?"

"I haven't slept in four days. Laronda, I'm trying to find our oldest child."

"Our oldest child passed on."

"I ain't forgot Lyle. You know I loved Lyle. But we gotta save Balinda's ass before she gets goin' on that dope again."

"Don't you talk like that in front of these kids."

Luther looked at me like a man being taken down by a shark. There was nothing he could do about any of this.

Aside from the murder and disappearance Monday night, there were other factors contributing to the volatility in this household, although I could only guess at most of them. Toylee, who'd trailed into the room behind Laronda and Luther and was hugging her grandfather's leg, was one factor. Balinda's history of drug abuse was another. The death of Lyle, Luther and Laronda's oldest son, another. I knew why Balinda was living with her mother, but I wondered why Laronda was living with hers. Surely, with her fast-track insurance company job Luther'd told me about, she could afford her own place.

Hanging his head like a schoolboy caught with a dirty picture, Luther said, "Come on, Thomas. We ain't goin' to get any more here."

"You're leaving?" Toylee screeched.

While Luther comforted Toylee and Shereffe tried to interest her distracted mother in the tunnel project on the coffee table, Pookie led me to the front door and motioned me close. We were standing in the same spot D'Witt's wheelchair had occupied earlier, except now the bar of sunshine was gone.

"Okay, listen carefully," Pookie whispered, her breath smelling of cloves. "A man lives on the twelfth floor. Every morning he takes the elevator down to the lobby and walks to work. Every evening he comes back through the lobby, and if he's alone or it wasn't raining that morning, he takes the elevator up to the seventh floor and walks the last five floors to his apartment. If it was raining that morning or if there is somebody riding with him, he proceeds directly to the twelfth floor and his apartment. Why?"

It took me a while to grasp that in all this hullabaloo Pookie was asking a parlor-game question, but then, guessing by the way she was looking up at me, the question might not be unrelated to what we'd spoken of tonight. It was hard to tell. And I didn't have an answer. I needed to ponder a riddle like this, and I couldn't do it with Pookie's sharp eyes boring into me. I'd been expecting intimate details about the family. I'd been expecting hushed confidences. I'd been expecting a gold mine, nuggets of deception, secrets to die for, not this lump of coal.

Luther burst through the doorway and motioned for me to follow.

"You figure that out, I got another," Pookie said as I stepped off the porch.

"Come on. Let's get out of here," Luther said, walking briskly to the hearse.

Luther drove away from the curb as unctuously as Jell-O

sliding off a plate at a picnic, smooth and fluid and easy and destined for the dirt. He was in a dark mood.

When I looked up at the house, Pookie was still in the doorway in her long burgundy dress and paisley scarf. Toylee was behind her, hugging her great-grandmother's thigh and waving to us with one small hand. Behind the heavy drapes in the living room a man's head appeared, but I couldn't tell which of the sons it was.

CHAPTER 8

Dodging all the arterials and threading the quiet shadows on the lake side of the hill, Luther said nothing for a few minutes. When he did speak, it was an explosion. "Damn! That woman *pisses* me off! And so does Shawn. He just doesn't get it. He's surly and he's rude and he's got no respect for adults. You seen him. What am I doing wrong, Thomas? You see the way that boy looked at me? All I want is for him to talk to me like I'm somebody."

"I guess maybe he's a typical teenager. It's too bad about D'Witt. What's he doing now?"

"D'Witt's in school. He's a good kid. He used to be more like Shawn. Until lately D'Witt's been a sore spot between Laronda and me. After she had Balinda, she said she didn't want any more babies. But then she had to get even with me when she found out about Patricia, so she had D'Witt. Remember Patricia? The heavyset one? Then after me and Laronda patched things up, we had Shereffe."

"Toylee and Shereffe are great."

Luther drove half a block without saying anything. "You're

right. Toylee and Shereffe are great. If I din't ever have any-body else in my family, I'd be blessed just havin' those two."

We drove another half block in silence before I said, "Pookie gave me a puzzle."

"About the two Arabs racing their horses?"

"About some guy in an elevator. You think it could have something to do with what's going on?"

"I think she likes you. What you gotta unnerstand, Thomas, is this is a house of women. They ain't never had no men or-derin' 'em around. I mean, Pookie had a couple of husbands, and I even knew one of them back when I was first seein' Laronda, but he was never nothin' but a pipsqueak in that house. He slept on a cot in his own little room in the base-ment. Pookie and them didn't pay him no mind. Years ago when Pookie's father came out from Chicago to live with 'em, it was the same. Didn't listen to a word he said. It's the women. They make the decisions and that's the way they like it.

"That's why I get so pissed off about the way they treated Lyle and the way they're treating Shawn now. From the boys they don't expect nothin', so they don't get nothin'. There's a whole different setup with girls. See, Laronda and them ex-pects their daughters to go to college and make something outta themselves. That's why Balinda was such a disappoint-ment. Balinda earned good grades. Was on the hoop team. Made all-city. She was *about* somethin'. And then she went and got herself messed up."

"Why don't you take Shawn into your house? He's your son, not Laronda's."

"He stayed with me two weeks. We ended up fightin' every day."

We drove in silence.

"So let's go at it from the other side," I said. "The Ben-jamin Aldrich side." Luther stopped the hearse in the middle of Alder Street. It was the only street we'd been on in the past few minutes that was empty of traffic.

"What are you sayin'?"

"Pookie told me Balinda was asking questions about the family. About when she was born. About when Lyle was born. Maybe Aldrich showing up precipitated that."

"There's a lot of hidden shit in that family, Thomas. Stuff I don't even know. I don't know what all Pookie done when she was young, but there's things she won't talk about. Now that I think about it, there's things Laronda won't talk about."

"Like what?"

"Laronda don't like the subject of her brother, Raymond, much. He's out now, but he's been in the joint three, four times. Last stretch was for manslaughter. Guy he killed? Raymond was in a convenience store down on Rainier Avenue and got into it with some Russian dude. The man barely spoke English. Raymond pulled out the heat and popped him. Bought a pack of Raleighs, collected his change, and calmly walked out of the store with the dude on the floor bleeding to death. Raymond's crazy."

"How long ago was that? When he went up for manslaughter?"

"Well, let's see. He's been out six years. He was in nine. That makes it about fifteen years ago. You want to see him tonight?"

"Yeah. Sure."

"Let's go."

CHAPTER 9

Luther had been too preoccupied with Mrs. Scott that morning to take me past the spot where Balinda wrecked her car, so we drove by it on the way to Raymond's. We'd both been to our share of accident scenes—Luther had been on the SPD accident investigation team for a couple of years—so it was possible we'd pick up something from the excursion.

Heading south, we crossed Yesler and went up a long, gentle slope on Thirty-first South, a row of town houses to our left, several residences high on the bank to the right, their front yards bunkered with concrete dikes to contain the hillside. We were only five blocks from Pookie's. Unless she was injured or disoriented in the accident, Balinda could easily have walked home from here.

After Luther parked on the hill, we got out and crossed the road to a long, empty sidewalk and, beyond that, a treed gradient that dropped down into the upper regions of Frink Park, one of the city's many greenbelts. Twice during my stint on the SPD we found bodies in Frink Park, young women both times. One had been raped and strangled by a former boyfriend who eventually went to prison for it. The other body was never identified. Homicide ended up calling her "Lucy" because of something written on the back of a sneaker found nearby, and I rarely drove past Frink Park without thinking about Lucy. I wondered if Balinda was being called Lucy by some other jurisdiction even as we searched for her.

There were a number of trees along the sidewalk, most young enough that the impact of an automobile would have uprooted them, yet none were damaged. Nor could we find any signs that a tree was missing or had been replaced. We hiked up the sidewalk to the top of the hill, scratched our heads, and turned around and walked back down slowly.

It was Luther who spotted the black tire marks along the curb. A car had careened down the hill, brushed the east curb for fifty feet, skipped over the parking strip, and shot down the hillside between the trees. Now that we knew where to look, we peered over the embankment and saw a path of up-rooted shrubbery and flattened saplings.

Digging the heels of our street shoes into the damp clay and hardpack, we descended the hillside. We found oil and fragments of broken window glass in the humus where we calculated the Escort had come to rest against a pair of thick trees, but even after Luther scrambled back up the slope to the hearse to retrieve a flashlight, we didn't spot any shell casings or anything else in the leaves and mulch. There were a multitude of footprints on the clay hillside, and down from where the car had come to rest we could see where someone had slid another twenty yards down the incline.

It would be interesting to know if it had been a cop, a rescue worker, or if the slide marks had been made by one of the occupants of the Escort. You would think a crash victim would go *up* the hill for help, not down into the dark woods. Heading down seemed to signify either extreme confusion or a desire to flee the scene, the latter being Luther's choice, simply because he wanted to believe Balinda was both uninjured and fleeing. If she were fleeing, she was probably fleeing whoever had shot Aldrich, which meant she hadn't done it.

Footing on the slope was precarious, so we gouged toe-holds with our shoes and each of us gripped a nearby tree for stability.

"This shoots down a couple of Haldeman's theories," I said.

"How's that?"

"One of his scenarios had the car crashing, Balinda climbing out, walking around to the rear passenger window, and shooting Aldrich through it. He was shot in the right side, wasn't he?"

"Three times in the right. Once through the neck from the left."

"Look at this hillside. Can you picture anybody walking around the car after crashing it on this steep bank? We can barely stand up. Plus, it was midnight, and there are no lights around here. We're having a hard enough time at twenty to eight, and we've got a flashlight. Haldeman was figuring on us not visiting the scene."

"You think he was going to send it to the prosecutors, knowing she didn't do it?" Luther asked.

"I hate to say this, but I'm not one hundred percent convinced she didn't."

Luther stared at me in the dark woods.

"Not on the physical evidence," I said. "Not yet."

Back on the sidewalk, we were slapping mud and twigs off our pants when Luther looked at me and said, "She's gotta be hurt."

"They said there was a broken windshield. People usually break that with their heads."

"I'm gonna call up and see if they used the K-9 unit."

When we got back into the hearse, Luther pulled a small supply of foil-wrapped alcohol wipes out from under the seat and tore a package open for me. Inhaling the pungent odor of medicinal alcohol, we wiped our palms off.

Luther spoke softly. "When he shakes hands, Raymond likes to hold you so you can't get loose."

"What?"

"Laronda's brother, Raymond. He'll grab your hand and hold it and then beat you senseless using his other fist. Lot of times he'll have an object in his left hand to help out—a bottle or something. Because he's left-handed and he's fast, it usually works. I ain't sayin' he's going to do that tonight necessarily. Especially not with me bein' there. I'm only giving you a preview before you see the movie."

"Thanks."

CHAPTER 10

It was clear by the way Luther's voice sometimes faltered when he spoke of Raymond that there was something between them he was reluctant to talk about. As young men they'd been friends. One had become a police officer and a productive citizen, the other a convict. I could imagine the frictions their divergent paths had generated, especially since they were bonded to the same family and would be forever—Raymond an uncle to Luther's three children by Laronda.

We drove half a mile west on Jackson to Twenty-third Avenue and headed north. Aside from Ezell's Fried Chicken on the corner of Twenty-third and Jefferson, and Garfield High School across the street, mostly what faced heavily trafficked Twenty-third Avenue were single-family dwellings. Between Cherry and Union the houses became run-down, and they were particularly shabby where Luther turned onto Marion. We parked and walked back to Twenty-third, crossing the busy avenue between clutches of cars.

Raymond lived in a tall, green house on the west side of the street. The yard was full of litter. A bicycle wheel was half buried in the sod like a piece of modern art.

Luther knocked. I watched traffic. Eventually a gaunt black woman with bloodshot eyes answered the door. She wore black leggings and a T-shirt, and her straightened hair stood up in back as if she'd been sleeping on it.

Luther said, "Raymond here?"

"Raymond?"

"He still lives here, don't he? Raymond Sands?"

"What you want with Raymond?"

"Is he home?"

"I don't know." She gazed at us with minimal interest and crossed her forearms over her faded cotton T-shirt.

"Could you check for us?" Luther asked politely.

She pushed the door closed against a stubborn piece of carpeting and wandered off somewhere toward the interior of the house. The smell of liver and onions came wafting out the door on a blast of hot air. I detected a vague odor of mildew and marijuana.

After five minutes Luther stepped into the house. Taking care to watch where I stepped, I followed.

We entered a trashed-out hallway next to a staircase so full of newspapers and broken-spined books it appeared impassable. The woman who answered the door was snoring on a sofa in a large, open living room to the left, the cleanest room in sight. A TV dinner tray sat on a low table in front of a television set broadcasting reruns of *Gilligan's Island*. An African-American man wearing Jockey shorts, galoshes, and a winter coat turned to look at us when Luther cleared his throat.

"Raymond here?"

"He probably down at the café."

"On Cherry?"

"You know he hang out there."

On the way down the front steps Luther said, "Damn, that makes me mad. We got Raymond walking around actin' all self-righteous and saying how he's cleaned up, and blah,

blah, blah, and there he is living with all them druggies and whores."

It was sadly ironic that his daughter had been caught up in drugs, because nobody had less compassion for addicts than Luther Little. It wasn't merely that he didn't like them—he *despised* them. Rightly or wrongly, I had the feeling it was because he believed that had his life been influenced by a few altered circumstances, he could have been one of them.

We got into the hearse and drove a quarter mile to Twenty-seventh and Cherry Street. When Luther and I had worked the area in patrol cars, drug transactions on the street could be observed at almost any time of the day or night, but it had been cleaned up since then and there was almost no action tonight.

Parking on the south side of Cherry, Luther got out and led me across the street to a small complex of single-story buildings.

Catfish Café was a humble little eat-in/take-out restaurant on the corner with a rectangular white sign over the entrance, eight or ten tables inside, and windows looking out over the street. A pink and blue neon sign in one of the windows promised SOUTHERN CATFISH within, and from the warm aroma reaching me outside, I knew it was true. The door was propped open, but the screen was closed to keep out flies and riffraff. I went in anyway.

Everybody but me was black. As conscious as I was of the color of my skin, it occurred to me that this was only one evening for me in a very small neighborhood in a rather large city, while Luther was conscious of the color of his skin every minute of every day of his life, no matter where he went. He'd told me so, many times. I had let myself entertain the conceit that if I could get inside that armor with him, I must be quite a guy. Except I wasn't inside his armor with him; I only thought I was, and it was brought home to me clearly when everybody in the joint turned to look at me and then turned away, dismissing me en masse.

Luther approached a table inside the diner where a man sat with his back to the door, a paper sack with a twenty-two-ounce bottle of malt liquor between his thighs. Two other men were at the table, one a distinguished-looking, gray-haired gent in his seventies, the other a husky, toothless younger man who looked as if he might have once been a heavy-weight boxer or sparring partner now gone to fat. An army of empty dishes and crumpled napkins held positions on the tabletop.

A young woman behind the cash register at the far end of the eatery noticed us and asked if she could help us.

Luther waved her off without even looking.

"We need to talk," I said.

She nodded but didn't look at me. I'd been in this situation before, immersed in a world in which I was the interloper, and I didn't much relish it.

"Raymond, you got a minute?" Luther asked.

With a deliberate and somewhat irritating slowness, Raymond Sands looked up. He was a smallish man with sturdy arms, not as buffed-out as you would expect of someone who'd spent so many years in prison. His stomach was crusading against his shirt, and his shoulders were rounded. He was about Luther's age, early fifties. His head was the rough shape of a bullet, and his short hair was combed straight back, a smattering of gray kissing his temples. He was a shade darker than his mother, Pookie, and a whole lot darker than Laronda, his sister.

He smiled, but then it vanished like a picture tube winking out when he spied me over Luther's shoulder. "What's goin' on, brother? Who's your friend?"

"Thomas Black. Raymond Sands." We shook hands without Raymond getting off his duff and without me getting clubbed. True to his reputation, his grip was a combination

Super Glue and manly horsing around, and for a moment I thought he wasn't going to let go. He did, though, and then did not look at me again.

"Could we talk?" Luther asked. "It's about Balinda."

"Balinda?" He sounded surprised.

After Raymond's friends got up and left, Luther and I sat in their chairs. I could feel the heat in the seat from the former occupant.

Luther said, "What happened Monday night?"

"You tell me, Luth. I was in California. Went down to see Sheryl and them. Got me a little piece." He smiled, but it didn't wipe the sour look off Luther's face.

When he continued to smile, Luther broke out of his mood for a moment. "Sheryl's sister? You got Sheryl's sister?"

"Naw. She wasn't even there. This was a gal works with Sheryl at the studio. Got me some fiiiine pussy. Ummm. Ummmmmm." Right then I decided, if I hadn't already, that I didn't like this man.

"You weren't here Monday?" Luther asked.

"Flew out Monday afternoon. Got back today."

"You know what happened with Balinda, don't you?"

"Dion filled me in on some of it. I don't think you have to be so worried."

"Wouldn't you be if somebody got hisself killed in your daughter's car and she disappeared?"

"Now, calm down, Luth. You're the last person should be worried about the *po*-leece. You *were* the *po*-leece."

"Who said I was worried about the police? I'm worried about her. And that police job was a long time ago."

"Yeah, but your cop friends will help you out with this."

"My cop friends weren't there a month ago when Benjamin Aldrich showed up at the house. They weren't there when you tossed him out."

"Who you talking about?"

"Benjamin Aldrich. The man they found dead in Balinda's

car. He was at Pookie's a month ago. They say you tossed his ass out."

"Oh, him," Raymond said, pulling a cigar out of his shirt pocket and bouncing it on end on the tabletop. *That's* the dude was in Balinda's car?"

"That was him. Why did you throw him out of the house?"

"He was annoying Laronda. They were arguing. Well, not arguing really, but they were headed in that general direction. I never talked to Laronda about it, so I don't know what all they said. I came in the back door at Pookie's, and they were in the kitchen, kinda squared off like Tyson and Holyfield, so I took him on outta there. I gotta tell ya, Laronda didn't even thank me."

Raymond seemed about as satisfied with himself as a man could be. And it wasn't only the story of Aldrich. It was in the way he sat, how he held his head and smirked, the manner in which his words came out in fits and starts. The way he did not look at me, not once after shaking hands. He was no-where near the beaten-down ex-con I'd expected.

"I still don't understand why you threw him out," Luther said. "You hear what they were talking about?"

"Why don't you ask Laronda?" Raymond said.

"You know Laronda."

"Never says boo to me either. By the time I got back in the house, she was in the bath. Stayed in there all night. I don't know what they were talking about, and it never came up again."

"It seems to me," I said, "that Laronda is plenty capable of throwing somebody out of the house by herself."

Until that moment, Luther had been asking all the questions. I could see right away it had been a mistake to inject myself into the conversation, because Raymond's attitude hardened instantly. He didn't answer me.

"Laronda didn't say *anything* about him?" Luther prodded.

"Said something about a wild goose chase."

"You ever see him again?" Luther asked.

"Saw him drivin' up the street with Balinda. Musta been last Wednesday or Thursday."

"What'd they look like? Were they sittin' apart? Did they look relaxed, or did they look like it was some sort of business deal?"

"You ask a lot of questions, Luth."

"My daughter's missing."

"She'll turn up."

"And you don't know anything about Benjamin Aldrich?"

"Only that he went out of the house real easy like. I believe he mighta peed his pants." Raymond Sands smiled.

"Dion working in back?" Luther asked.

"I ain't seen him."

Luther got up and walked past the cash register into the back of the restaurant, leaving me with a man who refused to look at me. Raymond Sands glanced out the window and took a sip from his paper sack. After a few moments his two friends came back and more or less edged me away from the table. I got up and began reading the restaurant reviews posted on the wall.

Getting shunned reminded me of a couple of incidents in my childhood, maybe a lot of incidents in my childhood. While I was thinking about this and reading reviews, yelling erupted from the back room.

"Luther, what the hell are you doing! Luther, get outta my freezer. Are you crazy, man? Get the hell outta my freezer!"

The cashier, Raymond Sands, his two buddies, and I all converged on the scene at about the same time. Luther and a man in a white chef's hat and apron were struggling in front of a large chest freezer. The door of the freezer was open and dozens of packages wrapped in foil were spilled on the floor at Luther's feet.

The man in the chef's hat said, "He's dumping out my freezer."

"Luther," I said, "what's going on?"

I might as well have been the man in the moon.

Intent on emptying the chest before he could be stopped, Luther broke free from the other man, leaned into the freezer, and threw out package after package, moving more and more quickly until he had his skinny rump up in the air like a dog digging for bones in the neighbor's backyard. He dug down to ice packs and a large, green canvas tarp spread out over a formless lump before the man in the chef's hat pulled him away.

Luther fought him.

Raymond and his friends jumped in to help the man in the chef's hat. Windmilling away from his captors, Luther fought them wildly, then halfheartedly, and then wildly again. Luther'd gone crazy. All five men danced over the frozen foil packages, a few of which shot across the floor like oversized hockey pucks.

"What the hell you doin', Luth?" Raymond said, gasping for breath.

"Look at that," Luther said. "Look what's under that green thing."

The veins on the side of Luther's head were pulsing, the muscles in his neck clearly delineated. His eyeballs began to protrude. The four men struggled to keep him from the freezer. I was thinking that when they took Luther to the nuthouse, I'd have to go back to my car on foot.

"What you doin' emptyin' out my freezer in this heat?" said the man in the chef's hat. "You crazy?"

"He want to jump in," said one of Raymond's friends, the one without front teeth. He smiled at the thought. "The heat got to him, and he want to jump in and cool his bones."

"Take that green thing out of there," Luther said, looking at me imploringly. "Take it out and look under it. Will ya, Thomas? If I'm wrong, we'll put it all back. Won't hurt nothin'. I ain't gonna hurt nothin'."

I glanced at the man in the chef's hat. The young woman

who'd been cashiering stood in the doorway, as did another employee in a Catfish Café T-shirt splattered with cooking oil. The man in the chef's hat nodded.

I reached into the freezer and pulled on a corner of a green tarp frozen to whatever lay beneath it. Everybody in the room peered in. I got a corner of the tarp loose and pulled it off. Underneath were more mounds of foil-wrapped fish, catfish one would assume.

I looked at Luther.

"I dunno," he said, dropping his head and relaxing.

"What'd you think was in there, Luth?" Raymond asked. He'd pulled a pair of cigars out of his shirt pocket and was inspecting them for damage. Luther said nothing.

Raymond's toothless friend rubbed Luther's biceps and said, "Man, Luth. You been liftin'? You're a wiry little fucker."

"Yeah," Luther said, jerking his arm away. "And you ever lay a hand on this wiry little fucker again, he's gonna kick your ass into next Tuesday."

"Luth? We were just tryin' to—"

"I don't give a flying fuck what you were doin'. You don't lay a hand on me. Are you listenin', Raymond?"

"I hear ya," Raymond said, putting a cold cigar into his mouth and another into his shirt pocket. He squinted at the man in the chef's hat and then turned to Luther smugly. "You were lookin' for Balinda, weren't you?"

"I wasn't lookin' for nothin'."

"You were looking for Balinda in that freezer. What'd you think? Dion capped her and set her in with the catfish and crawdads?"

Luther bolted the room. For a moment I debated whether to stick around and help restock the freezer or to follow him outside. I went outside.

"I expect you to be on my side next time somebody jumps me," he said as I pulled abreast of him in the street.

"They thought you were nuts, Luther. They were trying to help."

"They wouldn't have thought I was nuts if Balinda had been in there."

"Why don't we look for places where a *live* girl would be first. Okay?"

"I only hope to God she *is* alive."

CHAPTER 11

As soon as we got into the hearse, Luther fired up the engine and turned on the air conditioner. Sitting behind the wheel seemed to calm him. He placed his hands at ten and two o'clock, fingered the ridges on the underside of the steering wheel and stared through the windshield as if in a trance.

"Luther?" I said. "Who would have placed Balinda's body in the Catfish Café freezer?"

"Whoever kilt her."

"You think somebody killed her?"

"If she was in the freezer, she would be dead, wouldn't she?"

"But why that particular freezer?"

"Because Dion and Raymond both have access to it."

"Dion's her ex-boyfriend? Toylee's father?"

"He still works there. And you saw Raymond. He practically lives there."

"Luther, don't you think if somebody killed Balinda they would have thrown her body anywhere but a freezer in a busy place like Catfish Café? And why would Dion hurt Balinda?"

"She dumped him. He been playin' around with other

women, and Balinda found out and threw his punk ass out. His pride was injured. He took it personal. Guys are like that. I been expectin' trouble for a long time."

"You said you spoke to him?"

"I did, but he didn't convince me of shit."

"What about Raymond? What reason would he have to hurt Balinda?"

"Raymond been tryin' to get in Balinda's pants since she was in high school."

"Raymond's her uncle."

"You tell *him* that."

"You think he'd be likely to hide her body in the freezer?"

"Nobody's likely to hide her in a freezer. My brain turned around inside my skull a couple of times and came to rest backwards. Let me be."

Luther was watching a couple of young women maybe half a block away walking toward us on the sidewalk. A trio of young men on a nearby porch catcalled to them, but we were too far away to catch their words. The young women did their best to snub the men.

Once again Luther wheeled the hearse through the Central District while we talked. From time to time he would turn up a side street and cruise past a particular house or apartment building, as if hoping to catch a glimpse of someone he knew inside. It was hard to tell if he was actively searching for Balinda or driving the streets out of habit or for the sheer pleasure of sitting behind the wheel. Luther had always coveted fine cars, though the frugality he'd learned as a boy didn't allow him to splurge. The hearse was probably as close as he was going to get. The last time I'd seen him he was driving a Volkswagen bug with 450,000 miles on it.

"Can you tell me something, Luther?"

"Sure." He'd calmed down since leaving the café, his time behind the wheel acting like a sedative.

"Let's go back to that first night Benjamin Aldrich went up

to the house and Raymond threw him out. I got the impression from Raymond that Laronda was somehow incapable of getting Aldrich out of the house."

Luther's voice dropped. "He was white, Thomas."

"What are you saying?"

"She works with white folks all day, so she gets along with them, but she don't get along with them, if you hear what I'm tellin' you. See, she was raised to dislike white folk. Pookie taught her that. And that's no disrespect to Pookie, but that's always been Pookie's way. Raymond's the same. Laronda's livin' a charade. Pretendin' she's something she's not. She's the big insurance exec downtown, but when she gets back in the C.D., she don't believe none of that. What do they call that? Imposter's syndrome? That's her.

"You gotta understand, Thomas," Luther continued. "Laronda, when she was a girl, thought she was better than everybody else, me included. She never paid me no mind. 'Cause see, I'm so dark. You may not have thought about it, but most blacks are prejudiced against a brother who's darker than they are. So she was always a special challenge for me. You always want somethin' you know you can't have. But I didn't pay no attention to her at all. It was me and Raymond runnin' around together all through high school, and every time I walked into that house I didn't even look at her."

"What else did Raymond get sent up for besides manslaughter?" I asked.

"The first time he stole eleven hundred dollars from that restaurant we was just in, Catfish Café. Raymond worked there years ago, but he got fired—not for stealing the money. He did that after. Raymond was in a lot of trouble in those days. He almost got me in trouble with Harley Shoalwater's wife. Harley Shoalwater mighta killed Raymond and me. Or we mighta kilt him. Either way you and me wouldn't be sittin' here talkin' right now. And either way, Laronda never woulda had anything to do with me. You know, I think back on it, the only reason she turned over on me was because of the SPD. I think that impressed her. For a while there she thought I was *about* somethin'."

"You are about something, Luther. Who's Harley Shoalwater?"

Luther looked at me across the cab of the hearse for the first time in many minutes. "Harley was an Indian lived over on Twenty-ninth with his wife. A big old guy, taller than you, maybe close to three hundred pounds and meaner than a fat-back mama who just found out the moonshine she bought was gator piss. His wife was a sister. They lived right next door to Raymond's aunt Bertha—she died a long time ago. Geez, I ain't thought about Aunt Bertha in twenty years. She was a sweet old gal. What I mean by that is, she used to watch over us boys like we was her own. Never had no kids of her own. We used to go over there and stay on a Friday night and watch TV until we couldn't keep our eyes open. She'd bake peanut butter cookies. I can still smell 'em.

"Anyways, next door to Aunt Bertha lived this Harley Shoalwater and his wife. Harley was a fisherman, so he'd be leavin' his old lady to her own devices a lot of the time. Used to be gone up to Alaska. Raymond gets to goin' over there and mowin' her lawn and such. She turns out to be a lush, and Raymond figures if he can get a bottle of one-five-one into her, she'll about let Raymond do whatever he pleases. I think Raymond was sixteen. I was fifteen. She was our first pussy."

"Both of you?"

"I ain't proud of it. Raymond had her first. For weeks Raymond gave me every little detail, and then one afternoon he called me up, said he was with Harley Shoalwater's wife and did I want a go at it?"

"And?"

"I got to thinkin', and after a while my *little* head talked my *big* head outta what was smart."

The scene in the restaurant forgotten, Luther was relaxed now, handling the wheel and the turn signals with his left hand.

"So I go on over, go in the back so's nobody over at Bertha's would see. The house is all dark and the curtains are closed and Raymond is readin' the funnies, and I go in the other room and there's Harley Shoalwater's wife, naked as a jaybird, waving me over with a bottle of Bud in one hand and a remote control in the other. First time I ever saw a remote control."

"What'd you do?"

"I was fifteen. She was thirty-five, a growed woman. What would *you* do?"

"I probably would have run."

"I mighta too, but I didn't. She said, 'Come on over, big boy. It's time you was a man.' Just like that, Thomas. 'It's time you was a man.' I dropped my britches and got up there on it and gave her the ride of her life. After that, Raymond or me spent about every night over there. Raymond would drink with her, but I never. My mother caught me with alcohol on my breath, she woulda kilt me. I woulda married Harley Shoalwater's wife, she'd asked me. I never told Raymond that part.

"Then about the end of that summer, Harley Shoalwater comes back from Anchorage, and two days later he's drunk out on his front porch screamin' to all the neighbors somebody's been after his wife and he's gonna find 'em and fry up their balls like halibut eyes. The cops took him away in handcuffs, and that night his wife packed up and went back to her mama in Kentucky. She was all beat up.

"Old Harley Shoalwater, he spent the next coupla weeks turnin' over rocks tryin' to figure out who'd been with his wife. We heard he was lookin' for us, so we hid out over with a cousin of mine up by the golf course on Spokane Street, and sure enough, we saw him drivin' by in his Pontiac. Raymond said Laronda told him where we were, but Raymond was always tryin' to put shit off on Laronda. We tried to sneak home to Pookie's house that night to see if things were all right. So we were walking down there on Rainier near Borracchini's

Bakery and the Oberto sausage factory, and who shows up on Rainier but Harley Shoalwater himself? Jumps out of his Pontiac and tries to jump our shit right there on the sidewalk. Raymond and I keep pushing him over, and he's too drunk to really get up, and it keeps goin' on like that.

"Turned out a couple weeks after that he went to the hospital for some stomach thing. When he came out, he went back to Alaska, and we never saw him again. Me and Raymond were bad. We broke into houses. You know. An old guy dies. The house is vacant for a few months while the estate clears. We'd break in and take whatever we could carry. It was this lost period right between bein' a kid and bein' an adult. Right between knowin' right and knowin' wrong. I straightened myself out. For some reason, Raymond never did."

"But he's working now?"

"He runs a little house-painting business, him and those two you saw him with tonight, Buster and Earl. Buster used to be a fighter. He's got a temper, so I want you to stay clear of him."

"They're not the ones started Pookie's house?" I said.

"That was me. I scraped part of it last summer, and then I hurt my back and couldn't get Shawn and them to lift a finger. Balinda and I were gonna do it this year when the weather turned solid. Maybe the last part of June. It woulda been nice spending them warm weeks painting the house with Balinda. Toylee and Shereffe was gonna be our helpers, bring us Kool-Aid and shit."

"Maybe it'll still happen. Let's hope."

CHAPTER 12

Friday night when I got back to the office, there was a band playing across the street at Doc Maynard's. Through the front windows I could see colored lights playing across a youngish, festive-looking crowd of revelers.

A block away a gang of bikers fired up their machines in front of the J&M Cafe, the motorcyclists twitching their accelerators to magnify the effect. Even half a block away I wanted earplugs.

A slight young woman in a police cruiser at the light smiled at me. I smiled back. Luther would have no use for her. She didn't look as if she could do ten push-ups. He'd always been extremely conscious of how dependable his backups were, taking an instant dislike to coworkers he suspected were lacking in sufficient strength, physical or otherwise, to back him up in a worst-case scenario.

I jogged upstairs to the office and collected the messages off the phone machine, glanced through the e-mail, and made a few calls. The first was to a contact at the phone company who had, at my request, prepared a list of numbers dialed from the Sands household during the past five weeks.

The second call was to Benjamin Aldrich's residence in Tacoma. He'd shared the phone number with a woman named Peggy Lindseth.

"Hello?" The voice that answered was girlish and subdued, as if she were not too long out of her teens and had been aroused from a deep sleep. The former seemed probable, the latter doubtful. It was Friday and not yet nine-thirty.

When I asked if I could drop by the next day, she agreed, but her voice took on a slight vibrato. "I don't know what I can tell you about the accident. I wasn't there. Are you working for the insurance company?"

"No. I'll explain tomorrow."

"Come in the morning. I have to be here in the morning anyway."

"Around ten o'clock?"

"I'll be here."

Not knowing what Aldrich's relationship with Peggy Lindseth had been, it occurred to me that if they were more than roommates and Aldrich had been fooling around with Balinda, Peggy Lindseth would probably have nothing to contribute, except to tell me he was a nice guy if she didn't know about it, that he was a louse if she did. On the other hand, she might have chased down a philandering boyfriend with a semiautomatic. The only problem with this last hypothesis was that the woman on the phone sounded as if she couldn't chase down a fly with a swatter.

I took the freeway north and crossed the ship canal. From these elevated freeways Seattle looked like a toy city. At the base of Queen Anne, the Space Needle was lit top to bottom. Lake Union was a dark mass below on my left. To the east in the distance, the University of Washington was mostly dark too. I exited the freeway at the Northeast Fiftieth ramp and was home a few minutes later.

Kathy and I lived in the same house I'd owned when we met, a bungalow a few blocks north of Fiftieth in an undistinguished neighborhood of small, older homes, many of which were rented as off-campus student housing. The neighborhood was close enough to the university that during the school year students walked past it almost hourly, and our mother-in-law apartment in the basement was usually rented out to a student. Kathy had once rented it from me.

The house had a front yard with a steep ridge across it that made it tricky to mow. Along the south wall a driveway consisting of two strips of concrete in packed earth ran back to a single-car garage at the rear of the property. On the south side of the drive stood our nearest neighbor's house, a two-and-a-half-story showpiece belonging to a retired railroad worker named Horace, the tidiest man I knew. From time to time he directed snide comments at my lifestyle, my profession, and, more recently, my dog. This week he was having a new driveway installed. The old one, he told me in all seriousness, was too hard to mop.

Our backyard was dominated by a crab apple tree, but I kept a garden plot in one corner and over the years had spiced up the property with roses: Whiskey Macs, Rio Sambas, Helmut Schmidts, Gold Medals, Amber Queens. I favored yellows and flashy bicolors—no sissy pinks for me. All summer our yard was alive with bright bumblebees and brighter blossoms.

I swung into the drive and parked at the far end of the driveway in front of the garage. When I got out, I heard music playing somewhere up the alley. L.C. came running from the back yard, and we roughed each other up for a minute or two. I'd fed him and was inside the back door when Sonya came quietly up our wooden steps. She wore shorts and a sleeveless blouse, no shoes.

Sonya Burmeister was our current renter, a Swedish foreign student at the U.W. She was a strange one, hiding out for weeks at a time watching television, taking three or four showers a day, and listening to the Grateful Dead or ABBA— doing whatever homework she had. If she went to classes or the grocery store, I couldn't figure out when she did it. I'd nicknamed her The Mole.

"Mr. Black?"

She petted L.C. as he ate.

"I told you to call me Thomas. Everybody does."

"Thomas. I was wondering if you could come down to look at the shower. It's still making that noise."

"I told you before. It's the water running through the pipes."

"I know. But I wish you could come down and look at it one more time." Her voice began to fade. "I'm not being too much of a baby about this, am I?"

"Not at all. I'll try to find some time this weekend. You going to be around?"

She nodded, then knelt to scratch L.C. behind an ear. Finished with his meal now, the dog licked his chops noisily and leaned into her. He was half shepherd and half mutt, but his soul was in the mutt half. I'd found him scrounging through the garbage bin at the Safeway over on Brooklyn Avenue, and even though I was really a cat kind of guy, he adopted me before I could figure out a way to appeal the decision. We called him Last Chance, or L.C. for short.

Because the house was still warm from having been shut up all day, the air exchange in the doorway was close to gale force. We chatted at the door while I let the house cool. I asked Sonya about school. She asked me about work. We talked about Sweden.

Sonya Burmeister was tall for a woman, maybe an inch shorter than my six-one. She was lanky, with long, athletic-looking legs, although I'd never seen her doing anything even remotely athletic. Her hair, which tonight she wore pinned up, had a golden tinge. She had wide blue eyes, a long face, a good complexion, and generally wore little makeup and less expression. If she'd smile, she probably would be attractive, but in order to know for sure she would have to smile. I'd never known her to have a visitor, and several times late at night Kathy and I had heard her crying downstairs.

"Okay," I said, during a lull in our conversation. "A man

lives on the twelfth floor. Every morning he takes the elevator down to the lobby and walks to work. Every evening he comes back through the lobby, and if he's alone or it wasn't raining that morning, he takes the elevator up to the seventh floor and walks the last five floors to his apartment. If it was raining that morning or if there is somebody riding with him, he proceeds directly to the twelfth floor and his apartment. Why does he do this? Don't feel bad if you don't get it. It's a toughie."

"Oh, that's easy. He's a dwarf. He can't reach the elevator buttons past number seven. If there's somebody else in the elevator with him, he asks them to push twelve for him. If it was raining that morning, he has his umbrella and he pushes the button with his umbrella. Right?"

She crossed one foot over the other and glanced down at her bare legs as if she'd only that minute realized she was wearing shorts.

"You heard it before, right?"

"No."

"Sure?"

"I'm sure." She was looking down at her knees again.

Just then Kathy came up the stairs carrying a coat and the leather satchel she used to transport paperwork from office to home and vice versa.

"Hello," Kathy said, squeezing past Sonya. "How are you? Would you like to come in?"

"Oh, no, thank you," Sonya said. "I need to get going." She was down the stairs and into the backyard before Kathy realized she'd left. I noticed her face pinked up a little.

"I'll come down and look at that shower," I said.

"Sure," Sonya yelled back. From the sound of her voice, she was already in the concrete stairwell to her apartment in the basement.

"She seemed nervous when I showed up," Kathy said, hanging up her coat and slinging her satchel across a chair in the dining room.

"She's a nervous person."

"What'd she want?"

"Her shower again. She thinks it's making noise."

"Yah. Yah. It's the shower." Kathy mocked the Scandinavian accent Sonya did not have but which Kathy wanted her to have.

"What does that mean?"

"It means she's got her eye on you, Thomas."

"Don't be silly."

"Come on, Thomas. Didn't you see the way she blew out of here when I showed up?"

"She's lonely."

"If she were lonely, talking to two people would be better than talking to one."

When she finished telling me about her evening, Kathy asked how the meeting with Luther's relatives had gone. I told her about the Sands household, about the accident site, about Luther's crazed behavior at Catfish Café. When I was done relating these events, I gave her Pookie Sands's puzzle. It took Kathy a little less time to solve it than it had taken Sonya, which upset me, because I hadn't figured it out. Taking pity on me, she came over and sat on my lap at the kitchen table. It was late, dark outside, and the only lights in the house were in the kitchen.

We kissed. I said, "Did you have a good time at dinner with Mr. and Mrs. Boredom."

"Oh, but you're cruel. I did, actually. And then I got home and saw you were having a good time too."

"Jealous?"

"Of all that Nordic height? You bet. I'd give anything to have legs just half as long as hers."

"You do have legs just half as long as hers."

Kathy pouted playfully. "Did you give my puzzle to The Mole?"

"Well, it wasn't your puzzle when I gave it to her."

"How long did it take her?"

"Oh, a long time," I lied. "A real long time."

Late that night, after we'd made love, I lay awake thinking. Luther was worried sick about his daughter, and I was worried sick about Luther. Though we hadn't been as close as we might have been since our respective retirements from the SPD, I liked Luther a lot and didn't want to see him go wrong. For a few moments as he thrashed around with Raymond and the others at the café, I had the feeling he was losing his mind. To my uneducated eye, Luther'd always been on the edge, and I was afraid he was about to go over.

The house was still enough that I could hear the ticking of the regulator clock in the living room. Kathy rolled over and, half asleep, snaked an arm across my bare chest and mumbled, "Still thinking about The Mole?"

"Please don't call her that. Her name is Sonya."

"You're the one who thought it up. On Groundhog Day you were waiting to see if she'd come out of hibernation."

"I know, but her name is Sonya."

"Yah, yah, yah," Kathy muttered as she drifted back to sleep.

CHAPTER 13

The robin chirping outside our window Sunday morning sounded like a drunk trying to whistle and pee at the same time. It seemed as if I'd been listening to it for hours when Luther Little, still looking for a speck upon which to build a house of hope, telephoned at five before seven.

"Thomas, old man," Luther said. "What's goin' on today?"

"I'm going down to Tacoma to talk to Peggy Lindseth, Aldrich's housemate, girlfriend, whatever she is."

"When?"

"You want to come?"

"Well, yeah."

"Can you make the office by eight-thirty?"

"I've got something I'm supposed to do, but I guess I can put it off. You sure this isn't imposing, man? If you think you can find Balinda better by yourself, I'll stay home. I worry better at home anyway."

"This'll work. Besides, I've got some information I want to go over with you."

When Kathy stopped me on my way out of the house, I thought sure she was going to say something about the renter in the basement, but what she said was, "Hey, Bud, can you get me another puzzle?"

"I might if you keep treating me right."

"You know I will."

Outside, the sky was blue and the morning was already beginning to warm up. I took I-5 downtown, parked on the street, and discovered Luther standing on the steps of the Mutual Life Building. Despite the warmth and the promise of more heat later in the day, he wore dress shoes, gray wool slacks, and a starched, button-down white shirt under a dark green windbreaker zipped almost to the neck. There was a logo over the left breast on the windbreaker: DIBBLE'S FUNERAL HOME.

He looked at me expectantly, as if I had Balinda in the car and had only come around the corner alone so I could spring a surprise. Despite the leaven of hope in his dark brown eyes, his voice was flat and hollow. "Hey, Thomas."

I unlocked the front door of the building, and we walked through the cool air of the lobby. Once the elevator doors were closed, Luther said, "I want to apologize for last night. I went a little crazy."

"Don't even think about it."

He wasn't making eye contact, so I didn't either. Luther and I had spent the majority of our time together sitting side by side in a patrol car looking forward and out the windows. We'd gotten to know each other without looking into each other's eyes, and we'd become friends without looking into each other's eyes, and Luther still felt most comfortable that way.

"I didn't have any right placing you in that type of situation," he said.

I studied his reflection in the polished brass on the elevator wall and thought he looked like a patient in Dr. Kevorkian's waiting room, eyes bloodshot, face puffy. "You get any sleep, Luther?"

"Yeah. I woke up early, but before that I got good sleep."

"What's early?"

"Two, two-thirty."

"You've been awake since two-thirty?"

He nodded.

Upstairs he took a seat in my office, declined my offer of coffee, probably because he knew I didn't know how to make it, and looked over my list of long distance numbers dialed from the Sands household in the past five weeks. There weren't many. Their monthly bill came to a little more than forty dollars. While he examined the list, I used a CD-ROM phone directory to obtain names and addresses for all of the numbers but one, which wasn't listed.

"Goddamn it!" Luther exclaimed.

"What is it?"

"That damn Laronda been callin' Charlie Cole in California. She told me she don't never have nothin' to do with Charlie, and here it is in black and white."

"Who's Charlie—"

"The skinny little fucker Laronda was messin' with after Lyle and Balinda was born. D'Witt's father? He don't have nothin' to do with them. He never paid no child support. He don't even care about his own crippled-up son. And here she is callin' him long distance."

"There are a lot of people with access to that phone. Maybe it was D'Witt."

He mulled it over. "D'Witt don't have nothin' to do with his father. D'Witt's bitter against Charlie. And look at this here. They was talkin' seventeen minutes. God*damn!*"

"Does Balinda know him?"

"Everybody in the family knows the way he done D'Witt. He run outta state after Laronda got pregnant. For fifteen years he paid no attention to the boy. Then after D'Witt got hisself shot up, he come up here and visited him in the hospital. *Once.* One time, Thomas. Just enough to give the boy hope that maybe there's a spark of goodness in the man. That's why it hurts to see her callin' him."

Luther fumed while we discussed the rest of the names and phone numbers. Some Luther recognized; some he did not. One was an obese girlfriend of Balinda's now living in Everett. Luther casually mentioned to me that he'd had sex with her when she and Balinda were still in high school. When he'd visited last week looking for Balinda, she had, according to Luther, offered to renew their intimacy, but he'd been too worried to think about sex. I did my best to ignore the story.

In the four weeks prior to the accident, eleven calls had been placed from the Sands household to Benjamin Aldrich's residence in Tacoma. Oddly, each call had been placed between four-thirty and six P.M., the last at 5:55 on Monday, the day of his death. Most of the calls had lasted around ten minutes. The last one had been two minutes.

CHAPTER 14

When we got down to the street, Luther announced he was driving.

"Let me, Luther. I'm not all that thrilled about riding around in a hearse."

"It ain't the hearse. I got my Saturn right over there." He pointed to a small red car parked on Yesler with a huge lump of laundry in the backseat. "Work with me, Thomas. I get carsick, somebody else drives. You know that. Besides, I think better behind the wheel."

We climbed into the Saturn, drove over to Fourth Avenue, and headed south on I-5. Tacoma was about an hour away, and Luther was talking nonstop like a nervous man who'd just witnessed the birth of his firstborn.

He recapped his life history for me. Luther was raised in Mississippi by his grandmother on his father's side, a woman who had herself been raised by *her* grandmother on *her* father's side. His grandmother's grandmother was a slave until she was sixteen years old and bore two babies into slavery. During the Civil War she lost track of her babies and her husband, never to see them again despite classified ads placed in all the major Southern papers over a period of twenty years.

The day after Luther turned seven, his father was murdered by a woman he was having an affair with, or so went the story handed down to Luther. The local police in Mississippi knew who the killer was, but she was never charged, arrested, or even questioned. Luther's explanation was that in the South in those days when "one nigger killed another nigger it was just one less nigger to worry about."

One way or another, most of the males in his family had died before the age of fifty, and Luther always said he would too. Dying was always high on his list of conversational topics during our infrequent phone contacts over the years. Now that he was past fifty, he figured he was coasting along on borrowed time.

Shortly after his father's murder, Luther's mother moved with his two older sisters to Seattle to seek work, assuring Luther she would send for him when she saved enough money. Luther was in high school by the time she saved enough money, his growing years dominated by his strict grandmother, a woman to whom he was still fiercely loyal and whom he visited three times a year in Mississippi. It was his grandmother who instilled in Luther a churchgoing philosophy of thrift, hard work, and family. It was his uncles, father, and grandfather who instilled a legacy of going after any woman who looked at him twice. Married or not, all the males in his family chased women, kept girlfriends, and patronized the occasional hooker. It was expected.

Unfortunately, by the time Luther's mother mailed him a bus ticket for Seattle, he'd built up an unbending grudge against her, a grudge he played out for years afterward.

Luther said, "We was so poor we thought a birthday cake was *supposed* to be a pile of bread with peanut butter on top. The dogs on the white side of town ate better than we did."

Once at the Police and Fire Olympics after Luther'd won a

gold medal in table tennis, an embittered rival from another city announced that Luther was a "lucky" winner and if all the luck were removed from Luther's game he wouldn't have medaled. After some angry discussion, Luther voiced the opinion that his opponent was so clumsy he could beat him without a paddle.

The bet was taken up.

A crowd gathered.

Luther won two games straight using a frying pan for a paddle.

Afterward Luther told me that until he was sixteen he'd never played Ping-Pong with anything *but* a frying pan. They'd been too poor to own actual paddles.

We took the Narrows Bridge exit off the freeway and drove Highway 16 past Cheney Stadium, where blooms of Scotch broom along the road glowed nuclear-yellow in the sunshine. We got off at Sixth Avenue, headed west for a couple of blocks, and then north on Pearl Street. It was Saturday morning, but traffic was heavy.

The apartment complex was about a mile away on a curving residential road with low apartments on one side, houses on the other, all within sight of a nine-hole golf course. I'd grown up in this part of Tacoma and recalled that for most of my childhood the area had been a huge, deserted golf course overgrown with wild grasses and California poppies.

Aldrich's apartment was in a rambling, brown-shingled, one-story building on the east side of the street, with thick conifers towering over the units and walkways.

We parked between an immaculate light blue Nissan pickup truck and an older, beat-up Chevy pickup full of household goods in a partially covered parking area to the north of the complex. Luther mumbled something about the Saturn's paint job and then made a show of locking and testing the doors.

As we walked into the small maze of pathways and shrubbery between the various apartments, a large, pinch-faced man in his sixties or early seventies staggered past us with a television set in his arms. He looked as if he needed help, but for some reason neither Luther nor I offered.

"What you gonna say to her?" Luther asked after we'd passed him.

"I don't know yet."

"You ain't gonna tell her Balinda has a drug history, are you?"

"Do you not want me to?"

"Whatever you think."

A hot wind blew through the walkway and flicked pine needles against our legs. An evergreen stood inside the tall wooden fence that enclosed the entrance to unit eighteen. Next to the trunk of the tree stood a picnic table with a grouping of small plants in plastic containers. All but two of the plants had withered and died.

The door was open, and through the screen we could see a fireplace, a small kitchen to the left, and a living room to the right with a tan couch and two matching recliners facing a wooden console filled with stereo equipment. On top of the console was a large, rectangular patch of dust.

The woman who came out from the interior of the apartment when we rang the doorbell was tall and angular and wore round spectacles with wire frames that gave her a dainty look. She was younger than I expected, probably not yet twenty-five. Her cotton slacks were rumpled, but her white button-up blouse was ironed into military pleats. She wore spotless white deck shoes without socks or laces. Her dishwater-blond hair was pulled back into a bouncy little ponytail and exposed a pair of small, oddly shaped ears with tiny diamond studs in them. Her eyes were blue and unwavering. Her nose was fine-boned and long. Her mouth was wide, but her lips were mostly lipstick and pucker. She looked taller than Luther, but that turned out to be an illusion when I saw them next to each other.

"I'm Peggy Lindseth," she said, sticking out a hand, which,

despite the weather, was as cold as meat just out of the refrigerator. Her grasp was weak, and she was quick to disengage it.

She asked to see my ID, which I thought just a tad precious. It had been years since anybody had asked to see it. I showed her my driver's license as well as my P.I. license, and she studied them both intently. I might have brought out my library card, but I had a feeling she wouldn't have been amused.

She gestured for us to take a seat on a low sofa on the other side of the room. I sat behind the coffee table. Luther walked across the room with me but remained standing. Peggy Lindseth sat in a hard-backed chair near the window. Behind her we could see the picnic table in the tiny courtyard enclosure. She sat with her knees together, her heels up, only her toes touching the floor. She clasped her thin arms around her knees and leaned forward. The room had the same orderly yet slightly untended look she did.

"So. What is it you want to talk about?"

"First off, I'd like to tell you how sorry we both are that Benjamin was killed. This must be a very hard time for you."

"It is. Thank you."

"You were both living here?"

"Yes. We were going to get married. His father didn't like it, but we were. We met at school last year. I was student teaching at Truman, where he teaches fifth grade. He was a terrific teacher."

It wasn't until the pinch-faced old man we'd seen lugging the television set on the causeway came in that I realized the dusty patch on the console correlated with the television he'd had. The two recliners, lined up with the dusty spot, were tipped back as if their occupants had only gotten out of them minutes ago. I wondered if anybody had touched them since Monday night.

Without uttering a word, the old man glanced at Luther, then me, then stepped through the living room and into one of the rear bedrooms.

"Ben's father," Peggy Lindseth said, without emotion. "He's come to pick up a few things."

It seemed to me like a rather cold-blooded enterprise to be about so soon after his son's death, though Peggy didn't appear perturbed. In fact, the presence of Aldrich's father grubbing through his dead son's belongings bothered Luther and me more than it seemed to bother Peggy Lindseth.

"So you were both teachers?"

"Yes. At first the kids were told he passed away in a car accident, but then it got out that he'd been shot. It's so hard to accept. They've brought in a counselor to help the kids deal with it."

She was so matter-of-fact that she was about half a page away from not being involved at all. It was odd, in times of stress, how quickly most people learned to counterfeit normalcy.

CHAPTER 15

"**C**an you tell us what happened Monday night?" I asked.

Peggy took a deep breath and her voice dropped to a whisper. "I wish I knew. Ben said he was going to drive up to Seattle, and the next I knew I got a call from the police saying he'd been shot and to come identify him."

"You drove up there?"

"They had him in Harborview Hospital. In a room just off the emergency room."

"Do you know why Ben was in Seattle that night?"

"He didn't say."

"Did he often travel to Seattle?"

"He had been lately. A couple of times a week."

"How long had this been going on?"

"The last month or so."

"He never told you what he was doing up there?"

"No."

"You weren't curious?"

"He said it was complicated and he would explain later when he had it figured out."

A barrage of noises erupted in the hallway, and then all was quiet. We stopped talking, and a few moments later the old man marched past the fireplace with a cardboard box clasped against his barrel chest, unlatched the screen door with the fingers of one hand, and kicked at the door as if it were a stray dog trying to dirty his lawn. Again I found it interesting that there were three of us within spitting distance and none of us volunteered to help. I waited for the door to slam, but it closed slowly on a pneumatic mechanism.

"Can you think of anybody who might have wanted to kill your fiancé?" I asked.

"Of course not. Everybody loved Ben. He was the nicest, kindest man you could ever meet. The kids at school adored him." She brushed back a tear with her bony hand and said, "All I can think is that it was one of those road rage deals where somebody gets cut off or something and they go insane and start shooting."

I'd noticed Luther had left the interview to me, his only participation to turn his head a couple of times at noises in the rear of the apartment.

"Do you know a young woman named Balinda Sands?"

"Who?"

"Sands. Balinda Sands."

"I don't believe so."

"A young black woman about your age?"

"No."

"She's Mr. Little's daughter. It was her car your boyfriend was in when he died."

"What was he doing in her car?"

"That's one of the things we were hoping you could tell us. She's been missing since the accident, and the police think she was the driver."

"A detective told me some of this, but I was pretty shook up when we spoke."

"Arnold Haldeman?"

"Yes. He's been incredibly sweet."

Luther and I exchanged a look. The fact that Peggy Lind-seth was young and trim and blonde and, most of all, female, had no doubt influenced Haldeman's demeanor, because the Haldeman we knew was about as sweet as a pickle sandwich.

The old man came back in and strode through the living room and into the rear of the apartment without glancing at us. We heard a cardboard box being dragged around on the carpet.

"Would you rather wait to finish this until we're alone?" I asked.

She spoke in a whisper. "I don't know how long he'll be here. It's just . . . he never approved of our living together. He said it was immoral."

"To live together?" Luther asked, his voice climbing an octave.

"He didn't like it one bit when Ben moved out of their house."

"Ben didn't have his own place when you met?" I asked.

"He was saving money for the future. Living at home and saving money. Ben liked to plan ahead."

"You don't know anything at all about why Ben was going to Seattle?" I said. "Surely, he told you something."

"All I know is about a month ago Ben went over to see his mother and came back very upset. He stayed upset. But he wouldn't talk about whatever was bothering him."

"His mother lives here in town?"

"Over off Thirtieth above the bay."

"And that's when the trips to Seattle started? After this talk with his mother?"

"Yes."

"He didn't tell you what his mother said?"

"Ben wasn't talking a lot lately. He's been having problems dealing with his mother's illness. She doesn't have long to live."

"I'm sorry to hear that. Do you think his being upset after visiting his mother a month ago was related to her illness?"

"Maybe. Like I said, he didn't want to talk about it."

"The police found nine birth certificates in the car at the accident scene. Do you know anything about them?"

"I can't say that I do."

The old man announced his presence by clearing his throat. When I looked up, he was standing in front of the fireplace that formed a divider between the tiny kitchen and the living room.

He was a thick-chested man in a dingy button-up shirt and a pair of baggy, torn trousers that had been half of a suit maybe thirty years ago. A crop of gray hair bloomed at the neck of his shirt and ran around the back of his collar. His eyebrows looked like dust bunnies, and his thick features were scrunched together from top to bottom, as if somebody'd put his head in a vise and cranked down real hard. He had thick lips, large freckles, coarse skin, brown eyes, and thinning grayish hair. The landscape of his face was pitted with fresh shaving nicks. A drunk would have done a better job shaving. But then maybe he *was* a drunk.

He said, "I probably should get that ring now and the keys to Ben's pickup."

Peggy held up her left hand and eyed the engagement ring as if neither the ring nor the finger were hers. "This ring?" Her voice suddenly sounded like a girl's.

"Yeah. Give it here."

CHAPTER 16

The old man was so casual about it you almost wouldn't think there was anything aberrant about a father coming to his dead son's fiancée and removing the diamond from her knuckle.

Peggy took it off her finger and held it to the light for a few moments, then slipped it back on and said very quietly, "No."

"By rights the ring belongs to his mother," Aldrich said.

"I'm sure she's got plenty of rings." Peggy took a set of keys out of a dish on the table, removed one of them, and handed it to Aldrich. "Here's the key to Ben's truck. The ring belongs to me."

"I don't want to have to pay a lawyer over this. I'm just trying to make it as easy as possible on all of us."

Peggy said, "Do whatever you think is right."

Old man Aldrich disappeared into the back bedroom as if the conversation had never taken place.

Peggy looked from Luther to me. "Do you think you might stay for a while?"

"Sure."

"Thank you."

A few moments later the old man went outside with another box of his son's belongings.

"I know this is an awkward question," Luther said, "but did he ever do drugs?"

"Good God, no. Mister . . . I'm sorry. I forgot your name." Aldrich's father passed through the room again and left with an armful of clothing. He seemed to be rushing his pace, as if Peggy Lindseth's denying him the ring had given him the idea she might change her mind about everything else.

"Little," Luther said.

"Mr. Little, I don't know where you got the impression Ben was some sort of bad person, but nothing could be further from the truth. He was a fifth-grade teacher. He went to church. He had *me* going to church."

"Luther's daughter was involved with drugs at one time," I said, "and we thought there might be some point of intersection there."

Luther gave me a stony look.

She spoke quickly. "Ben never did any kind of drugs. He even chewed me out because I told him we smoked marijuana once in a while in the sorority."

"What about the old man? What's going on there? He's in there collecting everything but the spit off Ben's pillow," I said.

"He took his toothbrush," she said.

Old man Aldrich came back in and left immediately with another armful of clothing, again without making eye contact.

I noticed a photo montage on the wall near the hallway. More for the interaction with Peggy than for information, I walked over to it and said, "Is Ben here?"

Peggy walked over to me as if floating across the carpet and pointed him out. He was a youthful-looking thirty with short-cropped hair and dark eyes. He was a slight young man, not as slight as Peggy, but of the same body type, more bone and sinew than anything else. In the photos he had perfect posture, mild-mannered features, but an incredibly intense look. It was the look a teenage boy had when he was going through troubles, the look a lot of young men never outgrew. It was the look Luther'd had as a boy, the look Luther still carried much of the time. I didn't have to guess what sort of father the old man in the other room had been. Then again, he couldn't have been too terrible, not if Benjamin had been living at home until last year. Or had Benjamin been too dominated to move out?

Luther asked to use the bathroom and disappeared down the short hallway.

"Did Ben have any black friends?" I asked.

Peggy seemed more inclined to talk after Luther was gone, leaning toward me and whispering as if to keep her confidences from both old man Aldrich and Luther. "I've never thought about it. I guess he did. He was in a volleyball league where about half his team is black. We've had the whole team over for dinner at one time or another. They helped us move in together."

"Wasn't it odd that at midnight he would be fifty miles away when he had to be in school the next morning?"

"Actually, Ben didn't have to be at school until late. Monday and Tuesday were teacher planning days."

"What time did he leave Monday night?"

"I was watching television. I don't really know."

"Before or after dinner?"

"After."

"What'd you watch on television?"

"You'll have to forgive me, Mr. Black. This whole week has been a blur. To make it worse, our principal expects me to show up Monday and teach. I feel like the world has ended and I'm the only one who noticed."

"I'm sorry. When were you scheduled to be married?"

"This August, but we postponed it because of Ben's mother."

The phone rang. Peggy Lindseth let it ring twice before she moved, and then when she did, it was with a surprising torpor, as if she feared more bad news and didn't want to hear it any sooner than necessary.

The phone was in a small nook in a wooden shelf unit against the wall in the eating area. After listening for a moment, she said, "No. I don't think so. Not now. No. I'm not sure when." Then she turned her face to the wall in the kitchen, and I could no longer identify her words.

When she came back into the living room, she sat in the same chair in the same position she'd been in earlier. She was a clear-eyed young woman, and the glasses made her look intelligent, perhaps more intelligent than she actually was.

"Let me get this straight," I said. "Ben spoke to his mother about a month ago. He didn't tell you what they discussed, but it prompted some trips to Seattle."

"I guess. Yes."

"And then Monday night he said he was going to Seattle, left the house, and the next thing you knew you were getting a call from the Seattle police?"

"Yes."

The old man was in the room now, his back to the fireplace, studying the photographs on the wall, the same ones Peggy had shown me minutes earlier. He started to reach for one of them, but Peggy was across the room like a rookie stealing second base. She wedged herself between Aldrich and the wall, looked penetratingly into the old man's eyes and said, "No."

"I want those pictures."

"If you want them, you can ask like a civilized person."

He reached again, and again she moved in front of his arm.

"It's time for you to leave," she said.

"I got stuff to get."

"No. You're finished."

"I'm not finished."

"I think you are," I said, standing.

They stared at each other for a moment. He turned and glanced around the apartment. "I know he bought those chairs."

"I'm paying for those," Peggy said. "I have the bills in the kitchen if you need to see them."

Aldrich turned to me, glanced around the apartment one last time, and marched out. He'd been trying to take every last bit of his son that he could, and now, thwarted, he moved heavily, anger contorting his thick features. I could only guess how he might have reacted had Luther and I not been there, but I had the feeling it wouldn't have been the same.

After he was gone, Peggy laughed scornfully. "I don't want any trouble with Ben's father. I'm sure he's just . . . I'm sure it's the pressure of the situation. He was never like this before. They only had Ben. No other kids. You know, I'm beginning to believe he thinks I'm responsible for Ben's death."

"People get funny ideas when they lose someone."

"Don't I know it? Thursday I set fire to the stove."

Luther came out of the bathroom and said, "Did your fiancé know anybody in Seattle before last month?"

"He had a cousin up there, but I never met him. I don't think he was visiting his cousin."

Moments later I excused myself to use the facilities while Luther chatted with Lindseth. Situated at the end of the narrow hallway, it was a tiny bathroom with a tub/shower enclosure and a small pebbled-glass window that looked out onto the covered tarmac parking area where Luther'd parked his Saturn. The window was open two inches, and there was a large, shod footprint in the bottom of the tub where Luther had stood to peer out. I'd never seen anybody more worried about his ride. Luther's last personal vehicle had been a decrepit Volkswagen bug, so this Saturn must have seemed like a hand-built Ferrari to him.

In the parking lot, Benjamin Aldrich's father leaned against a panel of his pickup smoking a cigar.

As I washed my hands I noticed that the rim of the white porcelain sink was dotted with half a dozen fine, tightly curled black hairs. I took a tissue and wiped them off. Luther had been in here a long time, snooping, keeping watch on his car, combing his hair. I opened the medicine cabinet, but there was nothing in it that might belong to a man. On the back of the door two bathrobes hung like ghosts, a long one and a short one, his and hers. The old man must have had the door open and didn't see them.

When I came out, Luther was gone and Peggy Lindseth was standing by the half-open front door, a signal that I could either ignore or take as an invitation to exit.

"Listen," I said. "I know it's none of my business, but you can select what you want to hand over and give it to him on some neutral ground. You don't have to let him come back."

"I wasn't planning on it."

"And I'm sorry about your fiancé."

"Thank you."

I was halfway out the door when she called out. "Mr. Black?"

"Yes?"

"There is one other thing."

"What is it?"

"Ben told me he thought his father had been following him around. Ben couldn't figure out why he would do such a thing, and I still find it hard to believe."

"Neither one of you had a theory?"

"Nope."

"Did Ben seem frightened of him?"

"No, just puzzled."

"Thanks for talking to us."

"You're welcome. And Mr. Black? If you find out who killed Benjamin, would you do me a favor and give me a call?"

"I will."

She seemed like a pleasant, if somewhat passionless, woman of more than modest intelligence, and the subtext of our polite discussion was that her heart was broken and probably would be forever.

To my surprise when I reached the covered carports outside, Luther was absorbed in conversation with old man Aldrich.

CHAPTER 17

From their body language and facial expressions, I couldn't judge what sort of interchange they were having, but as I drew closer, Luther gave me a look he clearly thought signified something, though I could make nothing of it.

"Thomas, this here is George Aldrich."

We shook hands. A little more pressure and he might have broken my hand. His eyes were as hard as river stones. It didn't take a genius to realize the easiest handshakes to analyze were those bequeathed by people trying to analyze yours, and I thought about this as we wrestled.

He was an ugly man, almost completely bald, untended wisps rising like small clouds in no particular pattern off his shiny scalp. He had a bulbous nose, a large, formless mouth, and widely spaced teeth that were brownish-yellow, as if he'd been drinking coffee and smoking since he was eight.

"Thomas," Luther said, smiling, "this here's the former landlord of our church. He owned property all over the Central District. He owned that building Catfish Café is in. I think he still owns it."

"Yep," Aldrich said, moving the cigar around in his mouth again.

If he had at one time been a prosperous landowner, he certainly didn't look the part now. Or were his battered pickup truck and shabby clothes only props in an elaborate act?

"Mr. Aldrich here used to give me and Raymond work cleanin' up his rentals after people moved out," Luther said. "Mr. Aldrich? I just had Mrs. Scott in my car yesterday. You remember Mrs. Scott?"

"Can't say as I do."

"Frances Scott? She ran that church. She was the one used to send you the checks."

"I don't recollect the name."

Luther looked disappointed.

Aldrich turned to me. "Luther here tells me you're a private investigator."

I'd indulged quite a grudge watching him clean out Peggy Lindseth's apartment, and not wanting to give it up, I delayed interaction as long as possible. I shrugged.

He continued, "He tells me his daughter was driving the automobile they found my boy in."

After a few seconds I said, "It was his daughter's car."

Aldrich munched on his smoldering cigar, which smelled like a small, dead, burning animal. He was a man's man, the type who would make a good drill master or football coach at a youth reformatory, the type of man for whom the bureaucrats might find a thousand mechanistic uses during a war and almost no sociable ones afterward.

"I can't figure it," Aldrich said. "Nobody can tell me what my boy was doin' in Seattle at midnight. And that little Mickey Rooney look-alike from Homicide, Haldeman—he never even told me about Luther's daughter."

It took me a second to realize that what he meant was nobody had told him his son was with a black woman. The information seemed to unsettle him. It shouldn't have made any difference to anybody that Balinda was black, but if it made a difference to Aldrich, it was an angle that Luther and I should take into consideration. The younger Aldrich wouldn't be the first to get his old man's goat by crossing racial lines in the bedroom. Maybe that was why George had been following him.

I said, "If you don't trust Haldeman, you're in good company. But he does his job."

"I don't see anybody in jail."

"Mr. Aldrich," I said, "your son's visits to Seattle seem to have begun after a talk with your wife. Do you know anything about that?"

Aldrich looked genuinely puzzled. "Who told you that?"

"Do you think we could speak to your wife?"

Aldrich looked from me to Luther and back to Luther. "*Anything* Ben did would have begun after a talk with my wife. Ben came over and saw Mary every afternoon."

"Usually left around four-thirty, five?" I said, remembering that the phone calls from the Sands house to Aldrich's had been placed between five and six.

"How did you know that?"

"I figured he'd want to be home for dinner." Had Peggy Lindseth come home directly from school, or had obligations kept her away until six, which seemed to have been the cutoff time for Balinda's calls?

"So, you two are doing what?" Aldrich asked.

"We're looking for Luther's daughter," I said.

"How do I know his daughter . . ." He turned to Luther. "How do I know your daughter didn't have anything to do with Ben's death? Hell, maybe she shot him. I could very well be standing here talking to the father of the girl who killed my boy."

Luther swallowed his anger and said, "If you knew Balinda, you wouldn't say that. She's not capable of hurting anybody."

"Why? Is she crippled?"

He'd rendered Luther speechless.

I said, "She's got a little girl. She's a good person."

"I still want to know what was going on," Aldrich said, bottlenecking both of his large hands into his trousers pockets. "*My* son was with *your* daughter."

"That's what the police think," Luther said.

"On a date?"

"You don't have to look at me like that," Luther said. "Black people date white people."

"I didn't mean anything by it. Don't get touchy now. You're taking the wrong attitude here."

"I don't have no attitude," Luther said angrily. Although Luther would have denied it, I'd always thought of him as a man who spent his life waiting for whites to slip up and betray their innate bigotry. From what I knew of his life, he hadn't been disappointed too often.

I said, "Why don't you help us find Balinda, and then we can all ask her what they were doing."

"My wife is ill." Aldrich took the cigar out of his mouth and rolled the wet spot between his fat thumb and index finger. I wondered if he'd done that before we shook hands. "To tell you the God's honest truth, she doesn't even know about Ben."

"His mother doesn't know he's dead?" Luther was not only angry, now he was incredulous.

Aldrich looked at Luther and then turned to me, as if I might understand where Luther wouldn't. "She's been terminal for months. I'm afraid if I tell her, it will put her over the edge."

"You don't want us to talk to her?" I asked.

"You can talk to her, but only if you don't tell her about Ben."

"Doesn't she wonder where he is?" Luther asked.

"I told her he was taking a trip out of state for the school."

"What are you going to tell her when he doesn't come back?" Luther wasn't going to let it drop.

Stuffing the cigar back into his mouth, Aldrich chewed on it and stared at us wordlessly.

"So you haven't had a service?" I asked.

"I don't know what to do about that." He nodded toward the apartment we'd just left. "*She* wants one."

"It seems like when a fella goes on beyond, he deserves a service," Luther said.

When Aldrich didn't answer, I said, "Your wife's in the hospital?"

"Home. We got a nurse."

"We'd sure love to talk to her."

Casting a look at the apartments, Aldrich discarded his cigar stub onto the driveway and headed for his truck. "Follow me," he said.

Once we'd closed the doors of the Saturn, Luther muttered in a mocking tone, "*My* son was going with *your* daughter? *My* son? *Your* daughter? Lah-di-dah. He talked like Balinda was covered in horseshit."

"Keep calm. We have to be nice."

"When we was growin' up, Raymond and me thought Aldrich was a decent kinda guy. Jesus, that must have been thirty, thirty-five years ago. He gave us work. Paid good too. He even went to Raymond's first grown-up trial and spoke up for him. I always thought he was a stand-up guy."

"This isn't a great week to be giving him a character test," I said, wondering why I was defending the man. "His only son was just murdered."

"He's a goddamned racist."

"I imagine he is. He's also a tough old cob."

"He definitely is that. I remember a couple punks tried to rob him—he musta been almost forty then—he busted 'em up, broke their arms, I mean all four of their arms, put 'em both in the hospital."

Before Luther cleared the parking area, Aldrich was speeding down the residential street. Luther took a right turn and followed him but evidently didn't understand our situation. "He's trying to lose us," I said.

Taking a right-hand turn off of Highlands Parkway onto

Westgate Boulevard, Aldrich's pickup was already two blocks ahead. I didn't think it likely the old man routinely drove this way, but you couldn't go wrong overestimating how badly somebody else could drive.

Luther, of course, knew how to drive fast, a predilection city cops had by training, tradition, and inclination, but abusing his own car went against his nature. Losing ground, we trailed the pickup north on Pearl Street, and if we hadn't already believed Aldrich was intentionally trying to get rid of us, the breath of black smoke that came out his tailpipe when we were caught by the red light and he wasn't would have convinced us.

The whole thing made me uncomfortable, because it was a Saturday morning and we were parading through areas of heavy housing where kids might be playing. As I was about to tell Luther to call it off, the lump of laundry in the backseat shifted and crashed against the rear window in the midst of a particularly sharp cornering maneuver.

"That old bird," Luther said. "That old bird. He *is* tryin' to get loose of us."

"What was that in back?"

"That old bird."

"It sounded like somebody hit his head on the back window."

"That old bird."

At the bottom of the now-disheveled heap of laundry I spotted a pair of brown knit socks that looked almost as if they had feet in them. It scared me until I realized they *were* feet. I'd been wondering all along why Luther was driving around with two weeks' worth of laundry stacked on his backseat.

Twisting around, I dug under the clothes and uncovered a gaunt black man who had probably been close to eighty before he died. His eyes were open and his skin was ashen and he'd already stiffened up pretty good.

"Luther! You've got a dead man in the backseat."

"Huh?"

"Damn it, man. What's going to happen if you get into an accident and the police show up? Slow down."

He didn't answer me for a block or two. When he finally spoke, his voice was high-pitched, almost impish. Luther didn't have a lot of play in him, but for some reason dead people brought out what little he had.

"Thomas, meet Joseph Dixon. Joe? Thomas Black."

"That's not even remotely funny, Luther."

"Joe left us about five o'clock this morning. I didn't know what to do. It was my pickup. The hearse is having engine problems, so I couldn't use that, and the van was on another job, so I scooted on over there first thing this morning thinking I could get rid of him real quick, but then I called you and you were in such an all-fired rush."

We were crossing Orchard Street now, heading into Old Tacoma, an area of classic, stately homes and quiet, tree-lined streets. Puget Sound was about a mile away to the north, and even though Luther'd roped Aldrich now and was only a few car lengths back, the old man didn't slow. At one point I thought I saw the pickup tilt onto two wheels rounding a corner.

"What're ya gonna do?" Luther asked, intent on his driving.

"What can I do? I'm not taking a cab back to Seattle."

"That would cost a heap."

"I wonder what it would cost to send Mr. Dixon back in a cab."

"You can't send him back in no cab."

"How about a Greyhound bus?"

"That wouldn't be sanctified."

"And this is?"

"I got a license. I got me a license to transport dead people."

"Right." I began tossing loose laundry back onto the corpse. "Geez, Luther. I thought you guys used body bags."

"I forgot it. Like I said, you seemed in a big hurry."

"This is why we had to drive down here in your car."

"At least this way he got the air-conditioning. Instead of stuffing him in the trunk."

"The trunk? That's an idea."

"No you don't, Thomas. He rides with us."

"Yeah. I guess the trunk wouldn't be sanctified," I said sarcastically.

Aldrich led us into a pleasant neighborhood of turn-of-the-century homes just off Thirtieth high on the hill overlooking Commencement Bay, Dalco Passage, and Vashon Island to the north. The truck turned down a steep hillside and showed us brake lights as it swung into the driveway of a large old home on the side of a hill. The house was on a sloping corner lot, so it showed two stories approached from the street side on Thirtieth, three and a half stories approached from the downslope side. There wasn't room for us to park beside him in the driveway, so Luther was forced to go down past the house, turn around in the intersection, and drive back up the hill.

Stopping on the steep hill and rolling his window down, Luther said, "Where do you want us to park?"

From the look on the old man's face, he thought he'd ditched us. He gestured with his head. Luther drove up the hill and stopped the Saturn on Thirtieth beside a laurel hedge. Thirtieth was a wide, suburban thoroughfare with little traffic.

I got out of the car while Luther opened one of the back doors and fussed with the dead man for almost a minute.

"I put it all back already," I said.

"You don't put a pair of undershorts over a man's face. That was plain disrespectful."

"And hauling him all over the countryside is not?"

Ignoring me, Luther locked the Saturn and strode jauntily across the sidewalk into Aldrich's yard. Even as a cop, intimate contact with the dead had always brightened his outlook.

"I still can't believe you did this," I said.

"In my business you get used to dead people."

"Next thing I know, you'll be flying corpses down to Disneyland with you. Collecting frequent flier miles for them."

"Tell you one thing I do. If they're ridin' up front with me and the freeway's jammed, I unzip the bag a little and we ride in the car pool lane. It's always a nicer ride in the car pool lane."

CHAPTER 18

It was a huge brick house befitting old money: banking or
shipping or maybe horseless carriages. The shrubs in the yard
showed traces of previous professional care, though my guess
was Aldrich paid some kid up the street to groom them. I
couldn't help thinking how out of place the rusty old pickup
looked at the side of the house, and for a minute or so as we
waited, I entertained the notion that Aldrich had deceived us
and was merrily driving to his real home even as we cooled
our heels.

"He's probably unloading the truck," Luther said, for once
more optimistic than I.

"I guess if we were gentlemen, we'd go down and help,"
I said.

Luther looked at me and laughed. "All the money this
man's got, and he's over across town lifting a TV set from his
son's girlfriend. Can you imagine?"

"Grief does funny things to people." We both knew Luther
had been drunk for the best part of a year after Lyle died.

"That girlfriend. She's holding back. You could see that,
couldn't you, Thomas?"

"Yeah. I saw it."

"And this old bird here," Luther said. "A man this prickly doesn't raise a son who isn't screwed up."

"No, probably not."

"I looked all over that baffroom, but I didn't see any signs of drugs," Luther said. "She musta cleaned it up."

"Or he really was clean."

"You don't have to be a dirtbag to get all fucked up with crack, Thomas. You don't have to be anything but stupid for one minute. It don't take but one puff on the pipe and you got a fishhook through your gills. That's how it happens. One day you're a normal human bein' and the next day you're stealing grandma's car."

"Balinda took Pookie's car?"

"Drove it to Minnesota, where she tried to sell it to a state cop. That's how screwed up dope can make you. That's why I was lookin' for dope in the baffroom."

"I thought you were standing in the tub scoping out the parking lot. I saw your footprints."

Luther smiled. "I had to check out the window on Paul. I don't want nobody stealing him. He's my responsibility until I get him on over to Dibble's."

The front door opened and Aldrich appeared in the cool, shadowed foyer. He said, "Don't forget what I told you."

"We won't," I said.

Aldrich walked us through the dark interior of the house to a living area with a wall of picture windows looking out over Commencement Bay. To the north we could see Vashon Island, to the northeast Browns Point near where I'd once found a dead man on the beach. The sunny sky had a veiled haze to it so that in the distance the water and the air seemed to merge and become a mirage of gray. In the bay a pack of small sailboats tacked back and forth in the chop, and a far-away speedboat generated a small white wake.

The room we had entered was devoid of furniture except for a nightstand, a couple of sitting chairs, and a regulation hospital bed with a large canister of oxygen next to it. A woman in green slacks, a multicolored smock, and a white nurse's cap stood beside the bed, which had been angled so the patient could see out the windows.

The woman in bed looked as if she could be George Aldrich's mother rather than his wife. She was so small there seemed to be nothing under the covers, just a head on a pillow. She had wispy white hair, watery blue eyes, and sagging cheeks that looked too soft to touch. Her bare arm above the bedclothes was withered and bruised from needles.

When she opened her mouth to speak, her teeth were long and narrow and appeared to curve inward, as if they'd been meant for somebody with an even narrower head. I wondered immediately what she'd looked like as a young woman— delicate and pretty, I guessed, probably not unlike Peggy Lindseth. For some reason the curiosity of it nagged at me all during our interview.

"Who have you brought to me, George?" She looked at us without moving her head, then slowly rolled on the pillows stacked up under her so that we were square in her sight.

Aldrich said, "Mary, these men are trying to track down a friend of Ben's. They thought you might have some information."

"A friend of Ben's?"

Though it was reedy and croaking, her voice was stronger than I'd expected. She looked at Luther until she understood Luther wasn't going to be the one asking questions. It was interesting for me to recognize that Luther and I had fallen into a pattern we'd often used as street cops. He quizzed the black witnesses, I the white ones.

When she turned her eyes to me, I said, "My name is Thomas Black, ma'am. Did Ben ever mention a young woman named Balinda Sands?"

"Sands?" George Aldrich tucked the butt of the cigar into his cheek. "I thought she was *his* daughter. You said his name was Little."

"Her mother and I ain't married," Luther said. "I wish we was, but we ain't."

"George?" Aldrich stepped close to his wife's bed and took her hand in both of his huge, work-hardened mitts. "George, why don't you leave me alone with these gentlemen? Would you do that?"

"Mary, are you—"

"A couple of minutes, George. We'll talk later."

Aldrich left, and so did the nurse. He didn't seem pleased, but then, even though he'd agreed, he hadn't seemed particularly pleased about having us in the house either.

While they paraded out of the room, I took the opportunity to look around. The foyer had been crowded with plant stands, a hat rack and umbrella holder, and a lighted display case containing knickknacks, porcelain figurines, and a miniature tea set. The room Aldrich and the nurse had retreated through contained a cherry dining set, a china cabinet and sideboard. Yet, there was nothing in this enormous room but the bed, a nightstand, two chairs, and a small pair of binoculars perched on a window ledge.

"Mr. Black? Mr. Little?" Mary Aldrich said.

"Yes."

"You're police officers here about my son, Ben, aren't you?"

"Not exactly," I said. "We're here about Mr. Little's daughter, Balinda Sands. We're trying to locate her."

"I don't understand."

"Mrs. Aldrich, your son's girlfriend said he spoke to you about something a month ago, something important enough that she noticed a change in him."

"It was time for him to know some things."

"Can you tell us what those things were?"

Luther moved to the window and peered at the rooftops on the hillside below.

"You think this might be related to Mr. Little's daughter?" she asked.

"We do."

"Then look in that nightstand drawer."

The drawer was as messy as the room was tidy, jammed with newspaper clippings, pill bottles, pencils, paper clips, reading glasses, expired lotto tickets, old keys, and other items of no consequence. In the back I found a small manila envelope secured by a tie string. I took it out and offered it to Mary Aldrich, who said, "You open it."

Inside was a swatch of baby hair held together with clear tape, a small plastic band of the type hospitals put on a newborn's wrist or ankle, and a birth certificate, Benjamin Aldrich's, dated April 29, thirty years earlier. It listed Mary Aldrich as his mother, George Aldrich as his father. The swatch of hair was sand-colored and extremely fine, and I had no doubt it had come off a baby. The plastic band was identified as coming from Swedish Hospital in Seattle. The name had been scissored out.

"Benjamin just turned thirty?" I said.

"Yes. I'm going to tell you something now, and I want you to promise you won't tell my husband. Will you promise me that?"

"If that's what you want." Secrets seemed to be this family's stock-in-trade.

"I knew there were things that had to be said before I died or they wouldn't be said at all. So I showed Ben that envelope you're holding."

I was still trying to make sense of the nine birth certificates found in the car at the crash site. Clearly, we were getting close.

"Do you folks know what happens in this state when a baby is adopted?" Mary Aldrich asked. "They make a new birth certificate that looks as if the baby was born to the adoptive parents. They put the adoptive mother and the adoptive father on the certificate as if that child was actually born to them at that time and date."

"Benjamin was adopted?"

"Yes. I told him about it a month ago."

"How did he take it?"

"He told me he wanted to locate his birth mother and speak to her. It annoyed me, but I knew he would. My night nurse was adopted, and he told me how Ben would probably feel."

"Who were Ben's real parents?"

"I don't know. This sounds like some kind of fairy tale, I know, but out of the blue one night somebody rang the bell, and when I opened the door, there he was in this little wicker basket all wrapped up in his little blankets. You see, dear, all of our friends knew we wanted a baby. I thought somebody in our circle had an unmarried daughter or niece who'd gotten pregnant. I thought they'd decided to give the baby a good home but were too embarrassed to own up to it. Thirty years ago it wasn't fashionable to have a baby out of wedlock the way it is today."

"You didn't see who left the baby?"

"It was late. George was out of town on business. And there was this baby, couldn't have been more than three days old. I had Ben for two nights and two days before George came home, and by then I wasn't going to give him up for anything. We had our lawyer contact some people, and we eventually put through the paperwork that more or less turned it into a legal adoption. It cost a little, but George and the lawyer managed it."

"And you never told Benjamin he was adopted?"

"Not until a month ago."

"It must have been a shock."

"Yes, it was."

"There wasn't a note? Anything to give you a hint of who his parents were?"

"Only that Swedish Hospital wristband."

"Somebody's cut the name off the band."

"That's how it was when I found the baby. The parents must have cut it out so that we couldn't trace them, but I guess they wanted us to know his birthday, so they left the band. Ben and I didn't talk about it. He just took it out and looked at it. That's the pity of this family. Nobody talks about anything. George and I still haven't discussed my illness. We drive to the hospital. We listen to the doctors. We come home. We don't mention it. We haven't spoken of the adoption since it happened. That's another reason why I'd prefer you didn't mention this to George. I don't think he would look favorably on the fact that I told Ben."

"Did Ben find his birth parents?"

"He came back and asked more questions, so I have reason to believe he was working on it."

"What questions?"

"Oh, nothing I was able to answer for him. I don't know any more about his birth than what I've just told you. You know, the irony of this is that Ben resembled George in so many ways. The way he walked. The way he held his head. Even his mad-scientist hair. Sometimes the way he spoke. When he found out he was adopted, it was difficult for him. I tried to tell him young boys idolize their fathers and subconsciously pick up all sorts of traits and mannerisms."

"So you don't believe he found his birth parents?"

"Not that he ever told me. Now, may I ask you a question?"

"Sure," I said, glancing at Luther.

"Was Mr. Little's daughter involved in my son's death?"

I glanced at Luther again. "You know about your son's death?"

"Jim, the night nurse. We don't have many secrets. I wake up and need somebody to talk to. Jim and I talk. I'm still waiting for George to tell me. I think he just doesn't know how to say it, or else he thinks I'm not strong enough to hear it."

"I'm sorry about your son."

"I am too, Mr. Black. It seems like our lives are long, but compared to the rest of what's here, they're not. I'll be leaving shortly, and in the grand scheme of things, so will you. People like to push it out of their minds, especially young people, but it's an obligatory trip, and our tickets are all pre-paid. I feel bad for Peggy, because she would have had a good life with Ben. And she has so many more years to grieve than I do."

George Aldrich appeared in the doorway and motioned for one of us to come over. I stayed put while Luther walked behind the hospital bed and quietly conferred with him. After a few moments Luther gave me a beleaguered look and left the room with Aldrich.

"Mr. Black? Will you do an old woman a favor? Will you leave without telling my husband we've spoken of this?"

"If you wish."

"I do wish. Mr. Black, I know you're looking for Mr. Little's daughter and that has to take priority, but after you've found her, will you keep on? Will you find my son's killer for me? I'll write you a check for whatever it costs. You leave a card, and we'll mail it to your office."

"The police are the ones charged with finding your son's killer. They wouldn't be happy if they thought we were looking for him too."

"Please?"

How could I turn down an old woman on her death bed? I probably couldn't find her son's killer any faster or more efficiently than the cops could, but I was someone she could at least feel a sense of control over. She could pay me and ask me how it was going, and I would have to answer. This woman had control over nothing in her life, but she wanted at least the illusion of control over this. I removed a card from my wallet and placed it on the nightstand. "After I find Balinda Sands, if he hasn't been caught already, I'll do my best to find your son's murderer."

Mary Aldrich inhaled shallowly and said, "Thank you. Shall I write a check now?"

"Later. If it's necessary."

"Thank you. Ben came by every afternoon. We would sit and talk for hours. He was a wonderful son. From the very first, he was a wonderful son."

"I'm sure he was, Mrs. Aldrich."

CHAPTER 19

George Aldrich stopped me in the foyer. Luther was already behind the wheel of the Saturn, rocking his head to and fro like a blind man playing the piano. He must have had the radio on. It was good to see him loosen up. He'd been so tight yesterday I'd had the feeling his eyeballs might jump out of his head and roll down the street.

"You have a productive chat?" Aldrich asked.

"If I were you, I'd talk to her about your son's death. If she passes away before you discuss it, you're going to feel lousy."

"I were you, I'd mind my own fucking business. I were you."

"Fair enough. Just giving you my take on it."

"When I need a bunch of shit, I'll squeeze your head."

I wanted to say more, but there was little point in getting smart with an old man who had just lost his son and was standing in the doorway of his house waiting for his wife to die. I watched his jaws as he chewed on the cigar butt and stared malevolently past me at Luther. It was hard to tell whether he was angry at me, Luther, or the whole world.

"I can't visualize Benjamin running around with a nigger," he said.

Measuring my words, I said, "Luther's one of my best friends."

He gave me a hard look. "It was just an expression, son. Don't be getting on your high horse. Shit, fella. You're in my house. In my house we play by my rules."

I stepped out onto the covered porch and headed down the walk.

Aldrich followed. "Tell me the truth. Was Ben running with his daughter?"

"Mr. Aldrich, I don't know the answer to that."

"He had a perfectly good girlfriend. Why would he—"

"Who you disapprove of."

"What?"

"You disapprove of Peggy. You made that abundantly clear at her place."

"I was getting my son's effects. I wasn't over there to make her feel bad."

"You could have fooled us. Maybe you haven't figured it out yet, Mr. Aldrich, but she's in as much pain as you are."

"She don't know the meaning of the word. And neither do you. Wait until you watch somebody you been with fifty-one years wasting away like a sugar cube in a teacup. Wait until she calls to you in the middle of the night and asks you to put a pillow over her face because she can't stand it any longer. You want to know about pain, you got a little learning, son."

There was more to say, but I didn't have the heart or the wisdom to say it properly after his tirade. For just a split second something deep in my brain flashed ahead forty years, and I visualized Kathy in the hospital bed in the other room. Aldrich was a hard man, and circumstances hadn't made him any softer. From what little I knew of him, it seemed to me that his own pain and his own interests always had and always would supersede the interests of those around him. In fact, I had the feeling he felt worse about his own pain than he did about his wife's.

Mary Aldrich had given me material to think about. Benjamin had two mothers, one dying, the other lost. If he'd been on the trail of his birth parents when he showed up at the Sands house a month ago, it stood to reason we'd been lied to. He'd certainly been asking questions, not selling drugs or vacuum cleaners as Laronda had alleged, though what possible connection Laronda or Balinda Sands could have to his long lost mother was beyond me.

On our way to I-5, Luther drove wordlessly through the stately neighborhoods of Old Tacoma while I briefed him on what Mary Aldrich had said after he left.

Laboring under the mistaken notion that it would take his mind off his troubles, I gave him Pookie's elevator puzzle too. He solved it before I could adopt the smugness of a man who already knew the answer.

Then he said, "Aldrich was an all-right guy back when he owned property in our neighborhood. Always had a pocketful of brand new, shiny fifty-cent pieces. He used to pay us by the hour and then flip us one of those fifty-cent pieces when he thought we done a good job. We thought he was the richest man in the world, Raymond and me. Always drove a big Mercedes."

"Did you already know that puzzle?"

"What puzzle? Oh, no. But they're all the same. I wonder why Laronda and them hated Aldrich," he said.

"You mean why they threw him out?"

"I'm talkin' about the old man. We ain't seen him, none of us, in twenty-five, thirty years, but back in them days Laronda, anytime we'd mention Aldrich—Raymond or me— she'd say something nasty and leave the room. Something like, 'Why you wanta work for *that* man?' When that kid of his showed up at the house, it's no wonder Laronda threw a fit.

Maybe Pookie had some sort of trouble with the old man. She would have been in her fifties back then."

"You think Laronda might know something about Benjamin Aldrich's real father and mother?"

"I don't see how. Laronda mighta had a coupla white girlfriends in school, but I don't remember any."

"How old was she when you started going with her?"

"Twenty. I still remember bustin' her cherry. Right in that same bed that's in her bedroom now." I'd heard the story before and had always done my best to ignore it.

"Who would know about her friends from that time?"

"Raymond might. Pookie. Pookie remembers all that shit."

It was several miles later when I told Luther about Aldrich's "nigger" comment. Luther thought about it for a while. "That's funny. Raymond's always sayin' how he can sniff out a two-faced white man. Raymond couldn't sniff out a turd in a choir robe pocket."

What neither of us said and neither of us was going to say was that Luther had been fooled by Aldrich too. He'd been genuinely shocked by what he'd encountered today.

CHAPTER 20

Dibble's Funeral Home was in the south end of Seattle just off Rainier Avenue near Genesee Street. A white, stucco building, it was surrounded by a large, manicured lawn that could have doubled as a putting green. We swung around back, and I waited while Luther went inside, got a gurney, and began wrestling the dead man out of the backseat, a feat made more difficult by rigor mortis.

"You ain't gonna help?" Luther asked, breathing heavily, his own head and neck under the dead man's armpit.

"I'll let you and Mr. Dixon have this dance to yourselves."

"You *could* help."

"You ever hear that elevator puzzle before, Luther?"

"I told you no. Listen, you help me with Dixon and I'll take you over to Catfish Café and introduce you to Dion Williams."

"Balinda's ex-boyfriend?"

"Toylee's dad. Yeah. He should be over there workin' today."

"If he's over there workin' today, why don't I just go over by myself?"

"Come on, Thomas."

I took the old man's feet while Luther wrestled his head and torso, the cadaver as stiff and heavy as a mannequin made of clay. We put him on the gurney on his side, one arm jutting into the air, and Luther covered him and wheeled the gurney through the ramp into Dibble's.

When he came out, I said, "When we go to Catfish Café, maybe you should let me do the talking."

"That's 'xactly what I had in mind. I already talked my guts out with that boy. I don't want to talk to him no more."

It was almost one o'clock when we parked at the intersection of Twenty-seventh Avenue and Cherry Street and walked to the white-walled restaurant on the corner. The restaurant was again smothered in the aroma of deep-fried catfish. There were four customers in line and another eight or ten at tables. Everyone in the joint was black except me and a Japanese woman sitting with a black woman.

"You spot him?" I asked.

"He's in back. They're kinda busy. Maybe we should get somethin' to eat while we're waiting."

"Sure. What's good?"

"It's all good."

Luther ordered the catfish and mustard greens. I ordered the seafood gumbo. We took the last open table by the door and sat down with our plates. During our time in line, Luther'd gone into the kitchen to chat with Dion, a tall, handsome young man, straight-backed and clear-eyed. He wore jeans, basketball shoes, a white apron, and, like all the employees, a Catfish Café T-shirt.

As we ate, Luther briefed me on Dion's history.

He graduated from Garfield High School three years ahead of Balinda, had been all-state in baseball, all-city in football, and had been awarded a baseball scholarship to Washington State University. Two and a half years later he emerged from WSU with a sore pitching arm, flunking grades, and a contract with a team in the minors. Luther couldn't remember which club.

"Raymond would know," he said.

"He looks like a good kid."

Luther winced as if in pain, which was how he always showed disagreement.

"He ran into trouble in the minors. *He* claims he ended up with a bad elbow because they overworked him. You want to know the real truth, he couldn't take criticism. Got into trouble in high school behind the same problem. He's hardheaded. In fact, I'm surprised he's lasted this long workin' at the Café. He had big dreams, that boy, so this was a huge comedown."

"What sort of trouble?"

"He was a knucklehead. In high school the coach was tryin' to straighten him out one time during a game. They got into a beef. Started arguin' right out there on the field in front of God and the bleachers, the other team, the parents, everybody. Now, if you're an athlete in school, what's the first thing you learn? Don't argue with the coach, right? That's the *first* thing. So the coach tells him he won't be able to wear the uniform for two weeks; he's suspended. What he did, he stripped the uniform off right out there on the field, threw it at the coach, and walked back to the team bus in nothin' but his jockstrap."

I laughed. "You're kidding, right?"

"I wish I was."

"What'd he say when you talked to him about Balinda?"

"Says he don't know nothin'. I leaned on him kinda hard, so I almost believe him."

We'd finished our meal and were hashing over the old days when Dion came to the table. He was a regal-looking young man, twenty-eight by Luther's calculations, athletic, and maybe two inches taller than me. He had very short hair and large brown eyes that reflected pride as well as what I accepted as a token degree of fear. He seemed shy, but in spite of that he reminded me of the young Cassius Clay.

Before sitting at our table, he looked at Luther and said, "You're not gonna pull that gun again, are you?"

Luther gave me an embarrassed grimace. If he was wearing a gun, I hadn't been aware of it. "No, I ain't gonna do that.
This here's Thomas Black. He's helping me look for Balinda."

"I called over to her grandmother's today and Pookie said
she was out." Dion sat as straight as a rifle barrel. "Just told
me she was out. I thought you found her."

"Haven't found shit," Luther said. "That's because somebody's not tellin' the truth."

Luther looked at me.

I said, "When was the last time you saw Balinda?"

"Sunday. Sunday after church. I went over to the house.
Everybody else except Toylee was still at church."

"What happened?" I asked.

"We talked."

"Don't get into your usual bullheaded self here," Luther
warned. "You answer Thomas."

Looking irritated at being dressed down, Dion said, "I'm
not bullheaded. I asked her to come back to work. She gave
up this job over nothin'. I wasn't bothering her. That was all in
her head. Hal said he'd take her back any time."

"What else did you talk about?" I said.

"That cowardly white fuck."

"Which cowardly white fuck would that be?" I asked.

"The guy she was seein'. I don't know his name."

"You heard about him?"

" 'Course I heard about him."

"What did you hear?"

"That she was runnin' around with some white dude.
Making me look bad. Frontin' me."

"You ever meet him?"

"Why would I want to meet him?" His look was challenging.

"But you talked to her about him?"

" 'Course I did. I told her she better stop seein' him. Or
else."

"Or else, what?"

"Or else!"

"The police have spoken to you, right?"

He'd been spitting his answers out, almost breathlessly, but mention of the police slowed him to a crawl. "They talked to me. At my mother's house."

"Did you tell them you were making threats to Balinda?"

"I didn't threaten nobody."

Luther laughed. "Jesus, Dion. You're not even listening to what you're sayin' your ownself. You just now told us you told her to stop seein' him on Sunday. Monday he was shot. What do you think that's gonna sound like to the police?"

"They didn't ask me that."

"They will," Luther said.

"I didn't do nothin' to him. I never even met him. I just wanted to keep Balinda from seeing him again."

"Did you see Balinda on Monday?"

"Nope."

"What were you doing Monday night?"

"Now don't try to be puttin' this off on me. I told you, I didn't see her. Besides, if you really can't find her, you shouldn't be wasting your time talkin' to me. She's probably with that Cuban fuck."

"Which Cuban fuck would that be?" I said.

"Luther knows him."

"Fernando," Luther said. "I told you about him."

"What do you know about Fernando?" I said to Dion.

"I know he's no good for her. I know he used to get her stoned and take pictures of her. I know he was gonna end up pimping her. That's what I know. Her drug problems were his fault."

"No," Luther said gently. "She done drugs before him."

"He's the one got her back into it."

"You ever meet the Cuban?" I asked Dion.

"No."

The three of us looked at each other for a few moments. Finally Dion said to Luther, "You check *all* her friends?"

"Every one."

"You check Patrice?"

"You know I did," Luther said.

"You check Melissa?"

"Who's askin' the questions here, punk!" Luther snapped, his anger building even as he spoke, so that each word was louder than the last. The workers in the kitchen peered through the cutout near the take-out counter. Luther saw them and lowered his voice. "Don't be cross-examining my ass. You threatened her. You drove her outta this job. And now you're sitting here in a bib askin' me what I'm doin' to find her? You better pray to God I do find her, 'cause I don't, you're the first one I'll come for."

Dion moved his hands on the table nervously. "I ain't scared of you," he said, sticking his chin out.

"Let's agree on one thing," I said. "We all want to find her, right?" Neither of them replied. "Right?"

Dion nodded. Luther mumbled.

"Dion? Why did you and Balinda break up?" I asked.

"We had problems. She thought I was seein' other ladies."

"Were you?"

" 'Course he was," Luther said. "And he was beatin' on her too."

"I had a problem with my temper. It's gone now. I been workin' on it, and it's really not there anymore."

"Tell Thomas how many times you hit her."

"I never hit her."

"That's not how it reads in the arrest report," Luther said.

"Okay, I mighta popped her once, but I didn't ever use a closed fist."

"That's why Balinda doesn't work here?" I asked.

"Balinda and I are good together. She knows that; she just won't admit it. And I don't know why she left. She had troubles that didn't have anything to do with me."

"You realize, don't you, that sooner or later you're going to be the prime suspect in a murder investigation?" Luther said.

"What do you mean?" His voice had a whine to it now as

he tilted forward in his chair and put his palms down onto the table.

"The jealous boyfriend," I said. "Your woman running around with some white dude. You chase them down and shoot him. She runs off and hides. You'd be suspect numero uno in my book."

"But I didn't do nothin'."

"You have an alibi for Monday around midnight?"

He thought about it for a moment. "I was with Shawn. Raymond too."

"Shawn and Raymond, both?" Luther said.

"No, just Shawn."

"Raymond was in California Monday night," I said.

"No, he wasn't. I saw him Monday. Tuesday too. Tuesdays the special is gumbo. He never misses it. He's been here every day this week. Ask Shawn."

Luther and I looked at each other.

Dion glanced behind me and muttered under his breath, "Speak of the devil."

Behind us, Raymond Sands walked through the front door.

CHAPTER 21

"**W**ell, well, well, well," Raymond said, stroking his mustache and glancing from Luther to Dion and back to Dion. I might as well have been a knothole in a board. "What are you boys doing here?"

"I'm just taking a break," Dion said.

"We're talkin' about Balinda," Luther said.

"You still haven't found that girl?"

"I thought you said you were in California this week," Luther said.

"You talkin' to me?" Raymond made a show of feigning innocence. His act was almost comical, and if the circumstances had been different, we might have laughed. Or at least Dion and I might have. Luther quickly became incensed.

"You lied!" Luther stood up.

Faces appeared in the kitchen cutout again. There were three customers in the restaurant now, but they judiciously refused to look up from their food. "You stand there like a jackass tellin' me lies, and then you have the nerve to wonder why I haven't found Balinda. It's because of people like you."

"Don't you call me no jackass." Raymond glanced down at me for the first time. "You ex-cops are all the same."

"You were here in town, weren't you?" I said.

"It's none of your damn business where I was. What do you mean questioning me like some sort of back-room, jive-ass flatfeet? What makes you think I know anything? She's my niece. What am I gonna do to her, you fool? Yeah, I lied, and I'll lie again. You don't come to me askin' dumb questions."

Luther was clenching and unclenching his fists, while Raymond maintained a benign and rather superior look on his face. I wondered if he realized how close Luther was to an explosion. Perhaps he didn't care. Raymond was taller and, thanks to his pudgy midsection, a little heavier than Luther, but quite a bit softer in my opinion. In a fistfight, which I thought they were perilously close to, Luther would have made short work of him, yet I had the feeling from watching them that Raymond had always assumed he could whip Luther. For all I knew, he already had.

Glancing at Dion, who looked more uncomfortable than ever, Raymond said, "They bothering you, Dion?"

"I'm okay."

Luther said, "Why'd you tell me you was in California when you were here in town?"

"I answered that." Raymond dabbed at his heavy lower lip with his tongue, gave me a look of triumph, and after picking up a discarded regional black newspaper called *The Facts*, sat down two tables away. He was far enough away to put himself out of the conversation yet close enough to monitor most of what we said.

"I tole you before and I'll tell you again," Dion said, his courage bolstered by Raymond's attitude. "She's at Pookie's. You checked all her friends. She's gotta be hidin' out at Pookie's."

"Toylee couldn't keep that a secret and you know it," Luther said.

"Then she's with the Cuban fuck."

"Don't be talkin' about Balinda like that," Luther said, sitting back down.

At the other table, Raymond snickered aloud, possibly at something he read in *The Facts*, more likely at Luther.

"I'm just as worried about her as you are," Dion said. He had a certain roguish charm to match his boyish face and smile, and I believed him when he said he was worried.

"You never saw this white guy?" I asked.

"Never."

"*I* saw him," Raymond said without looking up from his paper at the other table. "I saw him, and I threw his funky ass out Pookie's front door."

Luther said, "Damn it, Dion. You're lyin'. What is it with all you?"

"I never!" Dion said.

"You tole me you followed her last week, from Pookie's up the hill and then downtown somewheres."

"I didn't say that."

"The hell you didn't. You think I'm so old I can't remember what you tole me three days ago?"

"Maybe I followed her once. But I never saw him. Not really. He came by the house in a little blue Nissan pickup, and Balinda ran out, got in it, and they drove off. I woulda seen where they went if my Saab hadn't been actin' up on me."

"You put some gas in it once in a while," Raymond said, still without looking up from the paper, "it might run when you wanted."

"Now you're changing your story," Luther said. "Tell me you weren't followin' her Monday night. Convince me of that."

"If I'd been following her Monday night, she wouldn't be missing, now would she? If I'd been anywhere nearby, wouldn't I have taken her out of there, got her to a hospital?"

"What makes you think she needed a hospital?" I asked.

"Luther told me there was blood all over."

"If you were there, you're probably a murderer," Luther said. "One murder. Two? What's the difference? If you were there, you killed my baby."

"I wasn't there."

I turned to look at Raymond but spoke to Dion. I wanted to watch Raymond's face while Dion answered. "Were you two together Monday night? You and Raymond?"

"No. I was with Shawn." Behind us, Raymond didn't crack his facade.

"Five minutes ago you said you was with Raymond," Luther said.

"I saw him. But I wasn't with him. I was with Shawn."

Ten minutes later as Luther was driving me back to the office, we spotted Shawn on the street along with three of his pals. Though the sun was shining and the air temperature was in the low eighties, three of the four, including Shawn, wore bulky, black Raiders coats. They wore sullen expressions too, as if their faces were as much a fashion statement as their jackets. They were all small for their age, and I felt guilty even thinking it, but I knew there were plenty of white people who, had they seen the four approaching on a dark street, would have crossed to the other side.

Luther pulled into a bus zone, set the brake, left the engine idling, jumped out, and went around the back of the car. He was smiling the way we all smile when we unexpectedly run into someone we love in public. I could see in the mirror that even though he'd been in a surly mood following our encounter at Catfish Café, he was attempting to be cordial and pleasant. He wasn't taking into account how important it was for a fifteen-year-old to be cool in front of his friends, and cool didn't include a big hug for Dad on the street, or even an acknowledging nod. Shawn backed away from his father. Twice.

I got out of the car and stood nearby.

Luther said, "We just talked to Dion. He said he was with you Monday night."

"Monday?" Shawn said.

"Don't pretend you don't know what I'm talkin' about. The night Balinda came up missing. Was he with you?"

"Dion?"

"Yeah, Dion."

"I guess so. If he says he was."

"You aren't alibiing him, are you?"

"No."

"You were together Monday night?"

"Yeah."

"Until when?"

Shawn shrugged.

"Until when?"

"I don't know. Late."

"Late? It was a school night."

"Oh, now I'm going to get in trouble?" Shawn rolled his eyes at his friends.

"You ain't gonna get in no trouble. Just tell me the truth."

"We was out late. Just late."

Luther was indignant when he got back in the car. "Damn kid. I do everything for him, and he treats me like a rag man."

Luther drove me back to the office, and we made plans. Luther was going to poke around to see if he could find ulterior motives for Raymond's lie concerning his whereabouts, while I was going to research Benjamin Aldrich. The following day Luther would approach Balinda's friends at church.

CHAPTER 22

Less than twelve hours later Luther telephoned to say he was parked down the street from Pookie's and he thought Balinda and "that Cuban" were sneaking around the neighborhood. Immersed in the sleep of the innocent, Kathy lay in bed next to me.

"Can you get down here?" Luther said. "I'm gonna need backup."

"What are you doing?"

"They come to rob the place, just like before."

"No. What are *you* doing?"

"I couldn't sleep, man. Thought I might as well keep an eye out on the place. Balinda and that Cuban robbed Pookie before. Took her TV, VCR, and some gold coins she had. Stole her car."

"You saw Balinda tonight?"

"I saw somebody around back. It's either them or it's not. If it is, I'm gonna need help. If it's not, I'm gonna need help anyway."

"I'm already out the door."

As I hung up, Kathy rolled over. "Who's that? Snake? Is he screwing Martian women again?"

"Luther Little. He thinks he's spotted Balinda. I'm going over."

"Come back soon," Kathy said drowsily. "I'm gonna miss ya."

There was no use asking Luther to call the SPD, because neither he nor I wanted Balinda in the hands of the police before we had a chance to talk to her.

I pulled on a pair of jeans, a T-shirt, and running shoes, kissed Kathy's sleeping face, and was out the door without a watch or a jacket or socks or binoculars or even the single article I was certain Luther was counting on—a gun. He knew full well I'd been a crack marksman during my time on the SPD, and he assumed, a notion I had not bothered to disabuse him of, that I still had a house full of pistols, subscribed to all the magazines, and loaded my own shells, none of which was true any longer. A year ago, after a shooting death involving an acquaintance, I got rid of every firearm I owned. It wasn't a political stand. It was a personal one.

It was just after one in the morning. The city was quiet, the streets empty, the night clear. Beyond the streetlights, I caught occasional glimpses of stars buried in a black sky. Tomorrow would be another unseasonably warm day.

Simply because it was the closest of our vehicles to the street, I took my old, blue Ford pickup truck. I rolled the driver-side window down in an effort to let the cool evening air spank me into a state of alertness.

I took Roosevelt south to Pacific Street, crossed the Montlake Bridge and traveled south on Twenty-fourth and then on Twenty-third to the Central District. The drive would take a little more than fifteen minutes, so I had time to think.

After parting with Luther that afternoon, I'd worked in the office for an hour, then pedaled my racing bike thirty-five miles in the warmth of the late afternoon sun. At home I mowed the lawn, showered, and helped Kathy fix burritos for dinner. Then we walked to the video store and rented an old Hayley Mills/Deborah Kerr movie, *The Chalk Garden,* watched it, went to bed, talked over our day, and made love. I was sleeping like a fossilized dinosaur when Luther's frantic call woke me.

Once again I was rolling in as Luther's backup.

The last time had been almost the same hour of the night. I'd thought about it often in the years since, though not for the reasons Luther did. There was an aspect to that night I'd never told Luther. Or Kathy. Or anybody.

That the department gave me a commendation, that Luther tirelessly and publicly credited me with saving his life only made it worse, or, as one of my young nephews liked to say, "It gets worser and worser."

When I turned east off of Twenty-third and crossed Martin Luther King Way, over the little hill and down the east slope of Yesler Way, I could see the moon riding high over the Cascade Mountain range, could see it again in Lake Washington. A smattering of car lights traversed the Mercer Island floating bridge.

Luther had parked his Saturn around the corner from Pookie's house, across the street from the Leschi Elementary playground on Spruce. He was nowhere in sight.

Nobody in the neighborhood knew my truck, so I drove around the corner and cruised past Pookie's house slowly. I heard shouting on the south side of the house, although I couldn't see anybody.

I parked and walked across the scruffy front yard.

There were five males at the side of the house, but only two of them were actually fighting.

The three standing out were young black males, one of whom had a gun in his hand, a small semiautomatic. Two of them, including the one holding the gun, were boys I'd seen with Shawn Brown that afternoon on Cherry Street. The third youth was larger than the others and was the only one of the three who looked inclined to jump into the fray. When I got closer I realized he was Dion Williams.

Shawn had his father in a headlock, was trying to walk him over to the side of the house, where I believed he would have slammed his head against the wall. Headlocks were dangerous holds and illegal in collegiate wrestling for a variety of good reasons, and Luther was struggling frantically. If he didn't break free quickly, I would stop it, but I didn't want to spoil Luther's chance to get out of it on his own.

I wondered how Shawn had gotten the jump on his father.

"Come on, you guys," Shawn gasped. "Gimme some help here. Come on."

Dion Williams moved forward tentatively, but Luther said in a measured cadence, "Don't you dare."

Only the quiet menace in Luther's voice and Dion's own second thoughts held him at bay. But then, anybody stepping into an altercation between a father and a son needed to have his head examined.

CHAPTER 23

I stepped to the right of the boy with the gun, tapped him on the left shoulder behind his back, and as he turned left, locked up his right arm from my side. I had the gun before he realized it was gone.

"Owww," he said.

"Who the fuck are you?" asked the boy next to him, bouncing nervously on the balls of his feet.

"They're both ex-cops," Dion said.

"He's my partner," Luther said, freeing himself.

Now that he was loose, he grasped Shawn's coat and slammed him bodily up against the side of the house so hard the window above him rattled. Luther was small, but Shawn was smaller, built like Luther must have been at his age. I'd been apprehensive for Luther a moment earlier, but now I was worried for Shawn.

I popped the clip out of the gun, ejected the cartridge from the chamber, and slid the clip and spare cartridge into my front pocket, the pistol into my rear pocket.

"That's mine," said the boy I'd taken it from.

"File a complaint."

"You give that back." He was indignant.

"Come on, you guys," Shawn hollered. "Gimme a hand."

"You're gonna need more than a hand, son," Luther said, slamming him into the house again. "You come after your own dad like some sort of slapjack street criminal, you're going to need more than a hand." He cuffed Shawn across the face. The blow made a loud, thwacking noise. Shawn tried to return it in kind, but Luther was too quick, fending his son's hands away, then swatting him two more quick blows to the face.

"You gonna hit your father? Your own father?"

"You ain't my father. You ain't nobody's father. You just screwed my mother."

"You shut up!" Luther shouted. It was noteworthy that his son's denial of his paternity would make him shout, while the threat of physical violence had not. "What were you going to do with your stupid friends here, huh? You gonna beat up your old dad, huh?" Each time Luther said "huh," he slapped Shawn, who now crouched low against the house with both arms up over his head, so his father's last blows struck only the top of his cranium. It was hard to watch, because I had a feeling neither one of them was ever going to come back from this.

"What the hell's going on?" It was a woman's voice.

Her hair in large rollers, and her body in an old-fashioned cotton nightgown buttoned to her neck, Laronda leaned out a bathroom window of the second story. I wondered how, in all this heat, she could be wearing something so warm.

"Let's get out of here," Dion said.

"Not till I get my piece." The boy I'd taken the automatic from placed himself in front of me. The arrogance of it made me want to level him, but then, he couldn't have been older than fifteen or sixteen, undersized at that, a full head shorter than me, and probably fifty pounds lighter than my one eighty. What did he think was going to happen here?

"You need a bigger brain and smaller balls," I said.

"What you say?"

"I said, be careful. You look like a slow healer."

"I'm not scared."

Dion laughed and said, "You should be."

Luther was still talking to Shawn, but I wasn't paying attention. Laronda had stopped yelling, but I noticed a couple more heads in the same window.

The boy stepped forward, chest-to-chest with me, and did not budge. I put my left heel behind his left and gently nudged him. It was the oldest schoolyard trick in the book, but down he went. He sprang back up and started swinging. I caught hold of his arm as it came past my face and twisted it behind his back.

"Go ahead," he yelped, struggling. "Break it. You better break it, otherwise you're going to have to kill me."

"Goddamn, Melvin," Dion said. "Don't you get it? You're losin' this shit."

"I ain't scared," Melvin said.

"That's 'cause you're too dumb to be scared," Dion said.

I pushed him away. This time he didn't come back.

One-handed, Luther pulled Shawn around by the collar.

"You boys get outta here before me and Thomas get pissed," he said.

"I ain't scared," Melvin said.

Dion laughed again. "Melvin, you're a nut. He's gonna stuff your head down in that coat, and we're never going to see you again."

I had the feeling if it had been just him and me, Melvin would have kept fighting until I knocked him out. It was the same attitude Shawn had exhibited against his father. These boys weren't afraid of anything.

A woman's voice came from behind. "Melvin! You get your skinny little butt off my property before I get in my car and drive over to your mother's house. You want me over to your mother's house?"

It only took a second or two for the boys and Dion to retreat past Laronda, who had covered her nightgown with a long, pink robe. Melvin turned back, pointed his finger at me and said, "I'll be back, and I'll get you for this."

"You'll be back?" Luther snorted. "You'll be back? Why, you stupid little punk. You're lucky he didn't break your arm and your neck both. This man's a champion shooter, boy. You could stand down there at the end of the street in the dark and he could put a bullet in each eye without even hardly blinking. You don't know who you tangled with here, boy."

"Fuck you."

After the three were gone, Luther said, "They're never scared. That's why they're going to end up in the joint." He turned to his son. "What was Dion doing here?"

"We hang out," Shawn mumbled.

Laronda said, "The question on my mind is what are you two doin' here fighting with these boys? What is the matter with you, Luther? You committed assault and battery on your son. You bring him over here for me to care for, and then you make like this. And *you*?" She turned to me.

"They was sneakin' out the back of the house here, Laronda," Luther said placatingly. "I come up on 'em, and Shawn started fightin'. What was I supposed to do?"

"You pushed me," Shawn accused, without meeting Luther's eye.

"Okay, maybe I pushed you, but that don't give you no right to be puttin' moves on your own father."

"You ain't my father."

"Shawn!" Laronda said. "You get in the house!"

"And you ain't my mother."

"Maybe she ain't," Pookie said, coming around the corner of the house, also in a long, pink robe, more faded than Laronda's and not long enough to conceal her skinny shins. Her voice was gentle and reasoning. "She fed you and housed you and took you in when nobody else would. Shawn, you give her some respect. Now, tell her you're sorry."

The boy thought about it and then said, incredibly, I thought, "I'm sorry."

"Shawn, why don't you go in the house?" Pookie said.

"Me and my friends—"

"Your friends are long gone. Go on in the house."

"What were you doing?" Laronda asked. "You have people in the house while we were sleeping?"

"No," Shawn said.

"He did so," Luther said. "Of course he did."

"I did not." Shawn stalked past me and the women and went around the corner.

"He ain't goin' in the house," Luther said before the boy was even out of earshot. "He ain't goin' to listen to you or anybody else. He's headed for the streets and juvenile hall."

"That's no way to talk about your son," Laronda said.

"After he just wrestled me and called his friends on me?"

Without warning or seeming reason, Luther sprinted past all of us, sprinted down the street in the direction of his car. We walked after him as far as the front of the house. Toylee and Shereffe were watching us from a closed living room window, D'Witt above them in his wheelchair.

A minute later Luther came back down the street pulling Shawn along by his ear. Shawn winced and grasped Luther's wrist with both hands to take the pressure off.

When they got into the yard, Luther glowered at Laronda and said, "What'd I tell ya? This boy didn't even have the decency to try to pull his shit off to the other side of the house where we wouldn't see him. No. He goes past us like we all of us got mud in our eyes."

"I was jus' goin' to say goodbye to my friends," Shawn said.

"You were just goin'—"

"You let go his ear," Laronda said.

This time Shawn didn't run, but rather, stood away from his father rubbing the side of his head. One of his eyelids was beginning to swell from the earlier pummeling. Despair had overcome defiance. Now that I thought about it, he seemed to carry a sort of general despair about him all the time.

"What are you doing out here in the middle of the night?" Laronda asked Luther.

"I thought I saw Balinda. Then I saw *him*. After he promised to be in by eleven."

Pookie looked curiously at Shawn. "Was Balinda around here?" she snapped.

"I ain't seen her," Shawn said.

"Are you sure?" Luther asked.

"Not since I saw her with that chickenshit white dude. Not since Monday."

"Don't you talk like that," Pookie said. "He's dead. In my house we respect the dead."

Shawn turned and went inside.

Luther and Laronda were glaring at each other fiercely. Pookie looked at me and stepped toward the porch. I followed while Luther and Laronda spoke in low, angry whispers.

When Pookie reached the top of the stairs, she turned around. "Shawn's a good boy. Luther can't be around him, and his mother's got a boyfriend moved in. An officer from the Bellevue *po*-leece. He's a hard man and don't get along with the boy. It ain't right a man moving in with a woman and displacing her child."

"There's something I've wanted to ask, if you don't mind."

Pookie looked at me and nodded.

"The police said there were nine birth certificates in Balinda's car."

"Birth certificates?"

"Yes. All around the same date thirty years ago. Apparently they were for nine different babies born in the same hospital."

"Thirty years ago?" She did some mental calculations, and then her eyes got loud. They quieted down almost instantly. "I don't know why there would be nine."

"Do you have any idea why there would be *one*?"

"Can't say as I do."

"Would Laronda know?"

"You'd have to ask her."

Laronda hustled past us up the steps and vanished into the dark house before I could say a word. Luther stood in the yard and stewed. Inside the house Toylee knocked on the glass of the living room window behind Pookie and waved to her grandfather. Luther's dim eyes brightened for just an instant as he waved back, then he looked down the street as if expecting more trouble. He walked out into the middle of the street and looked in both directions, standing as uncentered and unfocused as a drunk who'd stumbled into a closet.

"You *are* going to find Balinda, aren't you?" Pookie asked me.

"We're doing our best."

"She's had some problems, but she got a heart as big as all outdoors. I love that girl."

"Yes, ma'am. So does her father."

"I know."

After a moment or two of silence, Pookie looked away from the street and said, "You got an answer for my puzzle?"

"Yes, ma'am." I gave her the answer and asked for more.

She gave me a couple of word puzzles and went inside. I stepped off the porch and into the street.

"Luther," I said.

"Goddamn stupid kid! Did you see him? Damn, that pisses me off! I was puttin' moves on people before he was born. That no good little—"

"He's your son, and you know deep down you love him. It's the details that have to get worked out."

"The details?" We looked at each other, and Luther laughed at the look on my face. "I almost didn't get out of it. I was starting to see stars."

I laughed too. "Luther, you go get some rest. Sleep in tomorrow morning. Watch a ball game on TV. Have a beer. We'll find out what happened."

CHAPTER 24

Sunday went as quickly as a boy's summer.

A high, thin overcast drifted in and then burned off so that by mid-afternoon it was sunny and unseasonably warm, as it had been for over a week.

After two hours of thumbing through the morning paper at the kitchen table and eating biscuits with marmalade, I pumped the tires on my Eddy Merckx to pressure, filled two water bottles with Gatorade, pulled on my cycling togs, and went for a sixty-mile ride with three friends.

I lazed around the rest of the day, puttered in the garden, took a nap, and went for a walk with Kathy and the dog. Luther called and gave me a detailed account of his adventures at church. He was talking faster each time I spoke to him, more and more concerned over the tricks his imagination was playing. He'd been a cop long enough to envision just about anything that might have happened to Balinda, and the mental pictures were beginning to haunt him.

He gave me detailed descriptions of every conversation he'd had that morning, including another brief interchange with Raymond Sands, who'd shown up at church for the first time in many months. Luther speculated that Raymond was attending church because he was feeling guilty over something.

"He lied to me, Thomas. My daughter is missing, and he lied about where he was the night it happened. I can't take much more. I woke up at six this morning and laid there with my eyes open for three hours."

"Some exercise would help."

"I done talked to everybody I can think of. Nobody's seen her. And Raymond, that sorry, lyin' dog. Now, why would he lie except he's hidin' somethin'?"

"Maybe it's like he said. Maybe he didn't like the way you asked."

Our phone conversation lasted nearly an hour. I sat on the back porch listening to Luther and watching a trio of bees work over my Adolf Horstman. L.C. slept in the shade of our garage. Kathy was shopping with a girlfriend. It wasn't until we neared the conclusion of our conversation that Luther mentioned almost casually that Shawn was now missing also.

"We saw him just last night," I said.

"Shereffe told me that after we left, Laronda lit into him like you wouldn't believe. My guess is he never even slept there. I told you those women are hard on us. Why do you think I'm not livin' there?"

I thought he wasn't living there because he cheated on Laronda every chance he got and had since about the second week they were together, a circumstance Laronda could hardly have been ignorant of, but I said nothing.

Toward the end of the call Sonya came home dressed as if for church, went downstairs, and returned wearing a sleeveless shirt and skimpy shorts, no socks or shoes. Her long legs were pale in the sun. Right away I noticed she wasn't wearing a bra.

"You want me to look at that shower now?" I asked. Luther had just signed off.

"If you would."

Downstairs, I ended up replacing a washer and removing

some silt from the shower head. When we tried it out, the whistling was gone. Sonya jumped up and down at our success and took the opportunity of our passing each other in the tight hallway to clumsily grasp me in a hug of gratitude. At least that's what I attributed it to, gratitude.

We were talking in the backyard when Kathy came home, and Sonya disappeared into her basement stairwell within seconds.

"Was she wearing a bra?" Kathy asked, stepping close and kissing my cheek.

"How would I know?" I said.

Kathy gave me a suspicious look as she carried a pair of Nordstrom bags into the house.

"I never notice that stuff," I shouted after her.

After dinner that evening, after we'd finished cleaning up the kitchen and putting away the leftovers, Kathy settled in the living room on the couch reading a book about Chinese immigrants in the nineteenth century.

"I brought you a puzzle," I said, flopping into the easy chair in the corner.

It was a small living room and faced the street, our wooden porch and dinky front yard the only buffer between our lives and the occasional traffic out front. We had a fireplace of white brick on the north wall, a television set we rarely used near the front door, a long sofa facing the window and easy chair, and a couple of end tables and lamps on either side of the sofa. It was a modest room in a modest house. I had a small pension from the SPD, a skimpy income from private investigations, and a life I didn't want to change. Most of Kathy's criminal cases were poorly paid, and she still owed money on school loans.

"You got me a puzzle?"

"Actually two."

"Oh, boy."

To my astonishment, I'd solved the first one, but the second had me stymied. Kathy slipped a marker into her book, crossed her legs, and sat in the center of the sofa like a Buddha, her dark hair falling loosely over her shoulders. Her smile dimpled at the edges.

"On the lawn you find a hat and a carrot, but nobody placed them there. All right? You find a few rocks, but nobody put them there either. There's a scarf. Nobody placed any of this on the lawn, yet there's a logical explanation as to why it's there. Oh yeah, and a broom."

"That's way too easy."

"What's the answer?"

"A melted snowman. Why? Didn't you get it?"

"I got it."

"You don't have to snap at me. You have another one?"

"Okay. There are two boys born to the same mother on the same day in the same hospital, yet they're not twins. How can this be?"

"The same year?"

"Yes."

"They're not *identical* twins? Or they're not *fraternal* twins?"

"They're not twins at all."

"But they have the same father?"

"Presumably."

"Hmmmm," Kathy said. "Two babies born to the same . . . hmmmmm."

"I don't want to hear a bunch of wild guesses. Just think about it for a day or two, and then tell me when you give up."

"What if I get it?"

"Then I'll be your sex slave."

"Really? I've always wanted one of those."

Two minutes later Kathy leaned across the sofa against me and whispered into my ear, "They're not twins; they're triplets. Two-thirds of a set of triplets. Or one-half of quadruplets. Or—"

"You heard it before?"

"Nope."

I kissed the tip of her nose. "You sure?"

"Of course I'm sure. By the way, what does a sex slave do?"

"Whatever he's told," I said.

"For how long?"

"I guess as long as it takes."

"I'll let you off the hook this once, but next time we'll make it a real wager. In the meantime maybe we can practice some of this sex slave stuff and see what I'm going to like best."

"I already know what you like best."

She rolled into my arms. "So do I."

CHAPTER 25

Monday morning I sat down and went over Balinda Sands's criminal history as given to me by my researcher, Hilda. Seven years ago Balinda had been arrested for shoplifting at the Northgate Mall. During the next two years she was arrested for shoplifting, fraud, loitering, driving without a license, DWI, and seven times for prostitution. She'd worked the streets in Anchorage, Seattle, Honolulu, L.A., and San Diego. And then the year Toylee was born, it all stopped.

It would kill Luther if he knew I knew this.

On the night of Aldrich's death, the police found copies of nine birth certificates in Balinda's car, each with a birth date, according to Luther's informant, within days of Aldrich's own. Luther hadn't been able to get information more specific than that, and with Arnold Haldeman working the case, I wasn't going to get any more from Homicide, but it was clear to me that Aldrich believed one of those birth certificates was his.

My hunch was that since Aldrich knew when and where he was born, but not who his mother and father were, he had searched for names of babies born on the ward around the days he'd been there, had somehow obtained copies of their birth certificates, then looked them or their parents up—or was in the process of looking them up. Since he had the birth certificates with him while he was with Balinda, she may have been helping him in his quest. I didn't know if Aldrich's death and Balinda's disappearance were a direct result of this search, but it was all I had to go on.

I went to work on the computer and by ten-thirty had secured eleven names and birth dates—people born in Swedish Hospital thirty years earlier, each within four days of when Benjamin Aldrich took his first breath.

The third name on the list prompted me to phone Luther.

It took a couple of calls to track him down, and when I did, he was at Dibble's Funeral Home. I waited almost five minutes for a young woman with a thick inner-city accent to get him to the phone. I didn't ask him what I'd taken him away from.

"Luther?"

"Thomas. You find her?"

"Not yet. Anything new on your end?"

"No." Disappointment etched his voice like a bad tattoo.

"What about Shawn?"

"His mother and her boyfriend are out lookin' for him. He's their problem now."

"Been talking to anybody?"

"Naw. I been busy. Hot weekends like this bring in clients like flies. Especially when it's the wrong season for heat. Mrs. Freeman had her furnace going full blast when we picked her up."

"Luther, how many kids has Laronda had?"

"Total?"

"Yeah."

"Does this have somethin' to do with Balinda bein' missing?"

"It might."

"Four. Four kids. There's the three she had with me: Lyle, who died, Balinda, then Shereffe. And there's D'Witt, who she had with that asshole in California."

"When did she give birth to Lyle?"

"June eleven. It comes around each year, I just get me a bottle of one-five-one and don't answer the phone or nothin'. Know what I mean?"

"I know."

"Why are you askin'?"

"I'm not sure yet."

According to the records I'd obtained that morning, thirty years ago, when she was sixteen, Laronda had given birth to a baby, a baby even Luther didn't know about. She'd borne five children, not four.

It stood to reason that if she were a young, unmarried, scared new mother in an obstetrics ward, Laronda might seek out another individual in similar circumstances. Even if they had nothing else in common, such as race, they might share the normal trepidations of giving birth under the social stigma of illegitimacy. I found it curious that Laronda's family had known George Aldrich, and I wondered if they'd realized how badly he and his wife had wanted a child. If so, it was possible that Benjamin Aldrich's birth mother had been given this information by Laronda or one of her family and that she had left her baby where she knew he would be wanted.

I wondered how much Benjamin Aldrich had discovered about his birth before he was murdered, and if he'd learned of the past connection between the Sands family and his own adoptive father. I wondered if his reasoning then had paralleled my own now, and if he and Balinda had been searching for—or had found—a woman Laronda may have befriended thirty years ago on a maternity ward.

The one thing I knew was that Benjamin's search took him as far as the Sands household, and, in spite of being thrown out by Raymond, he developed a relationship with Balinda which ultimately resulted in his death and her disappearance. It was possible that after Raymond threw Benjamin out of the house, Balinda had rushed outside to apologize and it had gone on from there, an interracial flirtation blossoming in secrecy both from her family and his.

It was just after noon when I drove up Yesler over the hill to the Central District. The Central District was about as close as Seattle came to having slums, yet to call it a slum was to slander it, for the occasional broken-down house with its overgrown yard was almost inevitably sandwiched between well-kept homes maintained by fastidious owners who parked new cars in their garages.

The playground at Leschi Elementary was bursting with children, runaway baseballs, swinging tetherballs, shouting, and at least one teasing game of tag between two little girls and a boy.

The way I figured it, noon was the perfect time for a visit. Laronda would be at work, Shereffe would be in school, and Shawn, if he'd returned, would be in school too. It was warm, no rain forecast, so presumably Raymond would be off painting houses. D'Witt—I had no idea where D'Witt might be. Toylee might be around, but only if she was in morning kindergarten.

I'd had the feeling each time we met that, despite Pookie's stern demeanor and her daughter's efforts to get between us, I was courting a certain kind of rapport with her. Maybe this new information was the chisel I needed to crack open her bank of knowledge.

I parked my Taurus directly in front of the Sands house on Thirty-second and, as I got out, wondered whether the neighbors relished the sound from the playground as much as I did, or whether they even heard it anymore.

CHAPTER 26

The Sands house looked shabbier in the May sunlight than it had at night. All the blinds were closed again, and I had to wonder whether Pookie didn't want to see out or didn't want anybody else to see in.

She answered the door in a belted dress that dropped well past her knees, sturdy, brown walking shoes, and thin socks that were a dingy white. Her hair was wrapped in a linen cloth, a turban, which looked incongruous with her heavy black spectacles. It was the first time I'd seen her in daylight, and she still didn't look anywhere near the age I knew her to be.

She gazed at me quizzically and said, "You here for another puzzle."

Nothing in her manner or in her steady brown eyes betrayed it, but after I thought about it a moment, I realized she'd crafted a quiet joke. I smiled.

"Actually, it would be nice to get another one, but I'd like to talk for a few minutes."

"Laronda and them's not home," she said, preparing to shut the door.

"It's you I'd like to speak to."

She gave me a look through her thick glasses that was about the same as if I'd told her she'd won a million dollars and she had to decide whether to buy into it or call the Better Business Bureau.

"Well, I s'pose. Come *on* in."

The house was cool and dark when she closed the front door behind us and sealed off the cacophony from the playground up the street. D'Witt had left no tracks except a pair of badly worn and tattered cycling gloves on a windowsill.

She led me through the house and into the kitchen, where she offered me a hard wooden chair with chipped white paint. She went to the deep porcelain sink and began scrubbing a large collection of mason jars.

"Mrs. Sands," I said, "if—"

"Oh, don't call me Mrs. Sands. That's a misnomer anyway. Sands is my maiden name. My father's family traveled up to Chicago from Georgia, and most of them are Muslims now and have changed the name anyways. Sands was our plantation name. I never liked it. Call me Pookie."

"Pookie, I'd like to ask you about the child Laronda had when she was sixteen." Pookie stiffened but didn't look away from the rush of tap water. I continued, "A baby boy. Eight pounds, four ounces. Born to a Laronda Mayceptia Constance Sands on March twenty-fifth thirty years ago."

Without looking at me, she said, "Now, why on God's good earth did you want to go and dig up a thing like that?"

"I believe it was the reason Benjamin Aldrich showed up on your doorstep. It might also have something to do with Balinda's disappearance. During the three days Laronda was in the hospital, there were ten other mothers giving birth on the ward. Did she know any of them?"

"Son, I have no idea."

"I think Benjamin Aldrich's birth mother was on that ward. I think he was looking for her when he showed up here."

"You're sayin' he was lookin' for his folks?"

"Yes, ma'am."

"Luther told us at church yesterday he was George Aldrich's son."

"His adopted son."

"Laronda's the person you should be speakin' to."

"I'll get to her. Right now, I need to speak to you."

She eyeballed me from the sink for the first time in our conversation. "It was a strange time for her and me both, those years, and I'm not sure I ever got a proper handle on it, Mr. Black. She's a strong girl, Laronda is. These questions you're asking. You think the answers will help you find my granddaughter?"

"Right now, it's all I have."

As she mulled it over, Pookie washed out two more mason jars and set them on the strainer to the right of the sink. "I'll tell you some things, but I don't want you goin' to Laronda and blabbin' I told you this."

"No, ma'am."

"You're right. Laronda had her a baby when she was still in school. Kept it from us until she couldn't keep it no more."

"Who was the father?"

"Truth is, Mr. Black, Laronda never brought the father around. I never saw him. Never even heard his name. Not then and not now. Laronda was sixteen by then and old enough to make her own mistakes. She been makin' them pretty regular ever since."

Luther and Laronda had been together since almost before I was born, and I wondered if Luther didn't know more about all this than he was letting on. If so, he'd been bullshitting me for years, bragging she'd been a virgin the first time they had sex.

"What happened to the baby?" I asked.

"This is a hard thing for me to talk about, Mr. Black. I feel sometimes like it was my doin'. Laronda took a cab home with the baby. Didn't have no money to pay for it. Had to go to the neighbors beggin' for change. Here in the house by herself."

"Where were you?"

"My mother was dying, so I was in Chicago. I had a daughter about to deliver and a mother dyin' and callin' me. I had to make a choice. Laronda was havin' pains, but it was her first and you never know with the first. Coulda been a day or two; coulda been a week or two. Way I saw it, my mother would only die once. If things worked out, I could see my mother and still get back in time to do for Laronda."

"But that's not how it worked out?"

"No. By the time I stepped back on the bus in Chicago, my grandson was dead. My first grandchild, and I never did even see him."

"How did it happen?"

"Does it matter how any baby dies? Does Jesus care? Does it make it any more right? It's the same heartbreak, no matter."

The emotion in her voice surprised me. She clearly felt the loss as vividly as she had thirty years ago. "I'm sorry."

"Laronda woke up one morning and he was dead. She called the fire department, and they come and hauled his poor little body away."

"Did Laronda know anybody else having a baby around that time? Maybe she made some friends at the hospital?"

"Laronda was so upset by the time I got home, she would hardly say nothin', so I don't know what she mighta done at the hospital. Afterwards, she kept to her room, same room she's got now. That whole last year of high school she wasted up there moping. Still got straight A's, though."

"This was before Luther?"

"Oh, yes. *After* Luther, she had a whole 'nother lot to cry over."

"What was Luther like in those days?" Somewhere in the back of my mind I was beginning to suspect the baby Laronda lost at sixteen was Luther's, although I couldn't guess what difference it would make or why either one of them would try to hide it.

"This might surprise you, but Luther was a happy little man. Hardly had a care in the world. Always smilin'. Always with something pleasant to tell you. Then he and Raymond started doin' together, and he got my Raymond in Dutch and went off by hisself and hid like he didn't have nothin' to do with it. Luther was always hangin' around, but Laronda never paid him no mind till later when she was in college. If Luther woulda treated her right, he woulda had himself a nice little family. But Luther don't know how to treat a lady right. Luther doesn't deserve no family, much less comin' over here and bein' part of mine at all hours of the day and night."

She had known him for thirty years, had probably resented him the whole time, yet she couldn't disengage her life from his. He would be in the front row at her funeral, and there wasn't a thing she could do to stop it. Luther would probably pick her up and deliver her to the funeral parlor too, and if it was rush hour and the roads were gridlocked, he would put her in front and unzip the body bag and drive with her sitting up next to him so he would qualify for the car pool lane.

With men, Luther tended to nurture a few close relationships, but women were conquests, his affiliations skirmishes. He went so far as to keep records on a calendar at home, a running tally of women he'd had sex with, complete with ratings for each encounter. "I got me some four-star pussy," he would say. As far as I knew, he had tainted every love affair he'd ever had with the poison of duplicity, in each instance finding some way to put the blame on the woman. From what I knew of her, Laronda also considered male-female relationships a battlefield in which both parties went for the jugular and everybody kept score.

Breaking into my thoughts, Pookie said, "Sometimes I think my troubles with Laronda started right there, when I chose my mother over her."

"It would have been a difficult choice for anyone to make. And difficult for Laronda to accept."

"What was a body to do?"

"I don't know. Were you close to your mother?"

"I wanted to be. She was a singer, left when I was a baby and didn't come back until I was grown. My grandmother took care of me. She and her husband, Rupert, moved to Chicago after Rupert's brother brought his family up from the South. Rupert was working in a factory. Nana was working three days a week as a housekeeper for some white folk, the rest of the time watching me. Nana and I were home alone the night the riots broke, the night I saw a neighbor hung by the neck. I was seven years old. We lived on the second floor of a walk-up, and he was strung up right outside our window. For just a moment before the rope went snug, his eyes met mine. I can see him like it was yesterday. When I got older, Nana told me they cut off his privates and burned him before they hung him, but I didn't see that. I expect she kept me away from the window until she couldn't keep me away any longer.

"Whites was marching up and down the streets looking for coloreds to hurt, and they came back a couple hours later and actually came into our building. Looting and what have you.

"Nana and me didn't have time to get out the front. I remember Nana piling furniture against the door, the terrible yelling outside, and all the loud footsteps above us. I remember men shouting horrible things through the door.

"Then they busted in, and we ran to the bathroom and locked it. We could hear them in the apartment going through our belongings, breaking dishes. Nana helped me out that bathroom window and then reached down as far as she could and dropped me to the ground as light as a feather. She jumped after me, jumped just like a little girl, and we hid the rest of the night down the street in a stable. Lost everything we owned except a little blue dress I had on and some silver dollars Nana had in her pocket. We were poor before, but we had only the Lord after that."

"The riots of 1919?" I said.

"You know about them?"

"I've read about them. The experience must have shaped your thinking, to see that much hate directed against your family."

"Oh, hush. All I gotta do is go to a grocery store out in Kent or someplace to see hate. People like their own and not the other. That goes for me. Goes for you too."

"Your mother was a singer?"

"Yes." She appeared to drift off in thought.

"Benjamin Aldrich was trying to track down his family," I said after a few moments. "You were here the first night he visited, weren't you?"

"Young man come to the door asking for Laronda. Wanted to know where she lived. I told him she lived right here. Then he asked could he come in and talk with her. They set a spell in the dining room at the table. I don't know what all they talked about, because I wasn't listenin'. After a while, Laronda started arguin' with him, not real loud, just arguin'. Raymond come in and saw that and threw him out of the house. Dragged him out by the collar and tossed him off the porch. Shawn got all excited and thought he was goin' to help, kind of like a puppy dog helping a schnauzer kill a rat, but Raymond pushed him away. Shawn wouldn't talk to him for about a week after that. Shawn is prideful, you see. I have to admit, the young man acquitted himself well when Raymond tossed him out. He wasn't scared. He was awful good about it. He had a real way about him."

"Was Raymond always so tough?"

"Lord, no. I brought him up goin' to church, singing in the choir, fearing God, and reading the Bible. I asked Jesus for a hand with Raymond, but Jesus was busy somewhere else."

"What about his father?"

"Raymond's father and Laronda's was different. You have

to know this was before I got religion. Before I found Jesus. Have you found Jesus?"

"Not exactly."

"You have or you haven't. There's no 'exactly' about it."

"Then I guess I haven't."

"Time is shorter than you think. Look what happened to that Aldrich boy."

"Yes, ma'am. You were telling me about Raymond's father."

"Yes. Owned a little place in East St. Louis. Paid off the *po*-leece every week. Paid off the gangsters. Wore nice clothes. He was a gentleman, or so I believed at the time I married him."

Before she could finish her story, the back door opened and Raymond Sands came in, followed by the same two friends who'd been with him at Catfish Café on Friday, Earl and Buster. All three of them wore paint-splattered coveralls and walked in a labored manner as though they'd been working for hours.

"What are *you* doin' here?" Raymond said, shooting me an angry look.

"Same as before. Looking for your niece."

"So now we're doing a stand-up routine?"

"Mr. Black was just leavin'," Pookie said, grabbing my elbow and pushing me toward the front door. I was surprised at how strong she was. Over her shoulder she said, "There's meat in the icebox, bread in the drawer, sodas on the back porch. You know where everything is."

"Where's the beer?" said the older of Raymond's friends.

"Now, Earl, you know I don't keep no beer in the house." Once we were out of the kitchen, she said, "You just have to remember Raymond's had some bad times."

She got the front door open, stepped close to me and looked up. I noticed her glasses were smudged so that she could hardly see out. "Mr. Black? I'll tell you something I probably shouldn't be tellin' nobody. I don't know if it's related to Balinda's bein' missin' or not."

"What is it?"

She looked both directions up the street. "Raymond was after that girl."

"Which?"

"Balinda. Back when she was in high school, he lived right down the hall from her."

"What do you mean by *after*?"

"I believe he was considering unnatural relations with her. That's what she told me. He'd just got out of the joint, and he was bad mean in those days. You want to know the truth, I think prisons are turnin' our country for the worse."

"I think I agree with you. What happened?"

"I got him outta the house as fast as I could."

"You're telling me this for a reason."

"I think when he knew she was running around with a white boy, he didn't take it the way you or I would."

We looked at each other for a few moments. Suddenly I was aware that the playground to the south was quiet. A school bell rang, and the quietness seemed to expand like oil on water.

"Pookie, do you remember any of Laronda's white friends from when she was in high school?"

"I can't say as she had any."

"Did she have a white boyfriend?"

"Not that I knew of. Why do you ask?"

"Nothing special."

We were quiet for a few moments before Pookie said, "I 'spose you want another puzzle before you leave."

I was there to talk about more important matters, but puzzles worked as a social lubricant for Pookie and me in the same way that alcohol worked for others. Besides, maybe she would give me a puzzle Kathy couldn't solve.

I was standing on the sidewalk in front of the house trying to figure out either of the two puzzles Pookie had just left me with when Raymond came bounding around the corner of the house. At first I thought he was after me, but then I realized the tangent he was on led directly to an old blue van with two ladders tied to the top, rags tucked under the beams to protect the finish on the roof.

When he spotted me, Raymond looked at the ground and slowed to a walk. It was an odd reaction. Indoors he'd been bellicose, but out here he seemed almost timid. Against my better judgment, I followed him to the van and intercepted him.

"Raymond. Look, I know what you think . . . actually, I don't know what you think. But I'm trying to help. I owe Luther, and I'm sincere in trying to bring Balinda back into this family. Luther can't take another hit, and I'm not sure any of the rest of you can either. Any assistance you give would be appreciated."

Raymond stared at me. Even though he and his friends had obviously been at work that morning, I could smell liquor on his breath. I tucked a business card into the breast pocket of his coveralls when he wouldn't take it in his hand, turned and began walking away.

He said, "You stay away from my mother. She's an old woman. She don't need you in her life."

"She need to lose a granddaughter?"

He had no answer for that.

CHAPTER 27

For a long while I sat in my Taurus across the street from the empty school playground trying to balance things in my mind. Finally, reluctantly, I phoned Arnold Haldeman at Homicide on my cell phone. Haldeman was one of those people I preferred to deal with over the phone, because it seemed to me that in person he was somehow offended by my height and by the fact that I had more hair on my head than he did.

Haldeman was a small, round man who, if you'd put a bow tie on him, could have passed for Humpty-Dumpty. My supposition was that he didn't want to be a small, round man, and spent much of his life finding ways to get even with people who weren't. People who knew what they were doing seemed to annoy him as well. It was my feeling that if he had his way he would put most of the population in prison, but since he was a homicide detective and not a dictator, he made do with murderers and others for whom he could find reasonable grounds.

I got his voice mail and left a message. Five minutes later when he called back, I was still in front of Pookie's watching a pair of crows strutting around on the empty playground.

"Black? What the hell do you want now?"

"I just needed a friend to talk to."

"You are *soooo* full of shit. I would have loved to be your drill sergeant. You're not working on this Aldrich shooting, are you?"

"What makes you ask?"

"I spoke to the dead man's girlfriend. She said you'd been down there talking to her."

"Peggy Lindseth. A very nice young woman."

"The dead guy's folks said you'd been *there* too. You taking a census, or are you trying to interfere in a homicide investigation?"

"I'm trying to find Balinda Sands. I told you that last week."

"You didn't tell me you were going to be interviewing key witnesses in a murder investigation. What do you think? The black gal's hiding out with the dead man's girlfriend? Black, I don't know how you ever made it as a street cop."

"Mostly I used a Ouija board."

"You're a laugh a minute, buddy. The girl's hiding out. It was a drive-by shooting, and she's afraid they saw her."

"What makes you say it was a drive-by shooting?"

"Wake up and smell the coffee, buddy. It might even have been an attempted carjacking."

"Last time you told me *she* did it.

"Well, now, that's another possibility, isn't it?"

"Where's the car? I'd like to look at the car if possible."

"There's nothing there, Black. Not a damn thing."

"Humor me." The line was silent for a few seconds. Oddly enough, on the telephone Haldeman used silence as a weapon, a gambit he never employed in person. Face-to-face he couldn't get himself to stop talking long enough to blink. "You'll have your garage attendant right there with me. Is it in that garage off of James?"

"I don't know, Black. Our garage attendants can't be bothered by second-rate private investigators."

"Kathy's going to represent her. You charge Sands with something, I'm going to see it on discovery. Let me look now, and I might help you find her. If she did it, fine. If she didn't, she might lead us to whoever did."

"Go look at the damn car. But you're not going to find anything our techs didn't. I suppose you been talking to the missing woman's family too?"

"Some."

"The mother won't talk to us. Then there's the uncle. He's got a record as long as the toilet paper on your shoe. Murder. Robbery. Burglary. A couple of rape charges that never stuck. Drugs. He claims he's painting cars now."

"Houses."

"What?"

"He paints houses."

"That's what he *claims*. I bet I could drive down to Twenty-eighth and Cherry and get a suitcase of drugs off him inside an hour. It's a weird family. Did you know the old woman did a coupla months for beaning her old man with a lawn mower handle?"

"Pookie?"

"That's what she calls herself. Put her old man in the hospital with a lawn mower handle. This was back in the Fifties. I guess in her time she was a wildcat. I kind of like her. Every time I see her, she gives me a goddamn puzzle."

"She give you the one about the river and the boat?" I asked.

"Which one's that?"

"A man and his two sons need to cross a river. They have a boat, but it will only carry two hundred pounds at a time. The man weighs two hundred pounds. Each of his sons weighs one hundred pounds. How do they get across?"

Haldeman said, "The father rows the boat and tows his sons in the water."

"I don't think so."

"They take the boat, flip it over, and swim across underneath it."

"Nope."

"Okay. They all get in the boat, but they jump up and down alternately so there's never more than two hundred pounds in it at any given time."

The City of Seattle was paying this man to solve homicides? Even *I* had figured out the boat puzzle.

"What about the birth certificates?" I asked.

"How the hell are birth certificates going to help them get across the river?"

"I'm talking about the birth certificates in Balinda Sands's car."

"You need to give a person some warning before you go changing the subject on him like that, fella. What makes you think those birth certificates are related to anything? You stay away from the birth certificates. I'm going out on a limb letting you see the car."

"Was one of the birth certificates for a baby named Sands?"

"Black? Don't get too jacked up thinking there's a big mystery to solve here. It was a drive-by."

"Is that why you want Balinda Sands?"

"We want to question her."

That wasn't what he'd said earlier, but then, like the criminals he dealt with, Haldeman had a way of changing his story.

CHAPTER 28

It was a small brick garage run by Center Towing, and was on the corner of James Street at Nineteenth or Twentieth—I couldn't remember which, a one-story affair set up next to a tavern. They'd had a contract with the SPD for years and maintained a separate locked bay at the south end of the garage for impounds and evidence. There were a couple of down and out shops across the street, but other than that, the neighborhood was made up of one- and two-story apartment buildings and single-family residences. Years ago a block-watch captain told me she'd picked up over twenty dirty hypodermic needles on the parking strip across the street.

A small, wiry man in grungy denim coveralls, a flannel shirt, and long underwear met me and told me he didn't know anything about anybody receiving permission to look at the Sands vehicle. I tried to wisecrack him into letting me look at the car, but either he wasn't a genial sort or I wasn't funny. Probably a little of both. He said he didn't have time to stand around "bullshitting with every idiot who came in off the street."

Eventually I coaxed him into calling Arnold Haldeman,

who answered his phone without screening it as he'd done with me.

"You can't touch nothin'," said the garage man after speaking to Haldeman in monosyllables.

"No problem."

He led me to the south end of the dark building. As I walked behind him it became apparent that he hadn't bathed in a few days.

The crumpled blue Escort was in the northeast corner of the south bay under a skylight. The stall was roped off. My chaperon stood back with his arms folded, a distinct air of indifference stamped on his stubbled face. He was chewing something in the side of his cheek.

The two-door Escort was crumpled from the center of the grille halfway back to the windshield, vegetation and mud packed in the wheel wells and grille. The driver's door was badly gouged and jammed, as was the passenger door. Escape after the accident would have been problematic even without gunfire. The driver's door window was broken out, as was the passenger-side rear window, jewels of safety glass scattered throughout the interior. The steering wheel was intact, but there was a starburst crack on the windshield, probably made by the driver's head.

All in all, it looked like a medium-impact crash. Even though the sheet metal on the car was crumpled, the interior compartment was more or less intact.

I'd brought a powerful flashlight along and used it to probe the interior, placing my head and shoulders inside the broken-out windows while being careful not to touch anything. The interior smelled of gasoline, cigarettes, motor oil, and perfume.

From the color and from what Haldeman had told me about where the body had been found, I assumed the splotches on the backseat and floor were bloodstains. There were sizable stains on both front seats too—more blood in the front passenger section of the car than on the driver's side. There was also blood on the center console and on the black, plastic boot that covered the emergency brake. I wondered if someone sitting in the front seat might not have climbed out through the back, crawling over Aldrich and exiting through the broken-out rear passenger-side window.

I looked around the interior for bullet holes but found only more glass.

"You know if this door opens?" I said to the attendant.

"What?"

"This passenger door over here."

"Don't ask me. Richards brought it in. I didn't have nothin' to do with it."

Before he could stop me, I tried the door. It wouldn't open. "Anything else come with it? Like a busted-out window?"

"Nope."

The passenger in front, if there had been one, had either gone out the driver's window, or crawled over the dead man and out the missing rear window.

On the way out of the garage, I turned around to look at the Escort from thirty feet away. In half an hour or so a tray of sunlight from the skylight would hit it. Somehow, seeing the car up close made everything more real. Balinda was missing, maybe dead. Aldrich was dead. And the unknown third party, if there had been a third party, was missing as well. We weren't any closer to answers than we'd been three days ago.

Outside the garage, I stood in the sun for a few moments, walked across the street to a mom and pop grocery run by a toothless, gray-haired woman, bought a liter of chilled Dr Pepper, a Three Musketeers, and a bag of chips, and got into my Taurus. Except for two men talking outside the tavern next to the garage, the street was empty.

In my car, I ate and drank and thought for a few minutes and then called Haldeman back. I told him he was right; I didn't find anything in Balinda's car. I asked him about Benjamin Aldrich's vehicle. Did the techs find anything or did they just turn it over to Lindseth when she came up to ID the body?

Haldeman said, "Black, you ain't been paying attention, have you? We found Aldrich in a car registered to Balinda Sands, not his own."

"So the SPD didn't turn over Aldrich's car to Lindseth?" I asked.

"I don't know or care anything about his car, wherever the hell it is. Why are you trying to make a simple drive-by so complicated?"

"Forget it. It's nothing."

Next I phoned Luther and asked him if he'd been combing his hair in Peggy's bathroom during our visit. Luther said, "I ain't got enough hair, Thomas, I'm gonna be combing it all the time. Why are you asking?"

"Just juggling some things in my mind. We'll talk later."

Taking Peggy Lindseth at her word when she said she'd be back at school on Monday, I fired up the Ford and headed for Tacoma.

CHAPTER 29

Truman Middle School was only a few blocks from Lindseth's apartment. It was a sprawling school on a huge track of arid land in northwest Tacoma. As I drove to it, I could see the top portion of the suspension bridge across the Narrows, beyond that the Olympic Mountains gleaming brightly on the western horizon, their slopes still white from winter.

In the school office I was advised that Peggy Lindseth was in class. Like a truant, I waited on a small chair in a row of small chairs along a wall. Most of Washington State's middle schools were comprised of sixth, seventh, and eighth grades, and I was astounded at how tiny some of these kids were and at how others looked full-grown. Two girls came in crying for the nurse and were led into a back room. They'd accidentally butted heads in gym class. A talkative mother burst through the door and proclaimed she wanted to go through the lost and found.

When the commotion began to simmer down and the incoming phone calls slowed, the office secretary turned to me and tried to make small talk. I didn't mind, but I couldn't figure what gave her the idea I needed to be entertained. I'd brought a book and had been reading.

The bell rang, and the hallway filled with noisy kids like a balloon filling with air. A few minutes later another bell rang, and the noise ceased.

Aside from the old standard that a second visit was where you got all your information, I now had quite a few tidbits with which to prompt Peggy Lindseth. I had a fair idea what Aldrich had been up to and an even better idea of the odds he'd bucked.

Tall and lanky, Lindseth entered the office, spoke to the secretary, then turned to me while I slowly jackknifed out of the chair. She wore loose-fitting black slacks and a long-sleeve sweater that probably would be the focus of more than one pubescent boy's fantasies tonight. She seemed surprised to see me, even though she'd clearly received a message that I was in the building.

We shook hands, her grip damp and fleeting. "Did you find out anything? Did they catch the guy who killed Ben?"

The secretary was suddenly all ears.

"Is there somewhere we can talk?"

Lindseth led me to a small conference room, closed the door, and sat in a hard-backed chair against the wall. I took another chair and moved it until it faced hers. Once again she wore round spectacles with tiny wire frames. Once again diamond stud earrings winked at me from dainty earlobes. Her dishwater-blond hair was pulled into a ponytail. Her blue eyes wavered as if she had a premonition that I was going to do more prying than she would be comfortable with. Earlier, I'd tried to visualize her with Benjamin Aldrich, but it was only today that I got a sense of what they must have been like together: one of those all-American pairs you see strolling hand in hand in the malls, so anonymous and handsome and sleek they might as well have sprung from the pages of a magazine, two perfect people shopping for the best insurance policy, diet soda, Detroit steel, or indoor exercise machinery.

"You didn't tell the whole truth on Saturday," I said.

Her wide mouth pulled itself into a straight line, and I could tell her tongue was running scales back and forth across her incisors. Knees together, she lifted her heels off the floor and sat with her feet on tiptoe. It was almost identical to her pose Saturday morning.

"You said Ben drove up to Seattle the night he was killed. He owned that little blue Nissan pickup I saw in the parking lot to your apartment, didn't he? You gave George Aldrich the keys to it while I was there. If he drove it to Seattle alone, how did it get back to your apartment? You were with Ben in Seattle Monday night. You drove his truck back to your place after the accident in Balinda's car, and you brought Balinda with you. I saw her hair in your bathroom sink."

"Okay." It took a few moments of silence for her to begin. When she did, her voice was amazingly pinched and squeaky. "I didn't want to talk about it the other day because George was there and I was upset. Plus, I promised Balinda."

"You promised Balinda what?"

"That I wouldn't tell."

"She's hiding at your place, isn't she?"

"She was scared. I didn't know what else to do, so I let her come back with me."

"You were in Seattle with Ben a week ago?"

Tears began trickling down her bloodless cheeks. One of them rolled into her mouth, where she tasted it with the tip of her tongue. "Ben thought his father had been following him, and he took me along so I could keep an eye out for him while he drove."

"Why would his father follow him?"

"George thought he owned Ben. He couldn't stand the thought of Ben searching for his real father. I guess you must already know Ben's mom told Ben he was adopted and he was searching for his birth parents. I didn't know how much I should tell you when I saw you the first time. I was trying to protect Balinda."

"Was Balinda helping Ben find his real parents?"

"He got a stack of birth certificates—don't ask me how— and was convinced one of them was his. He went down the list one by one, and that's how he met Balinda Sands, or at least her mother. Balinda ended up helping him."

"Ben and Balinda were just friends? Not . . . more than friends?"

"Of course they were just friends. Why would you ask such a question?"

"Sorry. I didn't mean anything by it. Tell me what happened Monday night."

She swallowed, pursed her lips, and waited while more teardrops sped down the planes of her face. "Ben usually went to Seattle alone, but like I said, he thought his father was following him and he wanted me along. He was meeting Balinda. I had only met her once. She seemed nice."

"What was he afraid his father might do?"

"I don't know."

"Tell me what happened that night."

"We drove up in his truck and sat in this parking lot at the Promenade Market at Twenty-third and Jackson. It was late, Eleven, eleven-thirty. Ben said it wouldn't take long. Pretty soon Balinda showed up in her car and for some reason parked about a hundred feet away. Ben went over and got into her car and they sat and talked for a while. Ben was showing her the birth certificates."

"Did Ben's father follow you?"

"Ben thought he saw him on the freeway, but I didn't."

"What happened in the parking lot?"

"Well, they were in Balinda's car, and after a while another car came into the lot. I couldn't see it very well because it was behind a van that had been parked there all along. Anyway, this other car began creeping forward until it was close to Balinda's car. Like a cat creeping up on a sparrow. Then all of a sudden Balinda's lights came on and she raced out of there with Ben. The other car followed them. They all went east on Jackson."

"Did you get a look at the car or the occupants?"

"No. I assumed Balinda knew them. Later, she said she didn't."

"Were they white or black?"

"I didn't see."

"What kind of car was it?"

"A big American car. I don't know cars very well. I don't even know what color it was."

"Then what happened?"

"I waited for almost an hour until Balinda came back on foot. She was alone. She was crying. She said that the guys in the other car were trying to rob them, that she'd felt they were in danger, so she raced out of the lot. She said they drove up to Martin Luther King Way, went south, and then turned east into the side streets, this other car chasing them all the way. She said she eventually got back onto Jackson and began heading for her home. She went around a corner too fast and crashed. The next thing she knew there was a flashlight in her face. Then she heard gunshots and fell over and pretended to be unconscious. She was all bloody when I saw her, so they must have thought they killed her. When she looked up, Ben was dead. Thinking they would come back and shoot her too, she climbed out of the car and ran through the woods, then eventually wandered back and found me."

"Why didn't she go home? The accident site was only a few blocks from her home."

"She thought one of them might know who she was, that they would be waiting at the house."

"And you didn't tell any of this to the police?"

"I wanted to, but Balinda convinced me if she went to the police, the people who killed Ben would kill her too. I didn't know what to do, so I took her back to our place. We were both crying. I couldn't even see the highway. After we were home about an hour, I got a call from the Seattle police. I had to drive back to identify Ben's body."

"It must have been a long night for you."

Lindseth nodded.

"You said she was hurt?"

"She had a cut on her scalp, and her nose was bleeding. And she has some sort of glass cuts all over one side of her face."

"She told you one of these people might have known her?"

"She thought so, but she wasn't sure. She couldn't see. They had a light in her face, and she was disoriented from the wreck."

"Did they say anything to her to indicate why the chase? Why they shot Ben?"

"No."

"Where is she now?"

"She left last night. She called her place and spoke to somebody named D'Witt, a half brother I think, and then she just left. I have no idea where she could have gone."

"Do you know anything about her conversation with D'Witt?"

"No, she wouldn't talk about it."

"Was she using drugs?"

"I don't think so. Balinda is a very nice girl. She has some problems, but she means well. And she's scared. After I had time to think about it, I realized it was a mistake not telling the police right away. At the time I thought her life was in danger."

"You don't think so now?"

"I don't know. All I know is my Ben was murdered and she's scared of whoever did it. And she's scared of the police."

"She didn't recognize a voice at the accident site? Or the car?"

"If she did, she wouldn't tell me."

"How many people were chasing them?"

"She said two."

"Is that what you saw?"

"I think so."

"And you don't know where she went when she left your place last night?"

"No. I think she probably thought it would be safer if I didn't know."

"Are you going to the police now?"

"What if Balinda gets hurt because I went?"

"She's going to have the police, her father, and myself to protect her."

"Okay. I'll go."

"Just two more questions."

"Yes?"

"How many people were in Balinda's car when you last saw it Monday night?"

"Balinda's car, or the car chasing them?"

"Balinda's."

"Just Ben and her."

"And do you know if Ben and Balinda ever actually located Ben's birth parents?"

"If they did, neither of them told me."

When we emerged from the conference room, which I had decided was a detention chamber, the school secretary and two teachers began pestering us with questions about Benjamin Aldrich's death. I fled the office like a coward, and Peggy Lindseth slipped out behind me, disappearing down a hallway to the right.

From the car, I called a contact at the phone company and asked for a list of long distance calls placed from Peggy Lindseth's apartment during the last ten days. Then I left a message on Arnold Haldeman's voice mail telling him I was sending him a witness.

I called Luther and told him to recheck all of Balinda's friends in Seattle. "Why? What's goin' on?" he asked.

"As of last night, Balinda was fine. Only I don't know where she went."

"She on drugs?" Luther asked.

"Peggy Lindseth didn't seem to think so."

"Balinda's fooled wiser heads than a white-bread school-teacher."

"I know that."

CHAPTER 30

My afternoon was spent poring over the last six weeks of phone records from Peggy Lindseth's apartment, from which I learned next to nothing. On Thursday, Friday, and Saturday of last week, calls had been placed to the Sands household, yet none of the calls had lasted longer than one minute, which was the smallest increment used by her long distance phone company, AT&T.

During the dinner hour I canvassed the neighbors across the street from the accident site to see whether anybody saw anything significant. Of the five residences within viewing range of the site, the occupants of three stated they saw the police and fire units but didn't witness the accident. One homeowner said she heard the accident but fell asleep before the police and tow truck arrived. Until I mentioned it, she hadn't realized there'd been a death. Nobody recalled hearing shots. The fifth resident, though home, refused to answer the door, apparently having mistaken me for a religious pamphleteer.

Kathy and I were getting ready for bed when the phone

rang. Not wanting to answer it, Kathy scrambled under the sheets, playfully pulled the covers up to her neck so that only her face was visible, and gave me an exaggeratedly innocent look. I sank my weight onto the edge of the bed and lifted the receiver.

"Black? You bastard. You wanta talk or not?"

"Who is this?"

"What do ya mean, who is this? You know who this is."

"Raymond?"

"I been thinking about what you said this morning. We all want what's best for Balinda. Luther called over here a few minutes ago and said you still ain't found her. Why don't you come over, and you and me'll rap a little over some beer."

"It's pretty late. You gonna be around in the morning?"

"You want to learn about this family or not? The ball game's over. I got nothin' I'm plannin' to watch. Come on over and I'll pull your coat to some shit. You know where I live?"

"Luther showed me."

After I racked the phone receiver, Kathy said, "The president and the chief of staff need you again?"

"Balinda's uncle wants a powwow at his place."

"Oh, no," she said dejectedly. "I was hoping you and I could have our own little powwow right here."

"Oh?"

"Oh, yeah."

"Hold that thought. I'll be back as soon as I can."

It was almost eleven when I bailed out of a thin vein of traffic and parked in front of Raymond Sands's place on Twenty-third Avenue near Columbia. The rubble on the porch had been rearranged since my last visit. The overstuffed chair had been heaved over the handrail, and the supports on the handrail were broken off, their remains sharp and jagged like pungi stakes at the bottom of a booby trap.

It was hard not to dwell on all the reports Luther had given me about Raymond. That he was crazy. That he'd popped a man in a convenience store basically for looking at him the wrong way. There was a stereotype floating around about the angry black male: alienated, criminal, aimlessly bumbling about a staggered community while moving from one low-paying odd job to another. From the outside, Raymond Sands seemed to fit the stereotype pretty closely. He had his own business, but it seemed marginal, and he was as angry as a bee in a bottle.

The same skinny woman who'd answered the door Friday night opened it again tonight, as if she were in some sort of weird sorority and had door duty. Once again she looked doped and half asleep, eyes unresponsive, her golden face slack. She appeared to be wearing the same black leggings and T-shirt she'd had on Friday.

When I told her I was there to see Raymond, she led me into the hallway, still garnished with the same trash I'd seen on my first visit. Without a word, she crossed the large living room to the left and lay facedown on a sofa, her head directed at the television, which was playing an energetic advertisement for Mountain Dew.

Raymond appeared out of a dark door alongside the stairs that led to the second story, smiling as if we were old friends who hadn't seen each other in years. His teeth flashed in the mask of shadows. When we shook hands, I half expected him to club me with something, but he let go and led me to the rear of the house.

"You'll have to excuse all the crap," he said congenially. "I can't get my housemates around here to clean up anything, and I've about given up doing it myself. I just let it pile. I'm planning to move outta here pretty soon." He said the last as if he'd been saying it since the day he moved in.

He led me through a kitchen that was appreciably cleaner than the hallway and then into a back bedroom with a padlock arrangement on the outside of the door. In stark contrast to the rest of the house, his room was as orderly and spotless as a federal prison cell.

When he offered me a clear plastic cup filled almost to the brim with malt liquor, the lines around his eyes deepened and merged with his smile, and for a moment or two I glimpsed the Raymond Sands his friends saw.

"Thanks," I said. "But I don't drink."

"Well, that's all right. I don't mind drinkin' for two. Have yourself a seat. Take your choice." He laughed because there was only one chair other than the easy chair he had chosen for himself. He looked me over reflectively; residue, I thought, from the announcement that I was a teetotaler.

It was a large room with a bed in the far corner, a television in the opposite corner, and to the left as you came through the door, a small dresser, a closet door, and an easy chair set up at the foot of the bed in front of the television. The top of the dresser held four items: a wrist-watch with a metal band, a penknife, a silver money clip with a sheaf of bills pinched in it, and a worn wallet. The bed was made with military precision, although I could see an impression where somebody had rested on top of the spread. The ancient linoleum floor crinkled under our footsteps and looked as clean as the bottom of a gourmet's skillet. I sat with my back to the television while Raymond plopped into the easy chair and levered the footrest up with practiced ease.

He didn't have much, but it was tidy and organized and he seemed comfortable with it. For a moment or two I could visualize living in this room and being happy about it.

The television was perched high on a chest of drawers just past my right shoulder, and though he'd turned the sound off, during our dialogue Raymond peeked at it with irritating regularity. Throughout my visit he kept a twenty-two-ounce bottle of Colt .45 in his left hand, gulping from time to time.

His bloodshot eyes reminded me of white flowers in a vase filled with red ink.

"I used to live at Pookie's," he said. "But I had some bad jojos after me, and you never know when one of 'em is going to show up again. Even though I got shed of most of them, it's better I keep my own crib. Catch my drift?"

"Sure."

"What's goin' on with my niece?"

Ever since Pookie told me he'd had a sexual interest in Balinda, I'd been thinking about him differently. In fact, ex-con or killer, whatever else he was, none of those labels had accomplished what Pookie's story had. It took a lot for a mother to tell a comparative stranger her son had tried to molest her granddaughter.

I explained as sketchily as I thought practical where we were in our search. It was a relief to be talking to him *after* discovering Balinda was alive and at least marginally well, because no matter how difficult it had been for me to paint a scenario that implicated him in her disappearance, no matter how much he'd denied complicity, all along I'd harbored the eerie feeling that Raymond had been mixed up in the shooting and thus in her disappearance. Why else would he lie about going to California when he'd never left town?

"What's been going on with Balinda the past couple of weeks?" I said, interrupting a monologue he'd started about an old girlfriend. It was the kind of story told in a cell block, and I didn't care to hear it out.

"What do you mean?"

"You see her much?"

"I seen her. Sure. I'm over to the house every day. I have dinner with 'em."

"What kind of relationship do you have with Balinda? Does she confide in you?"

"We were close once. Then we had a misunderstandin'. Sometimes young girls get peculiar ideas."

"You knew she was seeing Benjamin Aldrich?"

"Yeah, I knew. Hey? I been thinking about that name. He related to the guy used to own our church and the building Catfish Café is in?"

"His son."

"Well, what do you know? I wonder why he didn't say somethin'."

"I'm sure he didn't think it would make any difference."

"He was botherin' Laronda, so I run him outta there."

"And you didn't see him after that?"

"Now, did I say that?"

"Not yet."

"Well, I ain't gonna say it because I did see him. Saw him a couple of times. I saw him with Balinda."

"And you didn't approve?"

"Balinda runnin' around with a white boy? I did not." I wanted to ask what the difference was between Balinda seeing a white man and him seeing white women, which Luther had told me were his preference, but I kept my mouth shut. He probably *did* think there was a difference, and I didn't want to hear what he thought that difference was. Besides, he was making what appeared to be a serious attempt to cooperate, and I didn't need to jinx it.

He said, "You know, this whole family been leadin' an interesting life. Pookie? She was a jazz singer just like her mother. You know that?"

"No, I didn't."

"Even cut a coupla records. They didn't go nowhere. She had three boys, and then she had Laronda by a club owner in Missouri. The Chickadee Club. She talks about my father, and she talks about the father of my two half brothers, but she don't ever mention Laronda's old man. He's dead now, anyway. I only met him a couple of times, but I steered clear. I'll tell you this. He screwed up Laronda's life. Just by bein' almost white. You see how light Laronda is? She been confused her whole life. *Thinks* she's white. *Thinks* she's black. Half the time she don't know what she is."

"Pookie's mother was a singer too, wasn't she?"

"Till she found Jesus. After that, she came out here to take care of us all, bein' as Pookie was gone most of the time. I guess she didn't do a very good job on one of us, did she?" He watched me to see how I took his last statement.

"She died in Chicago, right? Pookie's mother?"

"You been studyin' up, haven't you?"

"Pookie told me about it today."

"You're an interesting cat, Black, you know that?" His eyes flicked past my shoulder to something on the television.

"So your grandmother raised you?"

"Most of the early years. You think Pookie's tough, you should have seen her mother. Pookie would come home and stick around maybe six months. She'd get the itch and go back on the road. That's how it was. She'd send money, but we was poor. I remember going to school hungry and comin' home hungry. She didn't settle down and live with us perma-nent until about the time she had Laronda. She musta been forty."

"Must have been a hard life for a boy."

"It was. She stuck around after that. Stuck around and worked downtown cleaning buildings at night for different folks. In one year she went from being the star singer in a club to swabbin' out public privies. By the time Laronda came along, Pookie was feelin' guilty for not bein' a proper mother, so she spoilt that girl silly. Turned her into a bitch."

"Really?"

"Oh, yeah. She been a bitch since she was little. She's the one got me in prison that first time. Set me up. I'm pretty sure it was her. 'Course, there were others who mighta done it. Luther. My dead brother, Albert. Albert had a heart attack when he was forty, ran his car off the road and rolled over in a ditch down there by Fresno. It mighta been Albert. But deep down in my gut I put it on Laronda."

Suddenly Raymond's gaze fixed on my chest and his mouth twisted bitterly. "The reason I'm tellin' you all this is because if you're going to understand our family, you need to understand this one incident. It's at the very apogee of everything you'll see around our house."

"I'd like to hear about it," I said.

CHAPTER 31

Maybe he was right. Maybe I had to know all the secrets. Maybe, instead of being engaged in a love affair, Balinda and Benjamin Aldrich had been tunneling through all the family poses and subterfuges into the secrets. Maybe it was one of those secrets that got them in trouble.

"At the time, I hadda figured out who set me up, I woulda killed 'em," Raymond said. "I ever find out it was Luther, I still might. See, Black, every kid has a turning point. No matter how down on society he is, there usually comes a point along the line somewhere when he can look back and say to himself, 'This is the day I took the bad turn.' "

"I've always believed a man's life is determined by a whole raft of decisions he makes," I said. "Not just one."

"You're wrong. One decision'll do it. My turnaround came when I was twenty. I worked at Catfish Café for a time, but I was let go—said I was being rude to the customers. I knew they sometimes kept cash in the office locked in a drawer in the desk in an old cigar box. It was a damn fool thing to do. They was just askin' for somebody to take it. After I was fired, I come back late one night and lifted the cash outta that old box. It surprised me how much they had. Over eleven hundred dollars. Luther and me was hangin' out in those days, and I asked him to help, be my lookout, but he already found his turnaround point and said he wasn't goin' to have nothin' to do with it. I don't know what got us both in that state of mind just then. I mean, he'd already turned, and that was going to be my last bad thing. There was an Indian me and Luther tangled with. That mighta been it. He kinda threw a scare into botha us."

"But you stole the money?"

"Borrowed it. There was a big flap. They called the cops. They was lookin' all over the place. Askin' all the other kids. Then, for some of the reasons I already said, I broke back into the restaurant and put back every red cent. I took it out on a Sunday, put it back on a Tuesday. That very night the cops come into the house and tell Pookie they wanta search my room. They come up and woke me. Three in the morning. They started throwing me around. Pookie tried to get 'em out of the house, but by then it was too late, because—get this—they found eleven hundred dollars under my mattress. Some asshole named Hepplewhite lived across the street saw me climbin' back in the window at Catfish Café to put the money back. Didn't seem to matter to the cops or anybody else that it was the wrong day. The money turned up missing Monday morning. Hepplewhite saw me on Tuesday evenin'. Dates didn't make no nevermind to them fuckers. I guess you could say I was never the same after."

"But you *did* put the money back?"

"That's right." He sipped from his bottle and looked at me.

"Where did the money under your mattress come from?"

"To this day, I don't know. I told them, but they wouldn't listen. Why should they? They had eleven hundred dollars from under my mattress. How would a skinny colored kid get eleven hundred dollars without he stole it? That's what they said. That's what the prosecutor said, and that's what the judge said."

"You told them you put the money back?"

" 'Course I told them."

"What about the restaurant? What happened when they turned up the missing eleven hundred at Catfish Café?"

"Never happened."

"The restaurant got the money back and didn't say anything?"

"All I know is nobody from the Café ever reported it returned."

"Maybe somebody stole it after you put it back?"

"You tell me who and I'll put an ice pick in their brain."

"Is that why you hang around the Café?"

"I hang there because Dion works there and Balinda used to and Laronda used to and I used to and they got good food. It's pathetic, isn't it? That money was back at Catfish Café when the cops pulled another eleven hundred bucks out from under my mattress. I couldn't get anybody to listen. Couldn't get nobody to even check it out."

"But the money must have been found at the restaurant."

"They never owned up to it. Probably wanted to collect the insurance."

"What you're saying is, you stole eleven hundred dollars, put it back, and then another eleven hundred dollars turned up under your mattress just in time for the police to find it?"

"You got it."

"There was a total of twenty-two hundred dollars floating around?"

"Unless somebody went back to the Café, stole it again, and stashed it in my room. I didn't get a good look at it, but the money under my mattress was big bills. The stuff from the Café was little stuff. I don't expect you to believe me, Black. Even my buddies don't believe me. I know it's a crazy story. I don't even know why I tell it. Makes me sick to my stomach to think about it. It ruined my life. You know that, don't you? It turned me bad."

I'd heard a lot of if-only-this-or-that hard luck stories in my time, and had dismissed most of them, largely because I'd never been one to subscribe to the theory that one accidental act or omission could be the pivot to someone's entire life; the notion discounted human will and character. If Raymond Sands wanted to believe he'd been framed and it had ruined his life, perhaps it was some comfort to him, but as far as I was concerned, it was all self-delusion.

"You think Dion's heard from Balinda in the last two days?" I asked.

"Black, you ain't listenin'. You wanta unnerstand Balinda and her problems, you gotta go back to the beginning. And the beginning of the bad in our family was Laronda. Little Miss Laronda. Her Whiteness. Despite how light her own ass is, she especially despises whites who want black women."

"Meaning Benjamin Aldrich?"

"Exactly."

"And black males who date white women?" I said. "How does she feel about them?"

"I won't argue over it. Laronda and I never got along. Her Whiteness looked down on me from about the first time she looked in the mirror and realized she was lighter than I was. I'll tell you what it all stemmed from. I caught her pregnant. I knew before anybody. And I told her so. I told her I was going to rat her out at church during the testimonies. There she was all high and mighty, fifteen years old, little Miss Whiteness, looking down on me like I was a bug in the cider, and she was as pregnant as the dog down the street."

"Are you saying you think she framed you so you wouldn't rat her out?"

"It was that same week. It's possible. People were eventually going to find out she was knocked up, but at least it wouldn't be me tellin' 'em."

"You think she put eleven hundred dollars under your mattress?"

"Maybe."

"Did she have that kind of money?"

"Not that I ever saw. Maybe she got it out of the Café after I put it back. She worked there in those days. I don't know how she did it. She hated me. Now she gives me handouts. This chair I'm sittin' in. She wore it out and gave it to me like a Christmas present."

All I could think of was what Pookie'd told me about Raymond and Balinda and the reason Raymond was no longer living in their house. A man who would molest his niece might also molest his sister. I wondered what he wasn't telling me.

"Here's my thinking on the matter," I said. "If Laronda was determined to frame you, and she knew you'd taken the money and put it back, and she went behind you and took the money back out of the restaurant and put it in your room, why would she change the bills to larger denominations?"

"That's the thing I ain't ever been able to explain. I'll tell you the truth. I got outta Monroe that first time, I was gonna do her. She was seein' Luther, and I was gonna do 'em both, but there was something in the back of my mind that just didn't set right."

"Like who had eleven hundred dollars to frame you with?"

"Nobody had eleven hundred dollars but me. I had it twice."

Pookie had been giving him puzzles probably since he was six, and here was a conundrum at the very core of his life, one he'd been working on for thirty years and hadn't solved. I wondered how many hours he'd spent locked away in a cell going over and over the facts as he remembered them, or as he'd painted them. I wondered what sorts of self-serving distortions had crept into his narration over the years.

We talked for another hour. Raymond told me a couple of stories about Luther's shenanigans when they were boys, then spent half an hour grousing about his personal and business woes. He bidded out private houses for painting but lost money when his hired help misplaced supplies, splashed paint on windowpanes, mixed the wrong colors, and squandered sunny days gossiping and running spurious errands.

Before I left I said, "Was old man Aldrich around the neighborhood much back then?"

"Who?"

"George Aldrich. He owned the building Catfish Café's in."

"He was around. When you called him an old man it threw me. He wasn't that old, but I guess he must be now. That was thirty years ago. He testified at my trial. He came in and tried to talk sense to the judge. First and last time I ever had a white guy go to bat for me."

"I'm trying to think of people who had money who might have had it in for you."

"You want to think of somebody around the neighborhood who had a hard-on for me, think about the board of our church. I had me some trouble there. Mrs. Scott. She was the treasurer. Coupla times when the church got broke into she came after me like I had something to do with it." He was suddenly indignant. "No reason at all, but she's standing in my face pointing that finger of hers up my nose."

"Didn't she just die?"

"Last week somebody ran her down with a car. Right down here on MLK. Never caught the son of a bitch."

I had to consider his tone. He didn't sound sorry.

"Who was the father of Laronda's child?"

He paused. "I never did figure that out."

"You know anything about the baby's death?"

"I was in the pokey by then."

"You'd kill Luther if you found out it was him who set you up?"

"I would."

"What if it was your sister or one of your brothers?"

"Sis has kids. I don't know."

"Luther's got kids."

"That's different. He was a cop." Raymond took a sip of

malt liquor and thought about it for a few moments. "You think he mighta got that job with the *po*-leece for turning me in?"

"It doesn't work that way. It never did."

"Tell me something. Did you ever frame somebody? Come on, now, this is just between friends. Even for a parking ticket?"

"Never. And neither did Luther. Luther followed the rules closer than anybody I ever met. By the way, did Laronda have any white boyfriends in high school?"

"Are you kidding? Laronda? And Luther don't mind the rules because he's good. He minds them 'cause he's scared. Some people follow the rules because they can see things run better when everybody follows them. Some people because it's the easiest way to do. Others because the rules protect others and they're considerate of others. And then there's the ones who follow the rules because they're scared not to. That was always Luther."

"And you?"

"I make my own rules."

When I left the house at midnight, two little girls I hadn't seen before were sitting cross-legged in front of the television in the tomb-dark living room. If I'd had to guess, I would have put their ages at around seven and nine. Big-eyed and stunned, the girls looked up at me like startled fawns. Then they looked at each other and shyly returned my wave. Tomorrow was a school day, but I couldn't see how they were going to wake up in time to catch a bus. I went out the front door, locking it behind me.

It was a sign of how tired I was that I left Raymond's place thinking the incident with the stolen money from Catfish Café really did have something to do with the family, with Balinda and Benjamin Aldrich and the wreck and the shooting. But then I realized how crazy that would sound if I tried to explain it. For starters, there was no way Raymond had ever returned any stolen money.

Raymond was just another anguished ex-con dredging up excuses for why he'd flushed his life down the toilet. Over the years, I'd spoken to dozens of them, and every one had his own customized excuse. Down deep, Raymond Sands felt he could have been somebody, that what happened to him must have been the fault of another. Down deep, Raymond was the center of the universe and someday the rest of us would know it.

I wondered if he had come to believe his fantastic story himself. His thinking was wrapped in a delusional cocoon of paranoia in which he believed his sister, his best friend, or somebody else close to him had set him up, and now, over thirty years later, he still couldn't put his finger on who did it or why; nor could he trust his sister, his brothers, or his former best friend. Added to that stew was his general distrust of all authority and of the establishment. His world view was built on quicksand.

When I got home, I parked in the street and walked up the concrete strips in my gently sloping driveway to the back door. As I passed the lighted kitchen window in the basement, I happened to glance in and catch sight of Sonya, and for just a split second our eyes met. She was at the sink wearing, of all things, a see-through baby-doll nightie.

CHAPTER 32

Tuesday morning I hired a middle-aged African-American woman to do surveillance on Pookie's house. Constance drove a battered old Datsun onto Thirty-second Avenue, parked where she could maintain a sweeping view of the front yard, raised the hood, scattered some wrenches and screwdrivers around, and began her wait. There was no back street entrance, so if Balinda or one of her friends came to round up Toylee or collect clothing, my operative would spot them.

I'd given the birth certificate info to my researcher in Oregon, and during the course of the morning Hilda faxed me more information as she amassed it.

My plan was to call the surviving parents of these thirty-year-olds one by one and ask if anybody remembered Laronda Sands, had spoken to her, roomed with her, or knew anything about her predicament three decades ago. There was one certificate in addition to the Sands certificate on which no father was listed. It was for a male, and Rachel Robeson was the name of the mother. I decided to start there.

Hilda, genius that she was, figured out where her parents lived thirty years ago—Lakewood—and what her married name was now. We located her parents, but could not trace an address or phone number for her, so I called her elderly mother, Mildred Robeson, and gave her a long and carefully crafted story about working for an attorney who needed to find her daughter to help locate an old friend of her daughter's who was a beneficiary in somebody's will. An eager minion to authority, she gave me her daughter's address and phone number without thinking twice.

Rachel Robeson lived on Bainbridge Island, an eclectic community a short ferry ride across the sound from Seattle. She'd been married three times, and her last name was now Strandburg. She answered the phone on the third ring, and as I listened to her say hello, I tried to evaluate how she was going to take this less-than-surgical intrusion into her history and commerce. Over the phone her house sounded as quiet as the inside of a book. She'd probably be around fifty by now and sounded as if she worked at being dignified.

Without telling her about Aldrich's death, or saying anything about what happened thirty years ago, I explained who I was and slowly tried to introduce the disappearance of Balinda Sands.

"I don't understand," Mrs. Strandburg said.

"You were in Swedish Hospital almost exactly thirty years ago to give birth to a baby."

She took a deep breath and her tone grew defensive. "What do you really want?"

"I'm trying to help a young woman who's in serious trouble. I believe her mother was on that ward with you."

"I don't remember anything from thirty years ago."

"Do you remember a young African American named Laronda Sands on that ward?"

Another long silence. I had a feeling this would have been done better in person. Whatever demons were haunting Rachel Strandburg's past, she didn't want any fresh air on them.

"I remember a black girl. As I recall, she was quite shy."

"She must have been very frightened."

"I felt sorry for her. Her mother was out of town for some reason that escapes me. I think she was the only one on the floor who never received a visitor. I've always wondered what happened to her."

"She's a successful insurance executive in downtown Seattle. Unfortunately, her baby died just a few days after you last saw her."

"That's too bad."

"She has four other children, and it's one of those we're looking for."

"I don't understand."

"When Laronda's daughter disappeared, she was with a young man. He had a handful of birth certificates, and I have reason to think one of them might have been for the child you had in Swedish. This young man may have contacted you looking for his birth parents."

"I'm tempted to hang up on you, Mr. Black. There isn't any missing woman, is there?"

"There most definitely is. Perhaps if we spoke in person? Maybe—"

"That's not going to be possible."

"Mrs. Strandburg, you had a baby in Swedish Hospital thirty years ago."

"If you've got the birth certificate, I guess there's no point in denying it, is there?"

"There was no father listed."

Another long silence.

"I'm just trying to figure out if you gave the baby up for adoption. I know this type of situation can be delicate, and believe me, if a young woman's life didn't possibly hang in the balance, I wouldn't be asking. Did you adopt the baby out?"

Like a magician pulling rabbits out of a hat, I was bringing up events from her past, events her friends and neighbors and maybe even her husband didn't know about.

"Is this a trick? Are you trying to trap me into saying something?"

"It isn't any kind of a trick."

"That's not a . . . Did Hal send you? Are you working for Hal?"

"I don't know any Hal."

"I thought maybe Hal . . . Hal was my first husband."

"All I want to know is whether or not a young man contacted you sometime in the past month asking about his birth mother."

Her voice broke and she said, "You have no right to call me like this. You have no right. My husband's a lawyer, and I don't want to hear from you again. Is that clear? If I do, my husband's going to make you very sorry. I don't have to talk about this. I don't even know you."

"Just one last question," I said. "It doesn't have anything to do with you."

"What is it?"

"Do you know how Laronda's baby died?"

"I didn't even realize he had died until you told me."

There was another angle to this, another way to deal with it, and for just a split second some of the light from that angle glimmered somewhere in the distance as if at the end of a long tunnel, but like all light, I couldn't quite grasp it. It was possible she had spoken to Benjamin Aldrich. It was even possible Benjamin was her son. I wondered what her reaction would be if she found out her son had died trying to locate her. I decided to find out.

"I think you should know that the young man I'm talking about was killed a week ago."

The banging of the receiver in my ear sent a little shiver of shock through my system.

Besides turning up the addresses of most of the parents in the obstetrics ward in Swedish Hospital thirty years ago, Hilda had turned up another curious fact, one that bothered me enough that I asked her to double-check it. There was no record of anybody with the last name of Sands who died in Seattle or even in King County during the year in question.

Had the body been disposed of outside the law? Could I be looking into a thirty-year-old murder?

By two that afternoon I had reached six more of the eleven mothers who'd been on Laronda's floor at Swedish. Three of them recalled a young African American on the ward but remembered little about her. Two were determined to fill me in on their own grown children. I listened politely and extricated myself from the conversations as soon as possible. According to Hilda, one of the babies, along with the mother and father, had been killed in a car accident seven years later.

Only one of the women I spoke to admitted having had any contact with Benjamin Aldrich in the past month. She said a polite young man had telephoned and told her he was looking for his mother. The conversation had been brief, her memory hazy. She hadn't been able to help him.

At two-thirty I was on the phone with her when Luther reached me on another line. He said, "You gotta hurry. I don't know if I can hold her."

"Balinda?"

"She's at Bloomberg's Nursing Home. I don't know why I didn't check here before. Mrs. Bloomberg took good care of her when she worked here. Hurry. I need help."

CHAPTER 33

Bloomberg's Nursing Home was in the paper every once in a while. It was in an old house tucked up so close against Providence Hospital at Seventeenth and Jefferson that it looked as if it'd been pushed off the roof. Twenty years ago Bloomberg's had been a house in a block of houses, but now Adele Bloomberg was the lone holdout in a decades-long campaign by the hospital to own the block. In fact, a wing of the hospital had been built around the house.

Adele Bloomberg had been in that spot for forty-seven years, and if the hospital board was waiting for her to retire to Arizona or die, they were in for a ride. They'd offered Adele money, a new house, even a world cruise. What they hadn't offered were homes for her "people," and Adele wasn't about to sell her residents down the river.

When I pulled up on Seventeenth, the hearse was parked in front of the nursing home and Luther was standing on the front porch flapping his right arm in what he must have thought was a signal. Adele Bloomberg, an African-American woman with a kindly face, golden skin, and a skein of wild gray hair sitting high on her head, stood beside him telling him to get the hearse out of sight.

"It's a morale inhibitor for my people," she said, but Luther wasn't listening.

I parked next to the hearse and went up the porch steps.

Luther wore dark green slacks, wing-tips, and a black blazer with a yellow Dibble's Funeral Home emblem embroidered on the chest. I recalled years ago Luther boasting about getting Balinda a job at Bloomberg's, proud both of his daughter and prouder still of himself for having helped her out.

Balinda had worked here long enough to become part of the troupe of workers and residents that made up Adele Bloomberg's makeshift family. She'd been working at Bloomberg's when she met a man at a party who gave her the taste of crack cocaine that destroyed her life.

"Come on, Thomas. Let's get a move on. She locked herself in the damn baffroom." Luther was annoyed because I wasn't running. He turned to Adele on the porch beside him and said, "This is the guy I told you about. He's gonna help me."

He'd waited eight days to find her and was dancing around like a boy who had to pee after a long car trip.

Bloomberg's was orderly but crowded, full of gray skin and tired eyes, furniture with rounded corners and frayed seams. The rooms were filled to capacity with couches, bureaus, china hutches, dining tables, and, just off the front entrance, a television set with eight elderly people fanned out in front of it. Not one of them took notice of us as we passed between them and the television. The aromas inside the old house were a mystical combination of mothballs, old sweat, and the familiar smell of institutional cooking peculiar to cafeterias and school lunchrooms, a smell that seemed to cling to your clothing like a solvent.

Adele Bloomberg tried to follow us as we rushed through

one crowded room after another and made our way up a set of winding steps to the second story. In exasperation, she remained at the bottom of the stairs looking up at me.

The bathroom was at the end of a long obstacle course of a hallway with several armoires standing along the walls.

Threading his way down the corridor, Luther pounded on the bathroom door with his fist and hollered, "Balinda! You get on outta there, girl. I wanta talk to you."

No answer.

Even though I'd witnessed hostility from Luther in the past couple of days, Luther wasn't normally prone to tantrums. He hated displays and felt they demeaned the perpetrator. In fact, generally speaking, Luther was about the most even-tempered man around. That I'd seen him blow his stack two or three times now was a measure of his concern.

I said, "Luther, she's scared. You can't act like she's some wayward little girl in need of a spanking."

"I'm just so goddamned mad about this whole business. I didn't think of this place until a few minutes ago, and there she is, watchin' TV with Toylee like nobody's even worried. She sees me and runs like I'm gonna whip her."

"Listen, Luther. Why don't you go sit on that chair? Let me be the mediator here."

"She's *my* goddamned daughter!"

"Yes, and that's why I think I can talk to her in a way you can't right now. You called me so I could try. Let me try."

Luther stumped to the end of the hallway and stood next to a chair.

I knocked softly on the bathroom door. After a while it opened a crack. Balinda was fleshier than I recalled, but just as pretty, with full lips, flawless skin, a broad forehead, and, when she smiled, cheeks as round as doorknobs. Her hair was done up in dozens of thin braids that dropped from the top of her head in distinct waves, the upper waves beaded mostly gold and blue, the lower ones purple. Her perfume was the same fragrance I'd encountered inside her car in the towing garage.

Balinda waved two fingers at her father and said, "Hey."

"Hey," he said, without raising his arms from his sides. He seemed to relax.

I told her who I was and asked if she was all right. She assured me she was, although I could see an inch-long laceration on her brow. It looked about a week old. The left side of her face and neck was stippled as if somebody'd glued pepper fragments to her jaw. I'd seen that sort of wound before and had a pretty good idea what had caused it. When I asked her to send Toylee down the hallway to her grandfather, she gave the child a kiss and a hug before releasing her.

Balinda sat on the toilet lid while I leaned against the doorjamb. She wore black shoes that looked like slippers, black slacks, and a blue blouse. She wore five gold bracelets on one wrist, three rings on her opposite hand. Two small travel bags sat on the floor near her feet. She sat with her knees together and her hands folded calmly in her lap. It reminded me of the way Peggy Lindseth had posed when I interviewed her.

"Would you like to tell us what's going on?" I said.

"He's gonna get mad," she said.

"You're not on drugs, are you?"

"No." She was indignant that I'd asked.

"Then he's not mad. Are you, Luther?"

"I'm not mad," Luther said from down the hall, where he was standing just within earshot.

"I'm scared," Balinda said.

"We know. Tell us what happened."

Her rendition of the chase and shooting was nearly identical to Peggy's, so close, in fact, that I wondered if it had been rehearsed. The two grieving women must have discussed it endlessly in the six days and nights they'd been together.

"Me and Benjamin were sitting in my car talking, and this other car came up on us and started chasing us. We drove around like that for a while and then I went off the road."

"You were driving?"

"Yes. They were right on our bumper. Ben kept saying they were going to ram us, to go faster. So I kept going faster. And then we were kind of . . . I don't know . . . I was bleeding real good. Ben said he needed to get me to a hospital."

"You went over a hillside and got caught by a tree," I said.

"Is that what happened? I wanted to go back to see, but I was afraid. It was weird, because the headlights were still on and I was trying to figure out where we were when a voice came in my window right next to my face. He was all breathless like he'd been running. I tried to look at him, but he had a light in my face. There were two of them, but I never saw either one."

"What happened?"

"One of them shot Ben. That gun. I couldn't hear anything for two days. He said he was going to let me go but that he knew where I lived."

"That's why you've been hiding out? Because they knew you?"

"Yes."

"Did you recognize the car?"

"No."

"The voices of the men?"

"No."

"Do you know why they were chasing you or why they shot Ben?"

"No."

"Did Ben know them?"

"I don't think so."

"Were they white or black? The assailants?"

"I'm not sure. I think they were black."

"And you're sure you didn't know them?"

"That's just it. I probably did. But I couldn't see. And then after the shooting I couldn't hear, and that's when they did the most talking. I was waiting for them to shoot me. Only they didn't. I'm not even sure what all they said. After they left, I looked at Ben and I knew he was dead. I started to go home because Pookie's is only a couple of blocks from there, but I saw a car driving past the house a couple of times real slow, and I figured they changed their minds and were after me."

"That's why you didn't go to the police?"

"Yes."

"Balinda, what was your business with Benjamin Aldrich?"

"He was looking for his real parents. I was helping."

"Did he find them?"

"He thought he found one of them."

"Who?"

"My mother."

"Aldrich was white."

"He looked white, but he was my brother. We couldn't prove it, but we were finding all kinds of stuff that hinted at it. For instance, when he first came to our house and talked to Mother, she got really mad. *Really* mad. She doesn't do that unless you push a certain button. I think she gave him away and never wanted to be reminded of him again. Mother didn't want to acknowledge that she'd had relations with a white man."

"So you and Benjamin were looking into this together?"

"Yes. I found letters in the attic written from my mother to Pookie when Pookie was in Chicago. It was the week my mother had her baby. It was so strange reading letters your mother wrote to her mother over thirty years ago. Laronda was younger than I am now. She didn't know anything. These days I don't think there's much she isn't sure of."

"I thought the baby she had thirty years ago died."

"I did find a letter from my mother to Pookie that said that, but I don't believe it and neither did Ben. It was the same year my uncle Raymond went to prison the first time. A lot of things were going on."

"So how does this connect with Aldrich's death?" Luther asked, walking down the hall with Toylee in his arms. The girl looked drowsy. Balinda must have picked her up in the wee hours before my operative was in place.

"I don't know. I still don't know who shot him."

"Somebody goin' to shoot us, Mommy?" Toylee asked, coming suddenly alert.

"Nobody goin' to do anything," Luther said reassuringly. Toylee laid her head back down on her grandfather's shoulder.

"Look," I said. "We've got an attorney waiting. We want you to go to the authorities."

"The police think you're running from them," Luther said. He was behind me in the doorway now.

"But I wouldn't hurt Ben. Ask Peggy."

"I want you to see a doctor too," I said. "I want to get some pictures of your face. Those look like powder burns on your left cheek."

"I think we better take her over to see her mother too," Luther said. "We run her over to the cops first, Laronda'll be pissin' lemon soup."

Outside, Luther and I had a moment together while Balinda buckled Toylee into the backseat of my car. Luther whispered through clenched teeth. "Laronda didn't have no white man's baby. Jesus Christ."

"You think what they were doing was connected to the shooting?" I asked.

"No way. Somebody saw them in the lot and was spoilin' for trouble. In this town it happens all the time."

We drove Toylee back to Pookie's, and I stopped to thank and then dismiss my operative down the street. Then we drove downtown and parked in an underground lot off Second Avenue, hiking two blocks up the hill on Union, the three of us squinting in the sunshine.

"Mom isn't going to be happy about this," Balinda said.

"That you found out she had a baby when she was sixteen?" Luther said. "No, I don't guess she will be."

CHAPTER 34

There were questions I wanted to ask Balinda, little chinks in her story I wanted to pry into and tax, but there was a layer of icy apprehension overlaying our visit to Laronda that kept us all from speaking. Laronda, or so Luther had reminded me many times, carried a gun, which she had taken out and brandished three times over the course of their tortuous partnership. It wasn't that any of us thought Laronda was going to haul out her pistol today; it was just that we knew how mercurial she could be.

As we walked from the spring sunshine into the shadows of the building, past the security guard and into the huge lobby of the skyscraper, I suggested we call before going up.

"No dice," Luther said irritably. "That's only going to give her a chance to get up a head of steam."

We rode the elevator with a big-haired blonde in stiletto heels and with a bicycle messenger who smelled of cologne and dog. We got off on twelve and went down the hallway to a door designated PENSACK INSURANCE. It was a large office with dozens of partitions slicing individual work areas into mazes.

Balinda, who had been the shortest player on her high

school basketball team and who couldn't see over the tops of the partitions into the hopelessness of it all, was impressed.

The receptionist's desk was empty, so we waited a few moments, and then Laronda backed into view from a cubicle fifty feet away, where she'd been talking to a desk jockey.

Luther whispered, "Laronda run all this shit."

"All of it?" Balinda asked.

"Every speck."

Laronda spotted the three of us, gave a startled look, pulled her dress straight, and strode forward with long, artificial yet purposeful strides. She wore black shoes and a purple suit that highlighted her skin tone. In the breeze from her movement, her straightened hair flapped on either side of her head. She walked directly to Balinda and gave her what most people would have dubbed a dispassionate hug.

"How are you, baby?"

"I'm fine, Mother."

Before Balinda could explain where she'd been all week, Laronda took us down the long corridor she had come up, around a corner, down another corridor, and then down two flights to a lunchroom that was vacant except for two food servers in paper caps. We took a table in the rear, which Laronda polished with a handful of napkins. She worked so hard at it, I had to wonder if she was working over the table or her thoughts. When she was finished and the four of us were seated and calm, she pitched the wad of napkins onto the tabletop beside us, where it lay like a wounded bird. The place smelled like the inside of a coffeepot.

Balinda launched into her story, then comforted her distraught mother, patting her on the back without either of them getting out of their chairs.

Luther said, "You unnerstand what she was doing with that boy, don't you?"

"Doing?" Laronda asked suspiciously.

She'd seemed irritated by our intrusion, but more irritated by Luther's immediacy. I couldn't be sure, but I had the feeling she was embarrassed by Luther. Whether it was that or the funeral home blazer, or me, I couldn't tell.

"Don't you get it, Laronda?" Luther said. "Aldrich and Balinda was lookin' into the circumstances of your first baby when Aldrich got hisself killed."

Laronda gave Luther a long look. "Lyle?"

"The baby you had when you was in high school."

Laronda sat up straight. I'd always thought she was a peculiarly unattractive woman, had always felt guilty over the thought. Maybe it was the way Laronda straightened her hair almost like a bad wig, so that if you caught it from the right angle you could see high on her scalp. Maybe it was the scowl. Maybe it was just the fact that I knew she didn't care for me and, in particular, didn't care for the fact that Luther and I were friends. What made me feel even more guilty was that Luther had always told me how other men coveted her. She could have her pick, he said, and she'd picked him.

What made the needle of guilt run through the bone and into the marrow was that I really wanted Luther to be happy and felt certain, despite the three kids they'd shared together, despite their history, that he and Laronda would never be happy together.

"Okay," Laronda said quietly. "I had a baby before Lyle. What does that have to do with anything?"

Minimizing her part in the intrigue, Balinda explained what Benjamin Aldrich thought he'd unearthed, that Aldrich had been hers, that she had given him up.

For almost a minute after Balinda finished her stuttering tale, Laronda observed her daughter and then stared at the tiles in the lunchroom ceiling and at the joking kitchen workers at the far end of the room, as if she knew them and was trying to hear what they were saying.

She said, "There was a college girl I met in the ward who wanted to give her baby up for adoption. I couldn't see that myself. After all, a baby is something you carry in yourself. Part of you. Part of your blood. I love all my children like they're still part of me." She reached across the table to pat Balinda's hand, but Balinda nervously pulled back. Mother caught daughter's hand and held it. It was the warmest and perhaps truest gesture I'd seen from Laronda in all the time I'd known her. "I don't recall her name just now, but she wanted to give the baby a good home. A nice white family. We got to talking, and I told her about Mrs. Aldrich wanting a baby. Together we took it over there."

Hungry for confirming details, Luther said, "You left it on the porch?"

"We just found out where Aldrich lived and took him over. Left him outside and went away. All I remember is the girl cried all the way back. Like I was supposed to be sympathetic. My baby died."

I'd spoken with the woman I assumed she was talking about, Rachel Strandburg, and what she told me she remembered from thirty years ago was far different. I knew Rachel Strandburg hadn't told me everything, but while Strandburg recalled a young African-American girl, she did not seem to realize Laronda's baby had died. And she certainly hadn't admitted to giving her baby away.

"Do you remember the mother's name?" I asked.

Laronda gave me a sharp look, her tone chilly, her dark eyes dismissing. We were in an environment where she was used to being in control, and she clearly was not happy with our interrogation. So much of Laronda's life, at least the way I understood it from Luther, was about wielding or not wielding power.

"No, I don't remember her name. It was a long time ago, and I haven't thought about it in years."

At least not since the night Benjamin Aldrich showed up at Pookie's, I thought.

"The name Rachel Robeson doesn't jar your memory?"

"No. Do we have to talk about this?"

"Laronda, I'm not trying to put you on the spot, but I've been treading the same territory as Benjamin Aldrich, tracking down babies born in the ward where you were, and I've come up with a curious piece of information. We can't find a death certificate for anybody named Sands for the year in question."

"That's ridiculous."

"How did your baby die?"

Luther glared at me, and I could see a plea for temperance in his eyes. But being polite wasn't going to resolve the issues.

When Laronda felt we'd stared at each other sufficiently, she said, "Okay, the child didn't die."

"What happened to it?" Luther asked, incredulity straining his voice.

"I gave it away," Laronda said. "I gave it up for adoption. But not to the Aldrichs. My baby was black."

"Did you use an agency?" I asked.

"I don't see what any of this could have to do with anything. I just don't."

"Come on, Laronda," Luther said. "You been keepin' secrets. These two kids were diggin' 'em up. Now one of them's dead and the other one's scared to come home. Help us out here."

"My past doesn't have anything to do with what happened to that boy."

"You ain't gonna tell us, are you?" Luther said.

"It was a family up the street. All I remember is their name was Stimson and they had a little girl, but they couldn't have any more kids. They had a lot of money. About a year later they pulled up stakes and moved to Texas. I haven't heard from them since."

"I have another brother?" Balinda said.

"I suppose you do."

"Who was Benjamin Aldrich?" Balinda asked.

"I told you," Laronda said. "He was the son of a woman in my hospital ward."

"Where in Texas?" Luther asked.

"I have no idea," Laronda said.

The conversation dwindled down to a mother-daughter session in which the two women pretty much pretended we weren't there. Expecting nothing further, Luther and I sat patiently, he tapping a front tooth with a Dibble's pen he'd taken out of his blazer.

I was beginning to daydream and wonder whether I should call Kathy when Balinda said, "I only had one worry the whole week I was hiding out, and that was when Benjamin's father showed up."

"Tell me about this," Laronda said.

"Peggy didn't know he had his own key, and I guess he didn't know I was there, because one day while she was out he came in and was drinking beer out of the icebox like he had the place to himself. I came out of the back bedroom and he liked to call the cops on me. I had to convince him I was friends with Peggy. He finished his beer and then reached out for me like I was something on the shelf he could take. He said he liked 'dark meat.' I opened the front door and stood in the doorway and told him to leave. Even then, it was ten, maybe fifteen minutes before I could get him out of there. There were neighbors in the courtyard, and after I thought about it later, I realized that was the only reason he left, because he heard the neighbors and knew I had witnesses."

Luther had grown very still.

Jaw muscles knotted, forehead suddenly rutted with deep corrugations, Laronda asked her daughter to repeat the story and then mined it for details. Luther was watching his daughter too, but now he seemed to shrink into himself, like a house cat curling up on a cold winter porch waiting for his master to come home. It was hard to interpret this sudden change of attitude in a man whom I'd watched stand up to bullets and maniacs and who'd always been unflappable in the midst of any turmoil. I didn't think it was possible he was scared of old man Aldrich, but maybe he was.

When they had worried the subject enough, Balinda excused herself to visit the rest room. She seemed more and more brittle the longer we were around her. Moments later, saying she had plenty of work to keep her occupied, Laronda left.

"She mad?" I asked.

"Oh, yeah." Luther's voice was dry. "You better call your friend Aldrich and tell him to be on the lookout for her."

"Don't call him my friend."

"I'm sorry. I'm all het up."

Laronda's anger remained thick in the room like humidity in a house where somebody'd just taken a shower.

"You really think somebody needs to warn Aldrich?" I asked.

"She was that mad at me, I'd want to be warned."

CHAPTER 35

We took the elevator up two floors and retraced our route to Pensack Insurance. Balinda and I waited in the hallway while Luther went in to try to assuage Laronda's anger. He came back out immediately.

"She's gone for the day," he said.

"Where'd she go?" Balinda asked.

"I'll give you two guesses." Luther pushed the button for the elevators and looked at me over the top of Balinda's head. It was the kind of look he used to give me when we were grilling somebody on the street and we'd decided they were giving us some bad juju. "The receptionist said she took off outta here like a house on fire."

"Maybe we should head her off."

"Not this kid. I'm not getting between Laronda and her mad."

"Is Mother going after Ben's father?" Balinda asked.

"That's what Luther thinks," I said.

"I hope he doesn't hurt her," Balinda said.

Luther and I exchanged looks.

What made me uneasy about Laronda and her gun was that according to Luther she carried at least a hundred rounds of ammunition, sometimes twice that. It was one thing to carry a gun in her purse for protection, but even uniformed officers didn't carry a hundred rounds. What was she expecting? A coup at the office? An Armageddon at the cab stand?

After dropping Luther and Balinda off at Kathy's office, I called Aldrich's home in Tacoma, but all I got was his machine. Without labeling him an opportunity rapist and without calling Laronda a revenge killer, I tried to explain as precisely as I could that he might soon encounter some difficulty. George Aldrich operated on a curious set of standards. He'd told Benjamin it was immoral to live with Peggy, yet he'd propositioned Balinda.

I left my cell phone number along with the message and walked away with an ominous feeling that the answer machine tape would end up as an exhibit at a trial.

By eight that evening Laronda was home. Aldrich had not called back, but there had been no news reports of murders in Tacoma, so maybe we were okay.

Kathy and I had been invited to an impromptu party Pookie was throwing in celebration of Balinda's safe return, and after dining downtown at La Buca, we drove up Yesler. I wondered how I could get Laronda to tell us if she'd killed anybody that afternoon.

Kathy kicked her gray shoes off in the car and unbuttoned the top buttons of her suit.

"Luther and I had a little chat while we were waiting around at police headquarters," she said. "Luther told me he thought he was close to getting Balinda to admit it was Raymond who shot Aldrich."

"I thought she didn't know who."

"Luther claims she does."

"He didn't say anything to me about it."

"He told me Balinda went ballistic at the nursing home

and hid out in the bathroom because he had her about to implicate her uncle in the shooting."

"It was my impression she hid out because she was afraid of Luther."

"Why would her uncle shoot Aldrich?"

"Pookie told me Raymond made some advances toward Balinda when she was in high school. Sexual advances. He might have thought she and Aldrich were dating and become jealous."

"Oh, dear."

"He once shot a guy in a convenience store because he didn't like the way he looked at him. I had a long talk with him the other night, and we could have been just two guys talking. But I'm no mind reader. Who knows what he would do?"

"This should be an interesting evening. Raymond will probably be here."

We turned off Yesler onto Thirty-first, drove past the school playground, and went down Spruce to Thirty-second, parking in front of the house behind several cars I didn't recognize. I'd driven the route so many times in the past week it was beginning to feel like the way home.

At the front door Toylee welcomed us, giggling when I introduced Kathy, who pretended to steal her nose. Then Shereffe burst upon us, followed by two neighborhood girls I'd not seen before. Kathy asked for a piece of string and tied it into a loop and then made it look as if it had passed through her neck. We suddenly had four little girls who wanted to move in with us.

Laronda and Balinda had taken on the burden of hosting and were bustling to and from the kitchen, refilling plates and cups and stacking cookies on trays. Pookie and D'Witt sat in the living room and played word games. Shawn Brown had been found and for some reason was not nearly as sullen as he'd been the two earlier times I'd seen him. Kathy soon had him talking about the basketball playoffs, a subject I hadn't even realized she was interested in, and then one of his friends came in and the three of them moved to a corner and had a lengthy chat.

D'Witt had a young woman friend named Margaret— Caucasian, a little chubby, a little shy, a girl who seemed to relish running around getting things for him. Buster, one of Raymond's friends, was standing along a wall in the TV room. He looked a tad nervous and was apparently waiting for Raymond to show up before joining the celebration. He was watching an NBA playoff game on the television through the corona of noise and movement in the living room.

When Pookie met Kathy, she said, "So. You're Mr. Black's young woman?" Pookie peered over her spectacles. "I understand you like puzzles."

"Are you the one who's been sending me those wonderful puzzles?" Kathy exclaimed, her eyes lighting up. Pookie threw a new puzzle at Kathy, which she solved within moments.

D'Witt, who had wheeled into the room during the puzzle fun, was introduced to Kathy, as was his friend, Margaret. Except for a few minutes spent with Buster, Luther kept to himself. Raymond hadn't arrived yet.

After a while the party split into two groups. The adults and Shawn and his friends all settled down to watch the last quarter of the ball game. D'Witt, his girlfriend, and the four girls headed out the wheelchair ramp in back to visit the school playground across the street. Pookie shouted for them all to come home before dark.

The Bulls were up by four when Shereffe and D'Witt hollered at us from outside the front door. D'Witt couldn't make it up the steps in his wheelchair, but Pookie, Luther, Kathy, and I went out onto the porch. Moments later D'Witt's friend, Margaret, whom he had outdistanced in his chair, came jogging up the street from the schoolyard with Toylee and the other girls.

Everybody was talking at once, but the upshot of it was that the police had found a dead man on the playground. At first Shereffe and her two friends were nearly hysterical, and then they *were* hysterical. Pookie clapped her hands together to capture their attention, snapped at them to shut up, and herded them up the steps and into the house.

D'Witt and Margaret headed back to the playground. Luther glanced at me and we followed. Kathy gave me a wink that told me she was going to stay. Shawn and the others, who'd come out onto the porch during a commercial break, went back to polish off the game. Laronda didn't even look interested.

"Just his legs is all you can see," D'Witt said, working his wheelchair just enough to stay in front of us.

Doors winged open, engines running, lights flashing, two blue-and-whites were already on the playground. It was dark enough so their flashing blue lights cast shadows on the walls of the brick school. Leschi Elementary faced Yesler Way, so we were walking onto the playground from the rear. To the east of the school was a small park with brightly painted play equipment, and that's where the body was.

As we arrived, two paramedics carrying fishing tackle boxes full of drugs and equipment walked away from a small, brush-covered knoll. From outside the crime scene tape, which had already been stretched out, we could see, after D'Witt pointed it out, a pair of legs in thin, wool trousers.

When one of the young officers came over to us and asked if we knew anything, I explained that Luther and I were both ex-SPD. Luther, who had never asked for any special consideration in his life, wouldn't have done it in a million years, but I convinced the officer to let us through in the unlikely event that one of us might be able to ID the body. The officer took us to within twenty feet of the dead man.

He was African American, in his early fifties, lying on his chest, his face cocked toward us, eyes open. He wore a long-sleeve shirt that was bright orange where blood hadn't darkened it.

Luther turned his head sideways and said, "Damn, Raymond. What are you doing here?"

"It is Raymond, isn't it?" I said.

"You know this man?" the officer asked.

"Raymond Sands," Luther said. "His mother lives right over there. He was comin' to our party. I guess we know why he was late."

He had two gold rings on, as well as a necklace that was probably worth as much as my truck, so this probably hadn't been a robbery. As far as I could tell, there was nothing in his hands. From our vantage point I could see nothing in the vicinity that didn't belong. There were what appeared to be drag marks in the wood chips, but what with all the footprints from hundreds of children, it would take an expert tracker to figure out how far he'd been dragged, or even *if* he'd been dragged. Near the drag marks was a large, half-smoked cigar. It was in good shape, and I felt sure that, had it been there very long, one of the neighborhood kids would have either destroyed it or smoked it.

More police arrived.

Dogs and handlers searched the area.

The cigar was picked up and put into a plastic bag by an officer.

D'Witt and Margaret got cold and headed back to Pookie's.

The King County Medical Examiner's blue van pulled onto the playground. After we'd been there awhile, the officer we'd identified the body for came over with an open notebook and said, "We've got a sighting of the dead man talking to a white guy driving a gray Mercedes. Either one of you know anybody drives a gray Mercedes?"

Luther and I looked at each other. George Aldrich had a gray Mercedes.

Raymond had kicked Benjamin Aldrich out of the house largely as a favor to Laronda. I wondered if Raymond had been set to do another favor for Laronda, punishing George

Aldrich for predations on Balinda, ironically something Raymond himself had been accused of.

"You get any kinda license or description of the driver of the Mercedes?" Luther asked.

"No license. The kid who saw it just said he was a white man. Actually, he said he was an ugly white man. Said he was parked out on the street three hours ago. Around dinnertime. Anybody hear shots around then?"

Luther said he'd been having dinner at Pookie's and hadn't heard any gunfire. I said I'd been downtown. We told the officer George Aldrich was an ugly white man who owned a Mercedes. We told him that as far as we knew, Aldrich and Raymond would have had no reason to get together; that as far as we knew, they'd last seen each other thirty years ago. Luther told him about Aldrich's son's death eight days earlier only blocks from where we were standing. The officer took notes.

Soon a homicide detective I'd never met before came over and repeated most of the uniformed officer's questions. We repeated most of our answers.

When we left the playground, Raymond was still on his face. It was the second time that day I'd been reminded of *The Wizard of Oz*—the first was Bloomberg's Nursing Home sitting next to the hospital as if it had just dropped out of the sky, and now, Raymond's legs sticking out from the brush as if a house had come down on him.

I didn't really know the man and scarcely liked what I had known, so I was more upset over Raymond's death than I had reason to be.

What I was thinking was that if members of this family were being slaughtered, Balinda was no safer now than ever. I saw the same thoughts running through Luther's mind.

It was dark when we walked back to Pookie's house. A few of the emergency vehicles had left, and most of the neighbor kids had drifted off to other pursuits. Luther said, "I always expected Raymond to kick the bucket like that, but I never figured it would happen this close to home."

"Two deaths in eight days. This follows your cockroach theory, Luther."

Luther turned his sad face toward me and showed me his teeth. "You remember that?"

"Surprises are like cockroaches. You rarely get just one."

"It was one thing for a kid nobody knew to get killed. It's another deal entirely when Raymond gets it. Maybe Balinda was right. Maybe she needs to get outta Dodge."

"Was Raymond still hanging out with guys from the joint?"

"He had a couple no good friends. But I do too. We all do."

"You think Aldrich was up here?" I asked.

"Lot of people got Benz cars. Lotta people are white and ugly."

Luther laughed at the look on my face. He studied me for a moment and laughed again. Whether he wanted to admit it or not, Raymond's death was the mainspring for more good humor in Luther than I'd seen in days. I knew that part of him regretted it, but it had lightened his mood in a manner I could not explain other than to say one more of his contemporaries had left this plane of existence before he had. Unceasing pessimist that he was, Luther had always predicted he was going to die before practically everybody he knew, even his grandmother, thus he couldn't help but be delighted any time he was found mistaken.

"The cops are going to want to talk to George Aldrich," I said.

"If he *was* here and shot Raymond, he'll say he wasn't here. On the other hand, if he *was* here and *didn't* shoot Raymond, he'll say he wasn't here. Then again, if he *wasn't* up here, he'll say he wasn't here. About any way you paint it, he'll say he wasn't here."

"Maybe we should give this to Pookie," I joked. "Maybe she can figure it out."

"Pookie can't figure out nothin'. She gets those puzzles from a book. But listen up, Thomas. You gotta talk to her. And Laronda too. You gotta get to the bottom of this before anybody else gets hurt. You gotta help me, Thomas. Them women ain't gonna listen to my skinny ass. They're holdin' out. You and I both know it."

CHAPTER 36

As we walked toward Pookie's house we saw Dion Williams on the lighted front porch. Somebody opened the front door and he went in. Without a word, Luther broke away from me, sprinted to the house and ran up the steps.

By the time I got there, the place was in turmoil.

Having latched onto Dion just inside the front door, Luther was twisting the young man's arm behind his back and pushing his face up against the wall. It was almost comical, as if the two of them had a Vaudeville act—The Father and the Bumbling Suitor. Though Dion was taller and, presumably in better physical condition, it had taken Luther only seconds to get the advantage.

Using one hand to pinion Dion's wrist behind his back, Luther patted him down and then released him. Dion endured it with what I thought was reasonable grace, rolling his eyes and pretending it was funny. Balinda seemed annoyed at her father.

"Daddy, you just don't give up, do you?" she said.

"Did you invite him here? If you invited him here, I'll apologize."

"I just came over to see my daughter," Dion said. Luther let him go. "I didn't know you were having company."

"Daddy, Daddy," Toylee exclaimed, running from the other room and leaping into her father's arms. Luther turned his back on the show with a look that was a perfect merger of disgust and resignation.

Dion looked over his daughter's shoulder. "You gonna arrest me?"

"You gonna arrest me?" Toylee asked gaily.

A few minutes later Balinda asked Luther who the dead man was. Luther looked at D'Witt, who shrugged. He'd been in the house over thirty minutes without telling anybody Raymond was five hundred yards away on his face in the wood chips.

"Yes. Who was that man got shot over at the park?" Laronda reiterated. "I hope not anybody we know."

D'Witt grabbed the remote control off the coffee table and muffled the television. He looked at me and tightened his lips. The room grew quiet.

Luther looked around the room.

"You want me to do it?" I whispered.

He shook his head. This was Luther's family and Luther's job, and D'Witt knew it and so did I. Luther was the man with the hearse.

"Raymond got hisself shot over at the school," he said softly. "I'm sorry, Pookie, but he's dead."

The family was stunned. It was like a small bomb had detonated.

After the expected flurry of questions, which Luther fielded crisply and efficiently, Laronda sat down on the sofa next to Shawn and began weeping. For some reason, it surprised me. Shawn didn't know what to do, whether to put his arm around his guardian or not. After all, he was a guest in the house, and Laronda acted as a disciplinarian more often than a mother. Rightly or wrongly, I had decided a long time ago that most of what Laronda displayed as emotion was acting, but this wasn't. Her daughter, Shereffe, came over and put an arm around her shoulder. So eventually did Shawn Brown.

Pookie swiped at her eyes with a hankie she'd produced from the sleeve of her house dress. Her stern rectitude seemed to crack and wilt. Suddenly she looked much older. Pookie had lost children before, and grandchildren. She'd seen Raymond incarcerated, and she'd known the pain of realizing one of her sons was a killer, but this was defeat like no other.

Balinda began crying so prodigiously she got the hiccups. Toylee reached a small hand up and patted her back.

Buster moved in front of Luther and spoke slowly around a mouthful of missing teeth.

"Raymond was solving the riddle. He been figuring out all week how he got hisself framed back when he was a kid. I think he figured out who did it."

"Who?" Luther said.

"He wouldn't tell me. I guess I laughed at him once too often when he was recountin' his frame-up story." Buster glanced around the room guiltily. "It did sound like horseshit."

"Raymond was still thinking about that?" Pookie asked, looking at Buster through teary eyes.

"Oh, yes, ma'am. That's about all he did think about these last few days."

"That's not all," Dion said. "Raymond told me over at the Café the reason he lied about being in California was because he followed Balinda that night."

Balinda walked behind Dion and, tears still streaming down her face, gave him a look that I could not make sense of. She turned to her grandmother and tried to crawl into Pookie's thin arms, but Pookie was having none of it and more or less pushed her away. A moment later she reconsidered and pulled her granddaughter to her.

Luther turned to Dion. "Raymond told you he killed Benjamin Aldrich?"

"All he said was he was following Balinda Monday night."

"Was he in that car chasing her?"

"He must have been."

Luther turned to Balinda. "Did you know Raymond was following you?"

"Nobody was following me until the Promenade parking lot. And that wasn't Raymond."

"Dion says Raymond was following you."

"Well, I didn't see him."

"Balinda, if you're hiding something, now's the time to tell us," Luther said. "Now's the time."

Kathy made her way through the crowd and put an arm around the young woman's shoulders. "You know better than that, Luther. If Balinda has something to say, she says it to me and she says it in confidence."

"You act like I did something wrong," Balinda said. "All I did was try to save myself."

Luther began nibbling his upper lip in quick little bites. Finally, he turned to Buster and said, "What was Raymond's riddle?"

"Remember? He got busted when he was a kid. He said it was a frame-up. He told me by the end of the week he was going to know who did it."

Nobody had anything to add to that.

After a while Laronda went into the kitchen. I followed her.

CHAPTER 37

Laronda turned on the tap in the deep kitchen sink, rinsed her hands, and splashed water into her eyes with her fingertips, remaining at the sink long enough that I suspected she was doing it to avoid me. That notion was disproved when she turned around for a hand towel and jumped when she saw me. Cold water sparkled in her straightened hair like broken glass on a tar road.

"I'm sorry about your brother," I said.

"Yes . . . well . . . what do you want?"

"Answers."

"To what?"

"In the past eight days two people have been murdered within blocks of here. I don't believe in coincidence. I'm not convinced these deaths are unrelated. I think all of this has to do with your past."

"That's ridiculous. I work for an insurance company. I take night classes. I don't drink. I never even go out on weekends. I've had the same boyfriend my whole life. What could my past possibly have to do with any of this?"

"Your daughter and Benjamin Aldrich were looking into

your past when he was killed. Your daughter narrowly es-
caped with her life. Raymond was looking into *his* past when
he was killed. Listen to me, Laronda. It's one thing to keep secrets. It's another to sit on your hands when people you love
are dying. How would you feel if that was Balinda over in the
schoolyard?"

Without another word, Laronda walked out of the room.
From the drape of her shoulders and the sudden sag of her
back, I suspected she was considering what I'd said. She led
me out the back of the kitchen into a formal dining room
I hadn't seen before. The eight-place oak table had enough
polish on it that the dim economy lights in the chandelier
gleamed off the surface. A basket of fabric flowers sat on a
lace tablecloth. Each chair was positioned precisely, and although the furniture was of a style from thirty years ago, it
showed little wear.

Laronda sat at the head of the table while I pulled up a
chair next to her. She looked me straight in the eye and said,
"When Benjamin Aldrich came here, I didn't want it all raked
up. You know? About the baby and the adoption and that. I
wasn't ready to think about it."

"Where did your baby go?"

"I told you. The Stimsons."

"Laronda, Laronda, Laronda." Pookie came in the other
door and sat next to her daughter and directly opposite me.
Her eyes were rimmed red and her glasses were low on her
nose. Her lip quivered when she spoke. "I lost another son,
Mr. Black. I know you're not too bright and you're not very
good at puzzles, but if there's any chance at all you can learn
out what happened to him, I'm going to give you all the help I
can. And that includes not allowin' my daughter here to lie
her fool head off."

"Mother—"

"Now, hush up. We ain't got no family secrets that're
worth anybody dyin' over. You had a baby, and I don't know
what you did with him, but you sure didn't adopt him out to

nobody named Stimson. There wasn't nobody named Stimson around. That Aldrich boy was your son. In my gut I knew that the night he was here, but I didn't allow my head to know it until this minute. Why you didn't own up to it when he came here is beyond me."

"We don't know who he was, Mother."

Pookie pushed her heavy glasses back up onto her face and stared balefully at Laronda. "Did you or did you not have a baby that was as white as this man sittin' in front of us?"

"Mother!"

"Did you or did you not—"

"I had a baby. He wasn't—"

"Just as white as you are, Mr. Black, without that tan. Laronda never did fess up to who the father was."

"At the risk of being called stupid again," I said, "I don't understand the problem with a white baby."

The two women looked at each other, and then Pookie, her voice deep and gloomy, said, "It was Laronda's father. He wasn't living here then—fact, he never lived here—but had he found out, he woulda done serious damage to Laronda, to me, and no doubt to the father of the baby."

Laronda nodded reluctantly. "We only saw him a few times when we were growing up, but when we did, he didn't waste any time laying down the law."

"Carried a pistol and a straight razor," Pookie said, "and wasn't afraid to use either one. He was a hard man. He made it clear to Laronda the few times he seen her she wasn't goin' to be with no white man. He was telling her this when she was three years old. It was a strange point of view, because he was of the complexion that could pass for white whenever he wanted. I knew in my heart who that boy was when he came through the door. Had the same funny little way of cocking his head and blinking his eyes as his uncle Kenny, Laronda's older brother. I knew he was family, but I didn't want to interfere, so I put it out of my head. Then, when he got hisself killed, I didn't dare think it out loud."

"I knew too," Laronda said, surrender polluting her voice. "I just didn't want to see the look on his face when he found out I was his mother. People like him don't want to be related to people like me."

I said, "I think Balinda would tell a different story. He thought you were his mother and was eager to prove it."

Laronda began crying. It was all too much for her, Raymond's death. Her son's murder. The idea that he probably would have loved her if she'd given him half a chance. The fact that we were forcing her to admit events she'd been concealing for thirty years.

"Tell me about Raymond going to prison the first time," I said.

"Why do you want to know about that?" Laronda asked through her tears.

"Because Raymond was as obsessed with finding whoever framed him as Aldrich was with finding his real parents. They were both searching, and they both were killed doing it. I don't have any other trail to follow."

Pookie leaned back and heaved a sigh. She was a slender woman, but under the material of her dress, material thinned by time and washing machines, she had a little potbelly. "You think Raymond going to prison is connected to this?"

"All I know is, Raymond thought he'd figured it out, and now he's dead."

"I heard a knock at the door one night, and it was the *po-leece*," Pookie said. "They wanted to come in and talk to Ray. He was only a boy, so I let 'em in. Later on his father gave me holy hell for it, and I sure guess he was right."

"He had a different father than Laronda?"

"Till he passed away in 1980, Ray's father lived right here in town. We used to see him at church. Them *po*-leece. They came in and wanted to talk to Ray. When they learned out he was upstairs asleep, they marched right on up. It was three in the mornin', but they wouldn't let me go get 'im. They had to go on up. Right here in my own house. Next thing I knew, one of them had money in his hands, and they were haulin' Ray out the front door with his wrists in irons and no britches on, just his undershorts. I don't suppose Ray ever forgave me."

"Is there a possibility the police framed him?"

Pookie cleared her throat. "Even Ray said that's not what happened. But where that money come from, I'll never know. He had the oddest look on his face when he saw it. He said, 'Mama, I put it back. I took it, but I put it back. Mama, what's happenin'?' They used that against him. They used his own words to his mother against him in court."

"He admitted he stole it?"

"And then he put it back. He said, 'Mama, I saw my error and I did right.'"

"How many people had access to this house?"

"You mean who mighta planted that money? My first boy was growed and gone by then. Luther was over here all the time. There was Ray's other friends. Kenny, my other son, was living here. His friends. Laronda and her girlfriends. I couldn't even keep track of Laronda's friends in high school. She got no friends now, but in high school—"

"Mother, I have friends."

"Who?" When Laronda didn't reply, Pookie continued. "I was workin' downtown those days. I didn't have time to watch over Ray like I should have, so he ended up running in the street."

"And nobody's ever figured out who framed him?"

"No, sir."

I turned to Laronda. "What about you?"

"I don't know," she said.

"Okay. Let's talk about who Benjamin Aldrich's real father was."

CHAPTER 38

When Pookie looked at her daughter with undisguised curiosity, I had the feeling I'd asked a question even she had never dared. Without looking up, Laronda said, "It doesn't matter now, and it didn't matter then. He was white. I never told anybody who he was, and he never knew I carried the baby to term."

Pookie waved her hand casually and said, "It coulda been any boy at school. Laronda was the valedictorian. She was awful popular back in those days."

"Hush, Mother."

"You was."

"I don't know why it would matter," Laronda said. "Benjamin found me. He didn't find his father."

"Maybe he did. Or maybe in trying to find his father, he ran into somebody who didn't like him. What we've got here basically are two questions. Who was the father, and what happened at Catfish Café that made Raymond think he was framed?"

"Raymond stole that money," Laconda said. "He's never made any bones about it."

"For thirty years he's been sayin' he put it back," Pookie said. "It wasn't a game with Raymond. He didn't play games. I, for one, believe him."

Mother and daughter took careful measure of each other. They'd both been crying, and their eyes were puffy. Laronda looked at me as if to say, I don't have to tell anybody anything.

And of course she was right; she didn't.

"Let's look at this from another angle," I said, addressing Pookie. "I'm beginning to believe you. I'm beginning to think he was framed. Maybe there's a connection between the two secrets, Raymond's going to prison and Laronda's baby."

"This is silly," Laronda snapped, and as soon as she said it, she realized by the way she said it that she'd given Pookie and me enough fuel to keep this engine of speculation running all night.

Pookie said, "The only one around here I can think of who had money was a man owned the church until we bought it off him. Why, now that I think about it, he rented out the house right next door too. That was before the Andersons bought it. Ray used to run him errands for pin money. But he must have been in his forties back then." Pookie looked disturbed and confused. "Mr. Aldrich. George Aldrich was a very proper man. I can't see him framing Raymond."

I said, "Can you see him fooling around with a fifteen-year-old girl?"

"But he was the adopted father, not the natural father," Pookie said.

"Was George Aldrich the father of your child?" I said, looking at Laronda.

Breathing through her nose, Laronda attempted to wait us out. She'd been waiting people out for thirty years, so it was going to take a while for her to realize it had come to an end.

Still confused, Pookie said, "Aldrich?"

"He lied to me, Mother. I was fifteen. What did I know? He said I was his whole world. He said he thought about me every day and every night. He told me we were going to run away to Tahiti, just him and me. We were going to live in a grass hut on the beach in paradise. He'd been to Tahiti. He even showed me pictures. He knew all the words that would turn a girl's head. He fed me lies. And he was white, Mother. Is that so hard to understand? You had a white husband."

"I had a husband *passed*."

"What's the difference?"

Pookie didn't answer.

Laronda continued, "He had money and drove a nice car and owned things, and he said he thought about me all the time, and I was young and foolish and I needed to hear those things. One weekend you were out of town and everybody was gone and he was next door roofing the rental and he asked could he use our phone and he came over and we shared a beer. It was the first beer I ever tasted. And then he started sweet-talking, and one thing led to another. He'd been talking to me for weeks, and I was so stupid I thought getting pregnant meant we were going to get married and go away. But then he told me he had a doctor in Tumwater he wanted me to visit.

"Raymond thought he knew something. He saw me sick every morning after you were gone to work, and he knew I was pregnant. He was trying to mess with me. He said since I already gave it up, I might just as well give it up for him too. My own brother. I figured my only hope was to make his life miserable, so miserable he'd forget about me. I knew he took that money from the Café. Twice I searched his room hoping to get him in trouble, but I couldn't find it. So I had Aldrich give me eleven hundred dollars. I said it was for an abortion. He blew his stack, said it couldn't possibly cost that much money, but I threatened all kinds of repercussions, telling his wife, everything."

"Did he know you were planning to send your brother to prison?" I asked.

"I didn't think he would go to prison. I thought he'd go

over to the youth facility like before. Maybe for a month or so. I didn't mean for him to go to prison. It just got out of hand. And no. Aldrich thought I had an abortion with it. He thought I got rid of the baby."

"You sent Raymond to prison?" Pookie asked.

"You heard him, Mother. He took the money. All I did was bring it to the attention of the police."

"You called the *po*-leece on your own brother?"

"I put the money under his mattress and I called the police and I'm not sorry. Raymond proved me out. He was no good then and he was no good after. He tried to come in my room at night. He tried the same with Balinda, my own daughter. Raymond was no good. I only did what was necessary to get him out of this house. And then after he did his time, you let him right back in. I'm not sorry. Raymond going to prison was only a matter of when, and you know it."

Pookie was speechless.

"There was another reason I didn't want anybody to know who the father was," Laronda said, looking at me.

"What's that?" I asked.

"Mother would have thrown me out of the family."

"I doubt that," I said.

Pookie looked at me but didn't say anything. She didn't have to. The expression on her face endorsed her confession. Having a baby at fifteen wouldn't get her daughter kicked out of the house, but having a baby at fifteen by a white man would. I wondered if these two women hated me. It was easy to think all the racial bias in the world went in one direction. But it went in all directions. Every which way you could think of.

"So you gave the baby to his father?" I said.

"When I could no longer hide the fact I was pregnant, I stayed in my room. Mother told folks I was sick. Then Mother went to Chicago and I went to the hospital, and then afterwards I was here alone with the baby and—"

"You weren't alone," Pookie said sharply. "Aunt Bertha came in."

"Aunt Bertha did nothing but scold me. I called a woman I met at the hospital, and she borrowed her mother's car and drove me down to Tacoma, and we found the address and put him on their front porch. I was calling him Malcolm, but they named him Benjamin. It was funny, because I almost named him Benjamin myself. The next thing I knew he was on *our* front porch—asking questions."

"It was a long time ago," Pookie said resignedly.

After some moments of deliberation, Laronda said, "I framed Raymond for trying to pester me."

I would have played devil's advocate, but I wasn't certain she hadn't done what she had to. Her life had been lived in a harsh world, and I had no authority to judge it.

"Raymond took all those years to learn humility," Pookie said. "That was all it was—his damn fool pride. He wouldn't take nothing off of no one. And he kept going back to jail behind it. These last few years he was only just coming out of it. Painting houses. Doing for hisself."

The three of us sat at the table mulling over Raymond's life. Finally, Pookie said, "You know he went to that school right over yonder. I remember the first day I sent him off. He wore corduroy trousers and his favorite little blue shirt. He was born in this house, and he went to that grammar school, and now he's dead over there, and I feel all hollow inside like I haven't felt in a long time."

I didn't know what to say.

Before I could think of anything, Laronda said to me, "I need to ask a favor."

"What is it?"

"I'd like to talk to Benjamin's mother."

"She's not in very good health."

"I need to see her. Do you think you could arrange a meeting?"

George Aldrich would probably be there. George was a suspect in her brother's death, plus she'd been nursing a grudge against him for thirty years—and that was without taking into consideration Aldrich's recent attempt on her daughter's virtue.

"I'll contact her," I said.

"I'd appreciate that."

We went into the other room, where Balinda and Shereffe were crying, and before I knew it, Pookie and Laronda were going at it again too. Everything good Raymond had ever said or done was brought up by someone. Even with what I knew about him, he was starting to sound like a pretty good guy.

As we were leaving, a teary-eyed Shereffe cornered Kathy and begged her to look at her tunnel project, now completed, graded, and returned home, having bagged the highest score in the class. Toylee accompanied Kathy, Shereffe, and me to an alcove off the front entrance where the project had been carefully set up on a table, temporarily deposing family photos and knickknacks, which had been shoved to the back. It was obvious that Shereffe had set the project up where it might gain some attention on its own, but the evening's events had overwhelmed all of us, so she'd been forced to drop her nonchalant act and point it out. Basically, it was a papier-mâché rendition of Snoqualmie Pass and the two-and-a-half-mile-long Milwaukee Road train tunnel drilled through the mountain. She'd done a good job.

"When are we going to go see the tunnel?" Toylee asked, jumping up and down.

She was asking Luther, who had followed us and who looked dubious about the prospect of a trip anytime soon. He stuck out both thumbs so Toylee could hang on them and said, "I don't know, baby. Right now we're thinking about Uncle Raymond."

"We can take them up to the tunnel," I said. "Maybe this weekend. It might get their minds off this other."

"I think that's a good idea," Kathy said.

"You two don't have to go," Luther said to me.

"It'll be fun. We can take Toylee and Shereffe and anyone else who'd like to go."

After we made a tentative date for Sunday after church, Kathy and I left.

Five minutes later as we were driving surface streets toward the University District, Kathy laid a warm palm on my thigh and said, "I love those little girls. And D'Witt is a scream. Before they went outside, did you hear him telling jokes?"

"I must have missed that."

"So who killed Raymond Sands?"

"It might have been an ugly white man in a Mercedes."

"I heard Luther talking about that to Buster. What was that all about? You're not going to tell me Benjamin Aldrich's father drives a Mercedes?"

"He does. Plus, he's uglier than an outhouse wall."

CHAPTER 39

By Wednesday morning clouds had rolled in and fat raindrops were falling out of the sky onto Pioneer Square. I spent the first part of the day in the office on the phone. Luther called and told me he had stayed overnight at Pookie's as a bodyguard. He'd gotten almost no sleep and was frantic to know if the killer had turned up. I told him no.

"Me and D'Witt stayed up talkin'," he said. "Seein' Raymond shot like that gave him flashbacks to when he got put in that chair. He's havin' a hard time with it. You know, Thomas, he's always been the one child I felt closest to, and he ain't even mine."

"You want me to come over and stand guard tonight?"

"No. I'm doin' this."

I left four separate messages at Homicide/Assault before Arnold Haldeman got back to me. Haldeman was good at sensing who had the upper hand in a relationship, and when *he* had it, he played it out as deliberately as a cheap scenestealer in a high school play.

When I asked Haldeman if there were any leads on the

Sands killing, he said, "He was a bad apple, Black. A guy like that buys a couple of bullets, who cares?"

"I care."

"Yeah? Why?"

"Because somebody out there is getting away with murder, and people who get away with murder tend to repeat themselves."

"I didn't say I wasn't going to catch the slimeball. I don't know why you're so interested, unless you think your pretty little client offed her uncle. Is that it?"

"I know the family. I happen to think the Aldrich killing last week and this one are tied together, and I'm pretty sure you don't."

"Somebody said Benjamin Aldrich was related to them."

"It's true."

"In case you haven't figured it out yet, Aldrich was white."

"White enough. Laronda Sands was his mother."

"How the hell did that happen?"

"Same way it always happens. Two people have sex. The little spermatozoon swims up the—"

"You realize this dead man last night had a record? Theft. Assault. Drug charges. Manslaughter. He had two convictions for beating up girlfriends. Did you know that?"

"I do now."

"Why is it every black guy in the world needs to have a white girlfriend. *Any* white girlfriend. Even if she's three hundred pounds and losing her hair? They'd rather have her than the most gorgeous black woman around. Now, why is that?"

More to the point, why was it that some white guys were so concerned about every black man's love life?

"Other people's romances are none of my business, Arnold."

"You know what I mean. Maybe Luther never told you he was married to a white woman once. I bet he never told you that, did he?"

"Luther and I talk about everything," I said, though I'd not heard about the marriage and wondered if Haldeman was making it up. "One more thing. Do you folks have a time of death?"

"Right about when they found him. Maybe an hour before. You find anything relates to this, Black, you're going to call me, right?"

"I always do."

"And you're not going to mess around in my investigation, are you?"

"I never dabble in homicide. No, sir."

"Good, because I'd hate to have to cuff you and throw you in a cell."

"Me too. The excitement might give you heart palpitations."

CHAPTER 40

Mary Aldrich agreed to meet Benjamin's birth mother, Laronda. Had Benjamin been alive, I wasn't sure she would have been so accommodating, but he wasn't alive, and it was a chance to keep her son's name and memory burning, if only in conversation. She sounded incredibly weak and distant on the phone. I thought about talking to her husband while I had a line to the house, but decided to relegate that to a later date.

After playing phone tag throughout the lunch hour, Laronda and I arranged to meet at my office at four o'clock.

She arrived twenty minutes early, and we had a curiously pleasant drive to Tacoma, although the closer we got to our destination, the more nervous she became. We talked about Balinda's plans for the future, about Seattle's plans for a new football stadium, about the checkerboard weather pattern between Seattle and Tacoma.

She wore brown slacks and a matching jacket, a simple white blouse with a string of imitation pearls at her neck. She kept her knees together, and in her lap she held a black leather purse that didn't look nearly large enough to hold as much ammunition as Luther told me it carried. Even if her ammo supply had dwindled, I was entertaining serious doubts about taking her into the Aldrich household.

It was sprinkling in Tacoma, and the veins of rush-hour traffic were clotted with people trying to get home from work. To keep her mind off the impending encounter, I asked Laronda about Pensack Insurance, a topic she had no trouble delving into with great vigor, and by the time we pulled up in front of the Aldrich homestead over Commencement Bay, I knew more than I needed to about office rivalry, corporate back-stabbing, and inept underlings.

When I stopped the car and pulled the emergency brake, Laronda glanced across the parking strip at the brick house and said, "Is this it?"

"This is it."

"I don't remember it this way."

"You last saw it at night, didn't you?"

"I brought him at night, but whenever I could get a car, I used to drive down and look for him. The last time was Christmas day. He was twelve. I remember because Balinda was six. He had a new bike out here on the sidewalk, and his father was yelling at him. I couldn't stand it. I never came back."

I got out of the car and walked around to open her door. She remained sitting for a moment. "You don't have to do this," I said. "There's no rule that says you two have to meet."

"No, I want to."

As we walked to the house, her shoes sounded off on the sidewalk like hammers, and I noticed she'd begun breathing through her mouth. She barely came to my shoulders and was too thin to leave loose in a strong wind, but she took it all in—the huge brick house, the immaculate grounds, the expensive landscaping—like a soldier thinking about a fort she'd been assigned to assault. It occurred to me that Laronda undoubtedly earned a lot more money than I did, probably enough to finance a house such as this, yet she still lived with her mother. Maybe D'Witt's medical care had wiped her out.

Without being obvious about it, I stayed close. I didn't really think she was going to pull a gun out of her purse, but I kept my eyes on her hands anyway.

The same nurse who'd been here the week before answered the door, escorted us into the foyer, and told us Mary Aldrich was sleeping but had asked to be awakened upon our arrival. The nurse went into another part of the house and then a minute later came back and led us into the large, nearly empty room where I'd met Mary Aldrich the previous Saturday. In contrast to Laronda's drumbeat shoes, the nurse's gum-rubber soles whispered across the hardwood floors.

The furniture had been rearranged. The bed was next to the window, and the binoculars, which had been on the windowsill, were on the bedspread next to Mary's slight form. The bed was tipped up again, but it was angled so that without turning her head she could gaze north toward Vashon Island.

As a child I'd gone once to a display of Egyptian artifacts at the Seattle Art Museum, intent on seeing a genuine mummy, and what had struck me about it was how tiny and delicate it was. Even though I'd remembered her as unimposing, the Mary Aldrich I saw that afternoon surprised me with her smallness. She must have struck Laronda that way too, because she took her breath in and held it. After the nurse checked an IV that ran into her patient's arm, she nodded at us and left the room on a cushion of gum rubber and civility.

I made the introductions and stepped away, careful to keep myself on the same side of the bed as Laronda and feeling like a security guard stalking an innocent woman around a store because she fit the store's profile of a shoplifter.

"So you're Ben's mother," Mary said. Her voice was smaller than it had been five days ago."

"No," Laronda said. "You're his mother. I only gave birth to him."

"We're both his mother," Mary said pleasantly.

They thought about that for a few moments, and I could see a warmth spread across Laronda's face. "You're not surprised your son was black?"

"Honey, I'm one-sixteenth Cherokee. We're all God's children. I loved Ben, and I love you for giving him to me."

Laronda grew quiet; stunned, I thought, by the kindness in Mary Aldrich's voice.

"Thank you for giving him to us," Mary continued.

"There wasn't much choice."

"But you selected us. I've wanted to ask you about it all these years. Why us?"

Laronda looked at me questioningly. I shrugged and moved to the window, where I looked out over the cloudy sound and the islands in the distance. Laronda said, "I picked you because I knew you were a kind and loving person."

"But honey, you didn't know anything about me."

"I'd heard things."

"From whom?"

"I don't recall."

"What you're afraid to say is that my husband was his father. Isn't that right?"

Laronda looked at me again, but I had already decided this was a good conversation to not be involved in.

"How did you find that out?" Laronda asked, her voice cracking.

"There were so many clues. Ben had the same overbite as George. Their hairlines were almost identical. They both had a cowlick right here." She pointed to her skull, and the back of her veined hand, black and blue from too many IVs, flashed in front of us like a bouquet of bruised bones.

"It wasn't my intention to be cruel," Laronda said. "My plan wasn't to come here and tell you things about your husband."

I wasn't sure I believed her. There'd been a tension in her

ever since we'd crossed the Tacoma city limits, and I had the feeling her design had been to do as much damage to this household as humanly possible, though her sentiments must have mellowed significantly after realizing how close to death Mary Aldrich was.

Laronda spoke softly. "I know you took wonderful care of him."

Gathering her thoughts, Mary Aldrich looked past me and out the window for a few moments. "Were you with George just the once, or was it something else?"

Laronda looked at me again. Somehow I was surprised and pleased that Laronda kept turning to me for succor, though I remained about as helpful as a second tail on a cat, shrugging and looking out at the bay.

"It was a couple of times," Laronda said. "I never meant anything to him."

"I'm beginning to realize I never did either."

"I was a silly girl. I'm sorry."

They looked at each other, one dying, one riddled with guilt and something else I hadn't quite put my finger on. These two women from different spheres in different cities had a loved one in common, and for some minutes they chatted about Benjamin's youth, schooling, childhood illnesses, girlfriends, about his forfeited plans for the future, but not about his death.

Before we left, Laronda said, "Sometimes you do something, and it bothers you all your life. This was the one that bothered me . . . giving my baby to a stranger. I'll tell you now, it wasn't altruism. I was furious at your husband. And now I'm ashamed of myself. I want to thank you again for doing such a fine job of raising him. I could see he was a decent man. When he showed up at my door, I wanted to take him in my arms and hug him . . . but I couldn't."

"I wish you had." We were headed for the exit when Mary added, "You told me what it was on my husband's part. What was it on your part?"

The question startled Laronda, but she tried to answer it. "I don't even quite know. I was young and poor. He paid attention to me. Nobody else did." I noticed she left out that he was white and she was African American, which could hardly have meant less to each of them than their age or economic differences.

On our way out we bumped into George Aldrich by the front door.

"We had a detective from Seattle show up at the door here a couple of hours ago," he said. "We were talking about you, Black."

"A little, squatty guy with a chip on his shoulder? Looks kind of like a cartoon character?"

"That's the one. Said his name was Haldeman. Said I was to call him if you showed up."

"You remember his number, or do you want me to write it down for you?"

Aldrich grinned and rolled the stub of his unlit stogie around in his mouth. He was in dirty work clothes, and his hair was windblown, as if he'd been working in the yard. He barely looked at Laronda.

"I think you've got more important things to worry about than dicking around with me," I said.

"Like what?"

"Like becoming the major suspect in a murder investigation."

"Sure. I was up there. I already told the detective. I went up to talk to a few people. I was looking through Ben's things, and I saw the name Sands. I thought maybe the family had something to do with my son's death. So I went up and asked around."

Laronda, who was so stiff you could have laid her across a stream bed and used her for a footbridge, stepped forward and said, "I guess you don't remember me."

Aldrich's heavy lips played with the stogie while he dropped both hands into his trousers pockets and considered the woman in front of him. In the past week he'd seen Luther and he'd seen Balinda, and now he was obviously trying to connect Laronda to either of them. Suddenly, his eyes got big and the cigar dropped to the floor. He stepped back as if Laronda were something the cat had dragged in. Never one to shy away from enemies, Laronda took a step forward.

"I remember you as prettier," Aldrich said.

"Always the gentleman," I said.

"What you remember is a child," Laronda said. "A child you took advantage of. These days you could go to prison for what you did."

"Seems to me you were willing enough." He turned to me. "What are you doing, Black? What are you doing bringing her here?"

"We didn't come to see you. We met you on the way out."

"You were seeing Mary? You get out of here before I get my gun."

"You already got your gun," Laronda said. "You came up to Seattle and shot my brother, didn't you?"

I was keeping an eye on Laronda's hands.

"I never saw your goddamned brother. I left a couple of messages on his machine. I never got hold of him."

"Why did you want to talk to Raymond?" I asked.

"Because I figured he was the one person from that household I could bribe for the truth." He looked at Laronda. "I forgot about you. Eleven hundred dollars, wasn't it?"

"That wasn't a bribe," Laronda said. "That was for an abortion. An abortion I never got."

Aldrich looked at Laronda, his eyes clouding with doubt and bewilderment.

She continued, "Did he take a pretty good tan in the summer?"

We were out the front door and onto the porch when Aldrich stepped forward. "What do you mean by that crack? What are you talking about?"

"Your son. Did he tan?" Laronda asked.

"What does that mean?" He looked at me. "What does that mean, Black? What the hell is going on?"

"Laronda is the mother of your son," I said.

From the way Aldrich stared at us, I felt as if I'd just handed him one of Pookie's conundrums and told him to solve it or have some fingers cut off. His eyes lacked comprehension for quite some time; then he said, "I adopted my own son?"

"That's right," Laronda said sweetly.

"Your baby?"

"*Our* baby."

"But you got rid of it."

"No."

"Son of a bitch."

"You were contemptible *then*, and you're contemptible *now*," Laronda said as she pivoted on her heel and walked to the car. I wish I could say her stride was proud and graceful, but it was awkward, and as she crossed the grass parking strip, she nearly stumbled.

I started to walk away and then turned back to Aldrich. "By the way. Why were you following your son?"

"What?"

"You were following Benjamin. He knew about it. Why were you doing that?"

"He knew about it? I was trying to keep him out of trouble. I've had to follow him quite a few times. Benjamin didn't really know what was good for him. He was going to get into trouble looking for his parents."

"You knew about his search?"

"I had a notion."

"You pretty much tried to run his life, didn't you?"

"I was his father."

"I've got a father, but he doesn't follow me around."

Aldrich didn't have an answer for that.

It took an hour to get back to Pioneer Square, where Laronda had parked. After leaving her, I went to the Elliott Bay Book Company two blocks from the office and bought a collection of word puzzles, drove home, and hid it from Kathy.

CHAPTER 41

That night in the kitchen, Kathy and I discussed the events of the week while we prepared a dinner of white rice with stir-fried chicken and vegetables.

"Don't you have the feeling if we thought about it long enough," Kathy said, slicing a bell pepper, "we could figure out who killed Benjamin Aldrich and Raymond Sands without leaving the house?"

"Maybe *you* could."

"Now, come on. You're terrific at real-life puzzles. I know how your mind works. You're one of those players who doesn't bat well at practice, but then you go out and hit one right into the bleachers."

"Thanks for the undeserved confidence."

"It's not undeserved and you know it. Tell me about your trip to Tacoma with Laronda."

When I had finished the story, she said, "Wasn't it spooky listening in to all of that?"

"It sure was. I felt like a Peeping Tom on a ladder."

"Did George Aldrich look guilty when you brought up Raymond's death?"

"Like most murderers, he didn't bat an eyelash."

"Like most innocent people too."

"Yeah."

"Raymond thought he was close to figuring out how he got framed," Kathy said. "We now know it was Laronda and that George Aldrich was an unwitting accomplice. If Raymond knew either one of them was involved, he would have been furious. And if Raymond was furious at them, that might be reason to want him dead."

"It might. But other than the rather vague report of a white guy in a Mercedes hanging around the neighborhood, we don't have anything to tie George Aldrich to the crime. This morning Luther found Raymond's van parked over near Raymond's house on Twenty-third. So he was either walking over to the party or was driven by someone. Raymond didn't seem like a walker."

"Okay. Let's say Raymond knew Aldrich was involved in his frame-up. They get together. Aldrich drives him over," Kathy said. "Raymond accuses Aldrich, and Aldrich, thinking his life is in danger, pulls a gun and shoots Raymond. Then Aldrich hauls the body into the bushes."

"Another possibility is his sister, Laronda. You didn't see Laronda yesterday afternoon, Kathy, but she was hot enough to kill somebody. Raymond wasn't who I had in mind, but he's dead. I wonder if they tangled. Let's look at that scenario. Raymond walks over to the party early. He wants to talk. There are kids around. So the two of them take a stroll. Laronda has her gun. They go out to the playground, and Raymond, having found out she framed him all those years ago, gets rough. She shoots him."

"Or," Kathy said, "Raymond gets wind of who shot Benjamin Aldrich. He confronts whoever it was, and they kill him to keep him from going to the police."

"If Laronda shot Benjamin and then Raymond, it would explain one thing. I've had the feeling all along Balinda has been fudging her story. Balinda wouldn't turn her own mother in."

"You think Laronda's likely to get involved in a car chase?"

"I don't know, but it would explain Balinda's reticence. The trouble with all of this is that until the very minute he turned up dead, Raymond was my number one suspect for killing Benjamin Aldrich. We certainly can't eliminate him as a suspect in that shooting just because he's now dead, but I'd like to think the same person shot them both."

"Is there any chance Balinda shot her uncle?"

"Could be. Monday night Raymond chases Balinda and kills Aldrich," I said. "Balinda runs. She eventually gets back home, and Raymond threatens her if she won't keep her mouth shut. She's scared. Maybe she did shoot him. Haldeman seems to think she shot Benjamin, but you saw the powder burns on her face. Somebody fired a gun very close to her face. If she killed Aldrich and there were only the two of them in the car, those powder burns could have come from him firing back. I don't think he had a gun, though. Also, the burns are on the left side of her face. If she was driving and he fired at her, the burns would have been on the right side of her face. Wouldn't they? Peggy Lindseth says she was driving when she last saw them."

"'This is as bad as one of Pookie's puzzles," Kathy said.

"I know."

"And you don't like Pookie's puzzles."

"I take longer to solve them than anybody except a man who just got hit in the head with a brick, but I like them. By the way, she gave me another one. There was a man who had to swim across a river. He had to carry over a fox, a chicken, and a bag of grain. He could only carry one at a time, and he couldn't leave the fox with the chicken or the fox would eat the chicken, and he couldn't leave the chicken with the grain or the chicken would eat the grain. How did he do it?"

"Thomas. We're busy here."

"You can't figure it out?"

"We were talking about Balinda maybe having shot Aldrich."

"Okay. What we don't have is any evidence they weren't getting along. We don't have any evidence she had a gun. And if she *was* going to shoot him, why do it during a car chase? They were meeting at midnight to exchange information. You have to figure it was a friendly meeting—not romantic, or he wouldn't have brought Peggy Lindseth along."

"There's something else that's bothering me. Dion swears Raymond was following her that night. Why would Raymond tell something like that to Dion?"

"I don't know. You notice he didn't spill the beans until Raymond was dead. My impression of Raymond was that he trusted damn few people."

"Was Dion one of them?"

"Actually, he probably was. But Dion has a history of battery against Balinda. Luther says if he knew she was spending time with another man, particularly a white guy, he might fly off the handle. So maybe he followed her and killed him, and now he's trying to put it off on Raymond."

Later, much later, while we were being lulled to sleep by the sound of rain pounding the roof for the first time in ten days, Kathy said, "It's pretty clear to me that Laronda was seeking a father figure when she had her fling with George Aldrich, someone not unlike her own distant father. Unfortunately, George Aldrich betrayed her in the same way her own father betrayed her. Abandonment seems to be a running theme in her life."

"Yep," I mumbled.

I was almost asleep when we heard knocking at the back door. I got up and threw a robe on, realizing as I groped my way toward the back porch that only one person would use that door. Sonya looked as if she'd just come in from a date. I could smell her perfume immediately, along with a whiff of fresh rain. The spring storm was still beating on the back porch enclosure.

"Oh, you were in bed," she said in a whisper.

"I wasn't asleep. What's the problem, Sonya? Your shower again?"

"I bought a bicycle. I don't know anything about it. I thought maybe you could look at it sometime."

We talked bikes for a few moments. She'd spent some money and had a pretty good one, had bought it down the road at Gregg's Greenlake.

"I need some advice and so forth. Would you look at it? Not tonight, of course."

"Sure."

She fixed her pale blue eyes on me and then turned and went down the steps to her apartment.

When I climbed back into bed, Kathy was all arms.

"Okay," she said. "This is how it works. The man swims the chicken across first. He swims back and swims the fox across. When he comes back the second time, he brings the chicken with him. He leaves the chicken on the original side alone and takes the sack of grain over to leave with the fox. Then he swims back over and gets the chicken."

"You're good."

"I know. What did The Mole want?"

"Bought a bike."

"Of course she did. She knew that would be the key to your heart."

"Now now."

"Next, she'll be asking you to ride with her."

"I'll cut my wrists first."

"You'll do nothing of the sort. You'll go out with her and show her where it's safe to ride, and you'll be polite but very discouraging."

"Yes, dear."

"Don't patronize me."

"I didn't mean to. But I don't believe she's as artful as you think."

"I hope you're not really this naive."

I wasn't, but I kind of liked the way the pitch of Kathy's voice went up when Sonya's name was mentioned. The school year would end soon, so the situation would disappear on its own, but in the meantime it was kind of fun playing the dope. But then, for me, playing the dope had never been a whole lot of work.

CHAPTER 42

As with most events involving the Sands clan, our trip to the tunnel at Snoqualmie Pass metamorphosed from a casual day trip to a major juggernaut without any of us realizing it. We met at Pookie's house at noon on Sunday morning.

I had borrowed a van that would accommodate a wheelchair. Faced with the alternatives of being jammed into Luther's hearse or the backseat of Dion's car, Shawn and his two friends chose to ride in the van with us. Luther drove Laronda and their youngest, Shereffe. Dion, Balinda, and Toylee traveled in Dion's car, a Saab that had seen better days. We all agreed the venture was going to be great fun, even though I had misgivings about Balinda riding with Dion.

Having had several days to ponder it, I was more convinced than ever that the two killings were inextricably linked both to each other and to this family's history, and I viewed this excursion as another opportunity to probe the dynamics of the clan.

Over the last few days little new information had surfaced. Luther and Kathy had both interrogated Balinda again, but she hadn't yielded anything new. The police seemed to be stumped. Raymond had been shot three times in the chest and once in the head with a .32 caliber handgun. The bullets may or may not have come from the same .32 that had killed Aldrich. The police weren't saying.

Nobody seemed to know anything more about Benjamin Aldrich's last night on earth. I'd canvassed the neighborhood a second time and found no witnesses to the car wreck or to Raymond's murder.

Snoqualmie Pass was about an hour away from Seattle, and even though the road cut through the Cascade Mountains, it was made up of three lanes and was posted at sixty-five miles per hour most of the way, seventy on the lower slopes. After the small valley town of North Bend, mountains hemmed in both sides of the highway.

D'Witt's girlfriend, Margaret, was sitting beside me. D'Witt and Kathy were directly behind us, and Shawn and his two friends were on the bench seat in the back of the van.

Eventually our conversation turned to my role in the investigation of Raymond's death. Nobody seemed to care about Benjamin Aldrich, but Raymond's death was hot copy.

I filled them in on what the police had discovered in the past three days, which, as reported by Arnold Haldeman, was next to nothing, this later confirmed by Luther's downtown buddies who weren't as stingy with information as Haldeman.

"So who did it, man?" Shawn asked.

"I think I know who, but I can't prove it yet. I don't have that one last piece of information I need," I said. All three of the young men on the rear bench seat inched forward when I spoke.

"But you've got some sort of clue," Shawn said.

"Yeah, you got a theory," said one of his friends.

I looked in the rearview mirror. Shawn and his cohorts wore matching L.A. Raiders jackets. I'd watched them goofing around earlier, and it was hard to think of the three fifteen-year-olds as adults, yet I couldn't help wondering what they might be concealing under those long jackets in addition to

scrawny ribs. Melvin, the young man whose gun I'd confis-
cated during the brawl outside Pookie's house on Saturday
night a week ago, seemed to have forgiven me. I'd certainly
forgiven him.

"What I believe is this," I said. "Raymond's death was
probably related to Benjamin Aldrich's. And Aldrich's was related in some way to your family."

"Not *my* family. My mother lives in Laurelhurst, man,"
Shawn said. "I'm only visiting Pookie. Besides, how can you
know that?"

"Aldrich was investigating his origins when he was killed.
And his origins were here in the Sands family. Raymond was
also investigating the family's past when he was killed."

"That's all you got?" D'Witt asked.

"There's more, but I don't have it straightened out in my
mind yet."

"Jesus," Shawn said. "I thought most murder investigations were concluded within forty-eight hours. You don't find
the perp within forty-eight hours, you don't find him at all."

"Most cases, but not every case. We'll find him. Somebody's going up for both those killings."

"Are you sure?" D'Witt asked.

"Count on it."

The van went quiet. After we'd driven a few more miles
into the mountains, the three boys in back began speculating
about whether or not they were going to find enough snow for
a snowball fight.

I said, "Shawn, how much time do you spend with Dion?"

"Me?"

"You see him once a week? What?"

"About that. When I was at my mother's, I didn't see him
at all."

"What do you guys do together?"

"Mostly we hang out, and he asks about Balinda and
Toylee. Sometimes we talk sports."

"What does he want to know about Balinda?"

"Things like . . . hey? You're not gettin' on Dion, are you?"

"I'm only asking."

"He talks about if Balinda's seeing anybody. About Toylee, and are they takin' good care of her."

"Are they?"

"Sure."

"They don't chain her in the closet or anything?"

Shawn snorted out a laugh, but my questioning had made him tense. "Of course not."

"What do you tell him about Balinda?"

"Nothin' to tell."

"You didn't tell him about Benjamin Aldrich?"

Shawn's leg began shaking, a nervous kind of shake, as if he were trying to keep flies off. He didn't like ratting out his friends, but he was intimidated by me and I think by Kathy, who was half twisted around in her seat watching. When I looked at him, I saw a young Luther, the same flat nose, reedy body, and slightly bucked teeth, along with a feature I'd never really noticed in Luther but which, now that I thought about it, Luther had too, tiny ears that stuck out from his head like nickels.

Shawn said, "He knew about Aldrich. Dion knew."

"Did Dion ever confront Aldrich?"

"Not that he said."

"Did he meet him?"

"I don't think so."

"Were you there when Raymond threw Aldrich out of the house?"

"Yeah. Raymond pulled him up by his collar and walked him to the front porch and threw him off. It was hilarious. The dude rolled on the lawn and got up and walked away like it never happened. The guy moved like a cat with a can stuck on his head."

"Pookie said he was pretty cool about it."

"Well, yeah. Maybe."

"Did Raymond ever see Aldrich again?"

"How would I know?"

"You talked to Raymond."

"I talked to Dion more."

"What about Balinda? She say anything after Raymond's death?"

"Ask her."

"I'm asking you."

"Guy gets hisself capped, people talk. I don't know what she said."

"Has the family come to any conclusions about who might have done it?" I looked in the mirror at D'Witt.

"Buster served time with Raymond," Shawn said eagerly. "I bet you didn't know that, did you?"

Actually, having run background checks on both Buster and the older man I'd seen with Raymond, Earl Brown—no relation to Shawn Brown—I did know. Buster had served time for public lewdness, drunkenness, assault, and dozens of traffic infractions.

We were almost to the pass when D'Witt said, "I don't understand why you're keeping on with this. The police should be doing it."

"Thomas promised Benjamin's mother he'd find his killer after they found Balinda," Kathy said.

"I still don't get why you don't just let the police handle it," D'Witt said.

"For one thing, Luther and I don't think the family's safe until we find the killer."

"You mean Balinda?"

"Balinda. You. Everyone."

"Ain't nobody going to mess with me," Shawn said from the back of the van. "I got my homeboys. Ain't nobody gonna mess with me." The three young men slapped palms and bumped shoulders until D'Witt had to tell them to knock it off, that they were rocking the van.

D'Witt said, "I want you boys to be careful of the snowballs. There's women and children along on this outing. We
don't want anybody hurt."

On the other side of the summit we left the highway at
Exit 54 and bypassed the Hyak ski area. We parked in a small
lot overlooking Lake Keechelus on the Iron Horse Trail. In
wintertime this lot accommodated cross-country skiers and
snowshoers, but today it held powdery mountain dust, crab
grass, wildflowers, and six other parked cars. An abandoned
railroad bed converted into a hiking and biking path, the Iron
Horse Trail stretched along the lake and to the base of the
mountain to the west.

It took fifteen minutes for us to pile out, get organized,
distribute flashlights, decide which clothes to layer on and
which to leave in the cars, and then to file in and out of the
rest room facilities at the east edge of the lot.

CHAPTER 43

While the others got ready, I approached Dion. He had taken off his sweatshirt and was lying on his back on the warm hood of his Saab, his feet still on the ground. He wore jeans, basketball high-tops, and a sleeveless shirt that said CATFISH CAFÉ in small blue letters over his left breast. His arms were folded across his chest and his muscles rippled in the sun.

"I ain't been up in the mountains in years," he said.

"It's nice."

"Yeah. Especially being here with my family. Thanks for letting us drive up together."

I stepped aside so my shadow didn't fall across his face. "I didn't have anything to do with it."

"Balinda said you did it."

Though it appeared to be a simple thing, riding up to the pass with her ex, it could have been interpreted by Dion as a major repair step in an atrophied relationship, a misunderstanding Balinda had tried to forestall by saying it was my idea, not hers. I was sorry I'd said I didn't have anything to do with it, but it was too late to rescind it.

Dion said, "You coming to Raymond's service tomorrow?"

"Absolutely."

"I'm a pallbearer. Me and Luther and Buster and a couple others."

"A guy gets his life straightened around, and then he dies."

Dion chuckled. "I wouldn't exactly say he was straightened around."

"What do you mean by that?"

"Raymond been through a lot. . . . It marked him."

"You have any ideas who might have done him?"

"Me?"

"He hung out at the Café," I said. "You talked to him."

"Raymond told some sorry-ass stories about things he done to people in prison. Maybe one of those dudes came after him. I would have."

"Did Raymond talk to you last week after we saw you both at Catfish Café?"

"We talked."

"What about?"

"Balinda. He said I needed to get her out of there if I was going to keep her safe. He said that house wasn't safe anymore."

"What did he mean, the house wasn't safe?"

"He said too many people knew where she lived."

"He mention which people?"

"Just too many people."

"What was his slant on the Aldrich shooting?"

"He said he threw his own nephew out of Pookie's. I think he felt bad about it."

"He felt bad about throwing Aldrich out, or about Aldrich getting shot?"

"Both. I've been trying to talk sense to Balinda. She'd be safe with me. That house . . . that house is all women."

"You asked her to move in with you?"

"I asked last week, and I asked again on the way up here."

"What'd she say?"

"She's gonna think about it."

It was easy to see we'd underestimated the walking distances. It was at least half a mile along the Iron Horse Trail past a couple of state facilities for vehicle maintenance and a row of A-frame summer homes before we got to the tunnel entrance, and then the tunnel itself was over two miles end-to-end. Shereffe could walk it, but Toylee was going to need piggyback rides. Her father would be good for the lion's share, but with Luther's legs still bothering him from being run over years ago, the rest would probably be up to me. I'd been close enough to Toylee already today to realize if I carried her I'd smell like perfume for the rest of the day. She must have been playing grown-up before we left.

The bare ski hills were a five-minute walk to the west, but we were surrounded on all sides by peaks, most still spotty with snow. To the north the highway was so close we could hear the susurrus of traffic. Beyond that lay a shallow pass through the mountains that was open to hikers in the summer months and back-country skiers in the winter. The Cascade Crest Trail, which stretched from Canada to Mexico, bisected this area.

Toylee and Shereffe began collecting wildflowers. One of Shawn's friends picked up a rusted railroad spike, showed it around, and then pitched it into the trees as if he didn't care, although it looked to me as if he really wanted to keep it. It was tough being almost grown up.

Laronda and Luther were absorbed in a serious conversation and walked behind the rest of us. Kathy was heading up the trail, making sure everybody knew where we were going and explicating on the dangers of erratic bicyclists who sometimes rode the tunnel without lights. Anyone who hadn't been inside the tunnel before couldn't know how dark it was going to be, even with flashlights. After the first eighth of a mile a flashlight was good for maybe ten feet. Beyond that you were as blind as a mouse in a matchbox.

Guarded by two large wooden doors that had been

propped open for the season, the tunnel was tall and narrow, maybe thirty feet high and about sixteen feet across. Chiseled into the concrete arches over the entrance were the words SNOQUALMIE TUNNEL 1912–1914. We could hear water dripping from the ceiling inside. The way I recalled it, this end was the worst for dripping water.

CHAPTER 44

Outside the entrance we found clumps of snow so black we wouldn't have known they concealed any fun at all if earlier tunnel-goers hadn't already scraped off the crust of dirt and mined the innards.

As it was, Toylee and Shereffe hopped up onto a particularly large cache of blackened snow and began scuffing their shoes against it until they were showered in ice crystals and dirt. Toylee's hair soon took on a jeweled look. She was giggling hilariously.

While Balinda and Laronda tried to corral their daughters, Shawn and his two friends approached a clump of snow the size of a small car and began a serious snowball war.

"Stay behind me," I said to Kathy as a snowball whirred past my head. "I'll be your shield."

As I scrounged around for ammo, Kathy hit me in the back with a handful of snow, grabbed Toylee by the hand and dashed into the tunnel with her, Shereffe close on their heels. Their mothers followed at a more sedate pace. Shawn and his two friends threw a few more snowballs and went inside.

D'Witt rolled in, trailed closely by Margaret. Dion jogged along behind them in a shuffle of practiced unconcern, like an outfielder coming in from a routine inning.

Luther and I headed in last.

"I talked to Laronda," Luther said. "She's starting to feel bad about Raymond, you know, like maybe his bad times was partly her fault. She went and talked to our pastor, who put a real load on her. I don't know how she's going to forgive herself. She's sayin' she sinned and killed him. Oh, I don't mean she took a gun and did him, but you know. . . . The way she figures it, maybe he *was* getting his act straightened out when she turned him in all those years ago."

"She knew he put that money back, didn't she?" I said.

"Yeah, she did. Because she went to the Café and took it out again. She told me the other night."

"She stole the money out of Catfish Café after he put it back?"

"She looked at it as an exchange of funds. She'd put the money George Aldrich gave her for the abortion under the mattress to frame Raymond. She knew the Café would get that money after the trial. The other eleven hundred, the original loot from the Café, Laronda kept that. The way she saw it, George Aldrich gave her eleven hundred dollars, so she had eleven hundred dollars due."

"How did she know Raymond returned it?"

"Followed him. Saw him break back into the restaurant a couple of days after the robbery. All these years I been running around thinking he was a fool, and there he really did get framed. By Laronda of all people."

"You been thinking about who killed him?" We were dodging falling water, far behind the others. Luther had switched his flashlight on.

"Oh, I been thinkin' about it. It bein' so close to the house and all, you have to think it might have been somebody hangin' around the family. I heard Raymond was planning to fire Buster from that painting gig. Buster wouldn't have been too happy about that."

"What if Raymond knew Laronda framed him?"

"I was in her shoes thinkin' Raymond found out, I'd be plenty worried," Luther said. "Raymond had been threatenin' to take whoever did that and sink them at the bottom of Lake Washington."

"Let's suppose for a moment the report of the Mercedes in the neighborhood wasn't bogus, and the driver of the Mercedes was George Aldrich."

"I been thinkin' about that too, Thomas. It was pretty sketchy, but that don't mean it didn't happen. If Aldrich shot Raymond, it mighta been self-defense. But if it was self-defense, why drag Raymond out of the car and lay him on the playfield?"

"Maybe he shot Raymond, and Raymond dragged himself over there."

"After three slugs to the chest and one to the head? I don't think so."

I turned around and looked back at the tunnel entrance. We'd only been inside a minute or two, but already the entrance was the size of a thimble. Daylight refracted off the cut stone walls like a painting. I could see nothing in front but blackness, not people, not the other end of the tunnel, not flashlights.

"Damn!" Luther said as a large drip from the ceiling went down the neck of his jacket.

The tunnel was wide enough for one set of train tracks, but they had been removed and the roadway graveled. We passed four other parties, all coming out. A man and a woman who looked to be in their eighties hiked out with dimming flashlights. Then came a group of five women cyclists, all with lights.

The tunnel was almost two and a half miles long, but after a few minutes it seemed as if we'd been inside forever. There was a point, somewhere near the middle, where one knew by the relative sizes of the entrances at either end, each just a pinprick of light, that the center of the mountain had been achieved, but somehow we missed that point.

By hiking quickly we were able to catch the laggards of our group, Laronda and Balinda, with Shereffe between them, Shereffe pestering her mother to help her write an essay on the trip for school, her mother working hard to be vague about an answer. Luther dropped off and walked with his woman and his two daughters. Toylee was a few yards farther along, holding Kathy's hand in her right, a humongous flashlight in her left. Ahead I could hear D'Witt, lightless, talking to his girlfriend and, beyond that, Shawn chattering away with his two pals, also lightless. D'Witt was talking about a nuclear war and the probability that if Seattle was hit right then, we might be the only survivors in a two-hundred-mile radius. Since having been crippled, he'd become obsessed with survivorship.

Our expedition seemed to have honed the raw edges off this family.

I was glad we came.

I moved up next to Kathy and Toylee and took Toylee's flashlight and then her free hand. Looking up in the dark, she said, "Are you my daddy?"

"I'm Thomas."

She giggled and, for a while, swung between Kathy and me every third step. After another half mile I gave the flashlight back to Toylee and forged ahead alone.

The tunnel walls held widely spaced niches, about two feet deep and four feet wide, some empty, some containing scraps of lumber or what appeared to be old electrical panels. I couldn't tell what their original purpose had been, but each was barely large enough to conceal a man.

I walked quickly and soon was out of sight, searching for the next one. By squeezing into the niche against the rock wall, I became almost invisible, even to those with lights. It was a long wait.

Shawn and his buddies sauntered past talking about a young woman they knew. Their ribald speculations about her were crude and puerile, but I wasn't Shawn's father and I wasn't Shawn's friends' father, and they would grow out of it, or I hoped they would.

Dion walked past with Balinda. Then Laronda and Shereffe came by. D'Witt and Margaret and Luther. Having lost ground, Kathy and Toylee were last.

It was only in the periphery of Kathy's flashlight that Toylee caught a glimpse of me as I stepped out behind them. Walking directly behind Kathy, I drew closer and then was almost in her footsteps, which is where I would have stayed, stepping each time Kathy stepped, full of suppressed merriment, if Toylee hadn't begun giggling. I quickly cupped the rear pockets of Kathy's jeans in either palm and squeezed. She jumped forward and let out a howl that was probably audible in Seattle.

Toylee and I almost broke our belts laughing. Toylee had never had so much fun. Neither, for that matter, had I.

After about forty minutes our group straggled out the west end of the tunnel into the afternoon sunlight. After the dank, breezy cave, the sun was blinding and cat warm. We broke open the knapsacks we'd been carrying and distributed sodas and snacks. Luther and Dion stood off to one side and gazed down the mountainside at a small waterfall that drained down the hill alongside the tunnel entrance.

Watching the family had been instructional. Luther had spoken at length to Dion, to D'Witt, and had attempted conversation several times with Balinda, each attempt circumvented by Laronda, who apparently couldn't stand the thought of Luther spending a moment alone with his daughter. It was hard to believe, but Luther and Laronda were still vying for Balinda's attention.

D'Witt seemed the most cheerful and gregarious of the adults. I caught D'Witt alone, his wheelchair situated in an open area of weeds and wildflowers overlooking an outcropping of rocks below. Several stands of Douglas fir grew below that, and directly across the gorge loomed another mountain.

"D'Witt?" I said.

He cocked his head around, looked at me and said, "In my dreams I have legs that work."

"That must be weird."

"No, this is weird. In my dreams I'm always running. I'm running and they're shooting at me and I can never get away. That's how it happened, you know. They were chasing me in a car. They thought they capped me."

Luther told me D'Witt had been mistaken for a gang member while walking home from school. The young men who shot him had been arrested and incarcerated, but they were out already, and he was still in his chair.

"I'd like to ask you a question, if I could."

"Ask away."

"Did Raymond show up at the house this last Tuesday?"

"Not that I saw."

"Did he call?"

"No."

"Did Laronda leave the house before the party?"

"My mother? You think my mother shot her own brother?"

"These are only questions."

"My mother didn't do it."

"Then let's clear her. What was she doing before the party that evening?"

"Ran some errands. When she came back, she had groceries."

"How long was she gone?"

"An hour maybe."

A few minutes later Shawn and his friends traipsed out of sight down the slight incline of the old railroad bed and were gone twenty minutes, coming back with their jackets tied around their waists, all of them sweating and dragging their feet.

I caught Shawn's eye before he headed back to the tunnel entrance and said, "Mind if we talk for a moment?"

"Sure." His reply was sullen, and he avoided my eyes as if he and his friends had been up to no good.

His two friends stopped, but I gave them a nod that sent them on. "Shawn, did you see anything odd Tuesday evening before we found Raymond's body?"

"Uh-uh. No, sir."

"Shawn. Tell me the truth. Do you have any idea who killed your uncle?"

Shawn looked at his two departing friends as if they might help him answer the question. He had yet to look me directly in the eye. "Raymond wasn't my uncle, and I don't know who done him."

"What sort of relationship did you have with him?"

"We talked. He liked to know what I was thinkin'. Fact, he talked to me more than my father." For the first time, his voice had some life in it.

"You liked Raymond?"

"Yeah, I liked him."

"Did you talk about Balinda?"

"I guess we did."

"What'd he say about her?"

"He said she was a fool. He said she lied about him and got him in bad with the family."

"Lied about what?"

"You know. About messing with her."

"He didn't mess with her?"

"He said he didn't."

"Did he talk about Aldrich?"

"He thought Balinda capped Aldrich. Thought she ran off because they got into a lovers' quarrel and she shot his punk ass."

"They weren't lovers." Shawn looked directly into my eyes for the first time. There was no comprehension of what I'd said. I couldn't help wondering what his life was going to be like. He didn't seem particularly industrious and had an attitude you could spot a mile away. I didn't see any kind of a future for him, and it made me sad and pessimistic for the whole human race. If only he could have inherited a fraction of Luther's work ethic. I said, "They weren't lovers, Shawn. They were brother and sister, and they knew it."

"She shouldn't of been messing with him. That's what Raymond said. He didn't like it one bit, her messin' with a white dude."

"She was his sister," I repeated. "She wasn't messing with him." I still wasn't sure he understood.

"Can I go now?" he asked.

"Sure."

After forty minutes outside the west entrance of the tunnel, we regrouped and headed back in.

Dion wasn't carrying his daughter, wasn't anywhere close, and consumed by his need to patch up his relationship with Balinda, hadn't been the whole trip.

Kathy and I stayed at the rear with Toylee, who once again insisted on walking. Half a mile into the tunnel, when she started flagging, I knelt and without a word she climbed up on my back and rode piggyback.

When we were maybe half a mile from the east entrance, our starting point, we could barely see the faint beginnings of daylight creeping along the tunnel walls once again.

Suddenly a light flashed from one of the nooks in the tunnel wall.

It was directed at my eyes.

The flashlight was incredibly bright after the abject darkness Toylee had insisted we walk in, and I felt like a rabbit caught in a pair of headlights.

It was the gunshot that stunned me.

It missed, probably because I heard what sounded like the

cocking of a gun and, half in jest, dodged to the right even as I saw the muzzle flash, to the right again hard before they could fire a second round, and then to the right once more when they did fire a second round. The fireball from the muzzle had been brighter even than the flashlight. The speed of my movement and the adrenaline in my stomach almost took me down. I stumbled and did a three-point landing on my hands and one knee and then scrambled over against the wall of the tunnel, where I deposited Toylee, who had been clinging to me like a rag doll. The shots had been incredibly loud, and the noise echoed away from us eerily. A woman began screaming. Balinda? Laronda? Or was that Shereffe? Maybe it was one of the young men.

I whispered to Toylee, "We have to be very, very quiet."

Judging from the rigidity in her small body, she wasn't planning on making any noise for some time to come.

CHAPTER 45

I scrabbled along the trail on my knuckles and feet like a Stone Age man, thinking that if I got shot now it would probably be in the rump.

The flashlight wavered from side to side, and all I could think was that, a few moments before, the flashlights had looked feeble, but now one of them was brighter than all outdoors. Why anybody in this tunnel would want to kill me was another matter entirely. The beam caught and trapped Kathy, who was farther along in the tunnel than I was. My breathing stopped and I prepared to rush whoever was holding the flashlight. The light quickly moved on, and I stood up out of my starting-block crouch. The light flicked across D'Witt's girlfriend, Margaret, and moved on. A moment later the flashlight went off and the tunnel was dark. Another shot rang out.

In times of stress, Luther's voice gave out on him, and now it sounded as strained and raspy as a cheerleader at the end of a close ball game.

"Cut out that shit," I heard Luther say from a distance of about thirty feet.

Dropping to my hands and knees, I clawed at the gravel in the pathway.

The screams were farther down the tunnel—Shereffe, I thought.

And then suddenly more flashlights. Flashlights all over the place. And another gunshot. Another. The tunnel was reverberating with the sound of gunshots. From somewhere maybe half a mile away a stranger yelled to stop the shooting. If he'd been any closer, he would have drawn fire himself.

Luther called out, "He's shooting at your lights. Turn off your flashlights."

A moment later all the lights were off again, and we were in a place so dark you couldn't tell whether your eyes were open or closed, whether you were facing another human, a wall, or two miles of darkness. What kind of numbskull would endanger all these people? And where had the gun come from?

Before the gunfire my eyes had been accustomed to the inky core of the mountain, and I could see the pinprick of light emanating from the east end of the tunnel, but the flashlights and gunshots had, at least for now, left me blinded.

I moved.

Another shot. Judging from the muzzle flash, the shooter hadn't budged since the beginning of the assault.

Before the echo died, I moved again.

He was in one of the niches in the wall.

I was awfully close to him.

I zigged to the right, dodged left, threw a fistful of gravel hard at where I thought the shooter's face should be, and slammed into him as hard as I could. I hit something upright and soft, knocked my head into the stone wall and went down.

Two people were grunting. The louder, uglier sounds were coming from me.

I was on my back on the ground watching a plethora of

flickering stars somewhere behind my eyelids. At least I thought my eyes were closed. They might have been open. My skull hurt; my neck ached; my shoulder was numb.

Now was the time to turn on lights, but nobody knew that, and I didn't have the cognitive machinery to tell them.

For a few seconds my brain reveled in the incredible light show, and then I was dreaming I was in a coal car careening down a set of roller-coaster rails.

I woke up. I'd knocked myself out—a real goofball move.

It occurred to me that I had no clear idea how long I'd been unconscious or where I was. I could not recall any of our respective positions. Perhaps the others were gone.

I sat up and cupped my hand around my mouth in a sad sack attempt to throw my voice, but it came out sounding like an adolescent trying to imitate Santa Claus. "Everybody all right?"

Luther spoke from a greater distance than earlier, but I didn't understand what he said. A gunshot sounded. His voice, not mine, seemed to attract it.

Nothing had changed. It was still dark. We were still inside the mountain. Most of us still had flashlights, but all of us were afraid to use them.

Another shot.

I saw Toylee's outline in the flash. Immobile, rigid and big-eyed, she was standing by herself ten or twelve feet from me. I was beginning to get my bearings. It would be a miracle if everybody was all right.

"Kathy," I whispered.

"I'm all right. I've got Shereffe."

"On the starboard side of the tunnel. Head toward the Atlantic as fast as you can."

When I heard her footsteps, I stood dizzily, ran and caught Toylee in my arms, knocking the wind out of her, and then the three of us were sprinting down the right-hand side of the tunnel toward the entrance we'd all come in almost two hours ago, Kathy clasping Shereffe's hand, me packing Toylee under my arm like a running back with an oversized football. The farther I ran, the more my head cleared. Two more shots behind us. The shooter not only displayed a callous disregard for innocent lives, but it was obvious from the ricochets along the wall that he or she didn't know starboard from port.

CHAPTER 46

Twelve minutes later we passed through a spray of water pouring out of the ceiling and exited the tunnel into the sunny afternoon. I felt as if I'd been holding my breath for a year.

There were only four of us outside: Kathy, Shereffe, Toylee, and myself. None of them were injured, but they were all rattled, especially Shereffe, who was shaking and who, between the two children, seemed to more aptly comprehend the danger we'd faced.

Kathy inspected both girls, gave them each a hug, then stood and looked at my face. "You hurt?"

"I ran into the wall."

"Why'd you do that?"

"Must have lost my bearings."

Toylee laughed nervously.

"That was certainly a bizarre experience," Kathy said.

"That it was," I said.

"Did you get him?"

I shrugged. I'd made physical contact with the shooter,

but it had been an off-center body slam, and I'd caught him, or her, unawares and to one side, so that we'd both gone directly into the wall. Because of the angle of the impact, and because I'd undoubtedly struck the wall hardest, I couldn't be sure of his size. Or even his sex. All I knew for certain was it hadn't been D'Witt or I would have had a shin full of spokes.

My sense of it was that when they came out, and they all had to come out sooner or later, the shooter would be bruised, scraped, and dirty, the same as me. As I thought about it, I noticed two distinct handprints on the rear pockets of Kathy's white jeans. I could have told her, but I liked the way they looked.

The tunnel entrance fed out into a small canyon that only gradually flattened out at the sides and led to the parking area half a mile away. It was the nature of the tunnel entrance that we could see and hear anybody long before they neared the opening, so nobody was going to sneak past us. After some minutes, D'Witt and his girlfriend came into view. Neither was injured; both were shaken.

"Who the hell was shooting?" D'Witt asked. "Look what happened."

D'Witt leaned forward and showed us a puncture in the fabric of his wheelchair. Toylee put her finger through it and then was pushed aside in an uncharitable and certainly uncharacteristic move by Shereffe, who poked her own finger through. Shereffe, who'd been the most excited of us all, perhaps because the visit had been her idea, was easily the most disturbed over how the trip had panned out.

"Who was shooting that gun?" she kept saying in her squeaky little voice.

"Why would they shoot at D'Witt?" Margaret asked.

"Somebody was trying to stop the investigation," Kathy said.

"By shooting D'Witt?"

"Me and Luther," I said. "I think the bullet that singed D'Witt's chair was an accident."

"A shooting out here's only going to initiate another investigation," D'Witt said.

"No shit," Kathy said, who looked at the two young girls and added, "Excuse my French."

"Is 'shit' French?" Toylee asked.

" 'Course it ain't," Shereffe said. "None of the boys at school know French. Shawn doesn't know French."

After another couple of minutes we spotted a figure about three hundred yards away walking toward the entrance.

I said, "D'Witt? Why don't you take these women to the cars."

After the four of them were out of earshot, I turned to Kathy.

"Not on your life," she said. "I'm staying."

"I don't want you picking up a stray shot."

"And *I* don't want *you* picking one up. I'm not leaving. Besides, they're not going to shoot us both out here in broad daylight. That was just some sneak who thought he could get away with it in the dark."

"And because he didn't, he's going to be desperate."

"You know as well as I do, they're going to come out and pretend it was somebody else. That's human nature."

"That's what *I* think is going to happen. That's what *you* think is going to happen. But it's not worth risking your life over."

"Don't be so gallant. I'm not leaving you here alone. Do you think the shooter inside is the same person who killed Raymond Sands?"

"And Benjamin Aldrich. Yes."

"So you really think somebody was trying to stop the investigation by stopping you?"

"Waiting for somebody to catch you when you know you've done something wrong can be about the most nerve-wracking predicament on the face of the earth. I know. I've been there. Whoever it is, he's feeling a lot of pressure. And now that I've had a chance to think about it, I don't even really think it had much to do with this family's past. All that investigating, Laronda's baby and Raymond getting framed . . . we were on a wild goose chase. It was a lot more contemporary than that. But there's one thing a wild goose chase is good for, and that's flushing out pheasants. And I think that's what we did here."

"So you know who was shooting in there?"

"It was one of two people."

"One of two people? Who?"

"You don't know?"

"Come on, Thomas."

"No, no. You solved all those puzzles. You should be able to figure this out."

"But I don't have all the information you have."

"Yes, you do. I've told you everything I know about the case."

"So I could have figured it out?"

"I don't have it figured out. But I have it narrowed down to two people."

"We know one thing," Kathy said. "If the killer of Benjamin Aldrich and Raymond Sands is the same person who shot at you inside the tunnel, it wasn't George Aldrich. Because he wasn't in there."

"Right."

It would be another few minutes before the lone figure coming toward us would be close enough to identify.

Kathy caressed my brow. "You're getting a nice little lump." She walked over to one of the snow piles, scooped out a handful, and gave it to me.

"Thanks." It felt soothing against my swollen eye.

Kathy gave me a kiss on the cheek and held me.

I said, "I was knocked out for a good little while."

She kissed me again.

"Maybe a couple of minutes."

She kissed me a third time, longer.

"I mighta been knocked out for an hour."

She gave me a playful shove and said, "For an hour's worth, we have to go somewhere else."

CHAPTER 47

"**S**o, who did it, Thomas?" Kathy asked as we waited for the stragglers. "No, don't tell me. I can narrow it down too. It wasn't D'Witt, because if you'd run into a wheelchair I would have heard it. It probably wasn't his girlfriend. It wasn't Toylee because she was on your back when the first shots were fired. It wasn't Shereffe because she was next to me. We went in there with thirteen people. I've eliminated four of them. That leaves nine. Am I on the right track so far?"

"So far."

"Then we can exclude you and me."

"Noooo. We can exclude me."

Kathy laughed. "Right," she said. "You and me are out. That leaves seven suspects. Laronda, Balinda, Shawn, his two friends—Melvin and the other guy, neither of whom we know anything about—Dion, and of course, Luther. Shall we include Luther?"

"I don't see any free tickets out of this. I thought I heard his voice on the other side of me, but it was hard to figure where sounds were coming from."

"Would Luther do that?" Kathy said. "Let's say he killed

you. The cops would come up and drive in with a light truck and illuminate the scene. They'd find the shell casings, the footprints. Luther would know he couldn't get away with it. Besides, why would he have shot Benjamin?"

"There's a better reason to clear him. This was an ambush, but I don't think it was a planned ambush. Or if it was, it wasn't very long in the planning, say, from about the time we went in to about the time the first shot was fired. Somebody found himself—or herself—more or less alone with me and thought this was an opportunity to stop the investigation. Luther's figured out by now I don't carry a gun anymore. Without hardly trying, he could jump me just about anywhere. And without witnesses. This was somebody who doesn't have access to me on a daily basis."

"And somebody who's reckless."

"Right."

"Which would seem to eliminate Balinda. Whoever put the flashlight on you could plainly see you were carrying Toylee. Balinda wouldn't shoot at her own daughter."

"I think that's safe to say."

"Okay. Balinda's out. You would think Laronda would be out for the same reason, but I'm not so certain. So we're down to Laronda, Dion, Shawn, and his two friends. You're sure you don't know whether it was a man or a woman you ran into?"

"I'd swear it was a man, but not in a court of law."

"What about Dion? Would he shoot if he saw his daughter riding piggyback?"

"I'd like to say no, but I'm not sure about him either."

"So that leaves Dion, Shawn, Laronda, and those two boys with Shawn, Melvin and what's-his-name. I can't narrow it any further than that."

"Yes you can."

"With information that I already have?"

"Yes."

She thought about it but didn't say anything.

Luther was the next one out of the tunnel. True to my theory of exclusions, he didn't have any dirt on his clothes. As soon as he got into the light and saw there were only two of us, he said, "Goddamn."

"Did you see anything?" I asked.

"You were closer. I was way over to the other side. You came running by me with Toylee and about knocked me flat."

"How did you know it was me and Toylee?"

"We worked together long enough, even in the dark I recognize your stride. And Toylee been playing in her mama's makeup. You mighta noticed. She smells like an overturned perfume truck."

"Yeah, I noticed."

I was watching Luther carefully now, not entirely convinced he was on the side of the angels. It's funny how quickly paranoia takes over, even among friends.

"Man, I hope everybody's all right," he said. "I shoulda done something. I heard that shot, and I stood there like a post."

"Standing there like a post was the smart thing to do, Luther."

Disgusted with himself, he scrunched up his face and said, "You saved my life back in the department, and you did your best to save my family in there. You for sure saved Toylee. Man, I ain't ever going to get out from under owing you."

"Look, Luther. There's something I need to tell you, and now's as good a time as any. You always say I saved your life, but there's more to it. Remember that night? You were checking out a suspicious car. You drove past it and something didn't look right, so you went back and pulled them out and they started shooting."

"Now, don't get into this, Thomas."

"No. Listen. What I never told you, what I never told anybody, was that I drove past the same car. Twice. I saw them and I thought maybe I should take a look like you did, but it was so damn cold I decided to stay inside. That could have been me, Luther. That could have been *you* coming to save *me*. And the worst thing was, I let you call me a hero. I should have confessed to this a long time ago."

"You were on the shooting team. You never woulda got into the jam I did. You would have put them down."

"Don't make excuses for me. The only reason they were still there for you to pull over was because I ignored them. I let you down."

"I passed them up once too. Thomas, they shot me and run me over. I was dead, and you rode in there like Gabriel tootin' his bugle. I coulda kissed your lily-white ass."

"I think you did, Luther. I think you kissed it a couple of times."

We looked at each other for a long time, and then I laughed, and Kathy giggled, and after a bit Luther chuckled, albeit reluctantly.

After all these years of agonizing over it, I'd finally confessed, and to the one person it should have meant the most to, yet it meant nothing. I could tell from the look on his face and the tone of his voice that Luther thought my revelation innocuous, my remorse irksome. His dismissal of it, however, did not change how I felt.

Kathy finally broke the silence. "What happened in there after we left?"

"I just walked on out. I didn't see or hear a thing until I found you."

When the taller of Shawn's two friends came out alone, Luther threw him against a snowbank and frisked him. He found a wallet with three one-dollar bills in it, some ticket stubs from a rap concert two weeks earlier, and a crushed strip of condoms in foil wrappers that looked as if they'd been in his pocket since he was ten.

It took almost half an hour for the rest of the adults to straggle out. Luther searched the males, and each of them, knowing what had happened inside, knowing Luther had been a cop, submitted meekly. Only Dion looked close to throwing a punch as Luther tossed him around, but then, Luther was particularly rough on Dion.

Nobody had any visible wounds, and nobody had a gun.

Side by side, Laronda and Balinda were the last ones out, and were the only two Luther didn't frisk. Balinda didn't worry me, but Laronda, who was known to carry a gun, who was known to have a temper, kept looking at me with an expression I could only interpret as disdain.

Walking half a mile in a dark tunnel without a light after having been shot at was an experience nobody was going to forget quickly. Everyone was jittery.

Dion looked exhausted, Balinda disturbed and frightened.

Yet, Shawn and his two pals were openly contemptuous of the danger we'd faced, boasting how they might have stopped it if there'd been more light, how they might have put whoever was doing the shooting in his place. They reminded me of three crows waiting to get knocked off a fence.

Neither Shawn, his two friends, Dion, nor Laronda was particularly dirty. One of Dion's knees had mud on it. Melvin, Shawn's friend, had mud on both knees. Shawn had dirt smudges on the back of his shirt, but his pants were clean. Balinda, however, was a mess, looking as if she'd dropped to the ground and rolled. She had mud in her braids, on both elbows, her knees, and all over her bottom.

She gave mumbled replies to Luther's questions.

It wasn't until we'd all walked a couple of hundred yards together and moved from the shadow of the mountain into the sunshine that I turned and stopped Balinda, and subsequently the whole group.

"Look," I said. "This isn't a game any longer. You have to tell us what happened the night you crashed your car."

"Leave her alone!" Laronda said, coming at me like an attack dog.

Luther moved into the center of our lopsided triangle and spoke softly. "Let him do what he does, Laronda."

After an exchange of looks and some heavy breathing, Laronda stepped back and crossed her arms over her chest. Sweat was pouring off her face, and had been since she'd stepped into the sunshine.

I turned once again to Balinda. "It's one thing to be fearful for your life, but any of us could have been killed in there. Your mother. Your father. Toylee could have been killed."

"I thought those were firecrackers."

"Jesus!" Luther shouted. "Why you think I'm searchin' all these knuckleheads?"

"You searched them?" She hadn't seen that. She'd come out last.

"I heard slugs hittin' walls," Luther said. "There's a bullet hole in D'Witt's chair. Somebody was tryin' to shoot Thomas. It ain't no game, baby. You could be carryin' your dead brother or your daughter in your arms right this minute."

Head down, Balinda turned to me, her braids slapping her cheek with the movement. Laronda stepped forward once again and said, "You don't have to talk to him."

"Shut up, Laronda!" Luther said. I'd never heard him speak so harshly to her. Neither, apparently, had she, because she gave him a look that was close to stupefaction.

Dion stepped alongside Kathy. It occurred to me that Dion, even without a weapon, was large enough and probably agile enough to give both Luther and me a hard time. In the past couple of weeks, Luther had cuffed Dion around three times that I knew of, his weapons of choice: age, bluster, and intimidation. But if it got down to an all-out brawl, Dion was an ex-professional athlete, large, strong, and swift. There was no telling what he might do to us.

"I don't know who you're trying to protect," I said to Balinda, "but nobody's protecting you, or your daughter."

"I didn't want—"

"You know who shot Benjamin Aldrich, don't you?" I said.

"I don't know anything."

"Maybe reviewing the facts will refresh your memory. There's some evidence that there may have been three people in your car the night Aldrich got shot. However, only minutes before the accident, your car was seen by a witness, Peggy Lindseth, who saw only two people in it: you and Benjamin Aldrich. Did you pick up a third party?"

Balinda stared at my belt buckle and said nothing.

"You can tell us that, can't you?"

"There was just us two. I told you."

"Okay, there was blood in the front passenger seat. I don't think it was likely you were driving around with Benjamin Aldrich in the backseat. I think he was in front with you."

Balinda said nothing.

"I think you two crashed and somebody came up to your window with a gun. They shot at him through your window. That's how you got the powder burns on the left side of your face. The police thought he was shot in the backseat through the rear passenger window, because he was wounded in the right side three times. But if he'd been sitting in the front, he could have taken those same three shots as he turned around and tried to crawl past you to get out that back window. I think he took the first bullet through the left side of the neck while he was sitting in front, and then because he couldn't get out his door or window, he tried to squeeze out the back and took three more to his right side. Is that what happened?"

In earlier recountings of the incident, she'd remained vague about the mechanics of the shooting, but now she nodded reluctantly. We were making progress.

"You knew the shooter, didn't you?"

No response.

"I'm taking a wild guess here, but two people told us Aldrich was a coward. Pookie said he'd acquitted himself like a real gentleman the night Raymond threw him out of the house, so I couldn't figure out why they would say he was a coward until I started thinking about the placement of blood spots in your car. He got shot in the neck and then tried to crawl out the back while they were shooting at him. He was shot from two sides. He was moving. I'm guessing that because he was scrambling to get away, the shooter thought that made him a coward. I guess if somebody's pumping bullets into you, you're supposed to sit still and take it. The two people who said he was a coward were there, weren't they? Which of them did the shooting?"

Balinda looked at me with alarm and then glanced furtively around the group.

"Who said he was a coward?" Luther asked.

"Dion was one."

It was almost like watching a cocker spaniel attack a Saint Bernard, because when Luther marched up to Dion, he barely reached the younger man's chin. Luther said, "You say that?"

"Hell, no. Why would I say he was a coward?"

Luther cocked his head around at me. "Thomas says you did."

"He's wrong."

"You gonna call Thomas a liar?"

"Maybe I said something. I don't know."

"What made you think Aldrich was a coward?"

"He was."

"So you did say it?"

"I might have."

"Don't lie to me, Dion. This ain't a ball game where you get another chance to up your batting average tomorrow night. We're playin' for keeps here. You saw Balinda with a white guy, and you chased 'em down. You shot him. Right?"

"I didn't shoot nobody."

"Then tell me what *did* happen."

Silence.

I turned to Shawn, certain he didn't remember calling Benjamin Aldrich anything. He looked genuinely surprised.

"Me?" he said.

"Goddamn you," Luther said. "Don't tell me you had somethin' to do with this?"

"I didn't do nothin'," Shawn said.

"You were in that car that chased Balinda," I said.

"I never."

"You were," Dion said. "So was I."

Before any of us could stop it, Luther rushed over and slapped Shawn across the side of his face with an open palm. The look on Shawn's face was a hodgepodge of terror and rage. After he'd backed up a couple of paces, Shawn looked around at the astonished faces on the group, lowered his head and charged his father, slamming the top of his skull into Luther's sternum and pushing him backward, reaching around toward his waist in an effort to get hold of him. Father and son wrestled wordlessly, neither leaving his feet, dirt and rocks skimming out from under their shoes. Laronda yelled at them to stop, but anybody could see they weren't going to.

Dion's face ran through a series of pained expressions.

By the time Luther had control of Shawn, Dion was ready to talk.

"Man, I'm sorry," Dion said. "I'm sorry, Balinda. We didn't mean nothing. I never even took my gun with me. All we wanted was to follow you guys and put a scare into you. I thought you were *dating* Aldrich. I didn't know he was your half brother."

Twisting Shawn's wrist around so that Shawn bent over in pain, his face down near his knees, Luther addressed Dion. "Don't tell me you got in a jealous rage and took a fifteen-year-old kid out chasing after your girlfriend with you?"

"I don't know what I was thinking," Dion said. "We chased them around for a while, and then just as I was about to let up, she ran off the road. Me and Shawn went down to see if they were all right. The others stayed in the car."

"Which others?" I asked.

Dion nodded at Shawn's two friends, who had backed off and now looked ready to flee, having been implicated in a murder.

"Go on," I said to Dion.

"Before I knew it, Shawn had his piece out and was yelling at Aldrich. Aldrich said something back to him—I don't even remember what it was—and Shawn let him have it."

"It was an accident," Shawn said.

"Like hell it was," Dion said. "He said something, and you said 'bullshit' and let him have it. You said he was making fun of you. You said nobody makes fun of you."

"It was an accident," Shawn repeated. "I had my gun out, sure, but in that neighborhood you gotta have your piece or people are going to take advantage. I was holding it and it just went off."

Luther said, "You carry a gun?"

"Got to in that neighborhood. You don't know. You don't have people after you."

"They're after you because of your damn attitude, which I been tellin' you to change."

"It was an accident."

"One shot's maybe an accident. You almost shot your sister's face off. You put four bullets into a man. You killed him. What's the matter with you?"

"It was an accident," he said softly.

"You just now shot at me, didn't you?" I said.

"What?"

"That was you inside."

"No."

"Somebody's got some lumps," I said. "I hit somebody pretty hard before I went into the wall, so I know they must have some bruises."

"Take off your coat and shirt," Luther said.

"It wasn't me," Shawn said.

Luther pushed his son and shouted, "Take off your shirt!"

Luther's neck veins were standing up. His eyes were pop-ping, and his voice, hoarse to begin with, sounded like a dog that had been barking for two days and nights in the basement with a dead man.

"I ain't gonna take off no shirt."

Luther pulled Shawn's oversized coat off from where he'd been wearing it around his waist before he could resist. What followed was one of the sorriest spectacles I'd witnessed in years, a man stripping his son in an effort to prove he either was or was not a killer. It took longer than anybody wanted it to, because Shawn fought him every inch of the way and because nobody else had the nerve to help or to interfere. As angry as I was over having our lives threatened by a kid, I wasn't going to jump in.

Eventually Luther tore the shirt at the shoulder and then continued to pull at the torn piece like a man unwrapping a present he didn't really want. Shawn yelled for his buddies to step in, but they looked at me and then at Dion and didn't move. A couple of hikers came by, took in the spectacle, and rushed past. Shawn had a fresh abrasion the size of a silver dollar on the top of his left shoulder.

"You were shootin' at my friend Thomas?" Luther asked, still breathing hard. He clearly didn't want to believe his son was involved.

"I didn't."

"Don't you lie to your father. You did, and you know it. We're gonna run nitrate tests on your hands. And they're going to show you fired a gun."

Shawn looked at his hands. "I didn't."

"I don't understand," I said. "Why were you in the car following Balinda in the first place? What did any of it have to do with you?"

Realizing he was in probably the biggest trouble of his life, the taller of Shawn's two friends stepped forward and spoke contritely. "We didn't mean anything. We were ridin' with Dion to scare her new boyfriend. It was something to do."

"Something to do?" Luther snapped. "It was midnight on

a fuckin' school night. What the hell were you even doing out of the house?"

Nobody answered.

Shawn's friend continued, "And then we saw them in the parking lot at Promenade Market and they ran, so Dion took out after 'em. They shouldn't have ran."

"They threatened you," I said to Balinda. "Didn't they? That's why you went into hiding."

All eyes turned to Balinda.

CHAPTER 48

When Dion reached out pleadingly for Balinda with his huge, muscular, ballplayer's hands, Luther stepped between them. Luther didn't say anything; the look on his face was warning enough. It was incredible how much intimidation Luther wielded over Dion, and how little he had over his own son.

Dion looked past Luther's shoulder and spoke gently to Balinda. "He threatened you after I left?"

Near tears, Balinda nodded.

She began telling the story, slowly at first, and then more and more quickly, until we could hardly understand her words.

"I ran off the road and got all cut up. I remember being surprised because we were falling. For a minute I thought we were both going to be dead. Then the noise stopped and Ben was asking me if I was all right. He wanted to leave me and go for help, but I wouldn't let him. He took a rag from my car and pressed it up against my head. And then they were there, screaming at us, Dion and Shawn. Dion had the light. Shawn had the gun."

"That's exactly right. I never had no gun," Dion said.

"You shut up!" Luther said.

"But I didn't—"

"Shut up."

Balinda continued, "I don't even know if Dion realized Shawn had the gun. The way they were on that hillside, it was so steep, and Shawn was below and a little behind Dion. I was afraid the car was going to fall down the cliff, and here were these two screaming through my window at Ben. Ben yelled right back. Ben was real mad because they'd been chasing us and wrecked my car."

"What happened with the gun?" Luther asked, firming his grip on Shawn's arm.

"So Dion has this light in my face, yelling at me. And Shawn is yelling at Ben, and all of a sudden Shawn's gun goes off. And then Ben kind of mumbles something and it doesn't sound right, so I look over at him and there's blood coming down the side of his throat. That's when I realize he's been shot. Ben touches the blood on his throat like he can't believe it either. I can't hear anything in one ear. In fact, that ear's still funny. Shawn and Ben are looking at each other, and the next thing I know Dion is trying to grab Shawn, but Shawn has the gun all the way in the window by my face, and I'm ducking and he's firing and Ben is trying to get out the back because his door is jammed, and the car is bouncing and tipping from Ben's movement. I thought we were going to go end over end. I thought we were dead. Well, Ben *was* dead.

"After Ben stopped moving, Shawn ran off up the hill. Dion stood in the window for the longest time telling me we had to help Ben, but anybody could see Ben was past help. Then Dion told me to get out and run and pretend I'd never been there, like the police weren't going to know that was my car. Like I'd done something wrong." She looked at Luther. It was hard to tell what the look meant, but Luther gave a sigh and tried to smile. "I didn't go with Dion. Ben was my friend. He was my brother. So Dion left, and about a minute later Shawn came back. Alone. He leaned inside and grabbed me because I was all turned around in the seat, and he told me if I said anything to anyone he was going to shoot me like he shot Ben."

"And that's why you went into hiding?" Kathy said.

"Yes."

"You threatened her?" Luther said, slapping the top of Shawn's head. "You threatened my baby girl?"

Shawn had been kicked out of his mother's house because he couldn't get along with her new cop boyfriend. He was camping out with Laronda and taking orders from Pookie, two women completely unrelated to him, running around at night with a bunch of kids who carried guns. On a daily basis he was so angry with Luther he could barely move himself to speak to him, and now, trapped by his father's blows and our accusing looks, he seemed about as confused as he could get and still be conscious.

"I never threatened her!" Shawn said.

Luther continued batting at his son's head, then at his face, and then when Shawn covered his head and hunched down like a turtle under attack, at his shoulders and back. "You threatened her? After all the trouble Balinda's had, you came at her with a gun and threatened her? Your own family? Are you crazy?"

Luther's voice grew angrier and hoarser, his threats more vulgar. In his frustration, he began hitting Shawn with a closed fist. Before he could do any real damage, I stepped in, hooked his right arm with mine and pulled him away.

Shawn took advantage of the lull and started running. When he saw that he had a few yards on us, he turned on the afterburners.

Luther looked at me as if the entire situation were my fault and said, "Now look what you done!"

Dion chased him for twenty yards but then pulled up, grabbing the hamstring on his left leg. I followed at a more measured pace, Luther behind me. After a bit, Luther lost ground, then slowed down and stopped. Shawn ran straight down the trail. He was quicker than I was for fifty yards, quicker for a hundred yards, but I stayed behind him, and near the 250-yard mark he began showing signs of slowing, turning his head every few seconds to see if I had given up. By six hundred yards I was only a few feet behind him. I let him keep on another eighty yards to make sure he was worn out.

As we reached the parking lot, I caught him by the waist-band of his trousers and reined him to a halt. He was fifteen and he'd done something stupid, and a man's life was over and so too, for the foreseeable future, was his, and as we stood hunched over trying to catch our breath, he began cry-ing. I wanted to cry too. Here was a boy who'd driven a stake through the heart of his family, nails into the hands of his own future. What's more, he'd tried to kill me in the tunnel. He might have bumped off any number of family members and friends with errant bullets, but it hadn't deterred him. I couldn't understand that sort of recklessness. I was angry at him, incredibly angry, but my anger, I could see, paled in comparison with the future he faced.

We stood next to each other, hands on knees, huffing and looking back at the knot of family and friends in the distance. In the other direction, Toylee, Shereffe, D'Witt, and Margaret were exploring the trail toward the lake.

As we waited for the others, Shawn gradually got a hard look in his eyes and said, "Fuck it. What are they gonna do to me?"

"The problem is not what they're going to do to you, it's what you've already done to yourself."

"I ain't done nothin' to myself."

"I didn't expect you would think you did. You said some-thing to Raymond, didn't you? You said something to him to make him suspicious." Shawn didn't reply, but I could see from his reaction I'd hit a bull's-eye. "You must have thought because he'd been to prison that he'd be sympathetic to what you'd done, so you told him all or part of what happened.

Then when he figured out the rest and realized Aldrich was family, his nephew in fact, he wanted to talk to you about it. He showed up at Pookie's for that party, and you met outside. You went over to the school to talk. That's where you shot him."

"I didn't do nothin'."

"Why'd you even take a gun along when you went with Dion? If you hadn't had a gun, you wouldn't have shot Aldrich in the first place."

"He was frontin' me, man. Nobody fronts me."

I thought this statement odd coming from a young man who'd just had his ears boxed, his shirt torn off, and then been run down by a private investigator more than twice his age. It seemed to me he was taking guff from a lot of people and had put himself in line to take a lot more.

I said, "I have a feeling when we go back into that tunnel and locate the gun, it'll be the one that killed Raymond. Maybe even the one that killed Aldrich."

"Why do you think that?" Shawn asked.

"Because you have the audacity of youth. You think you're invincible, that nothing bad can ever happen to you. You didn't even throw the gun away, did you?"

Shawn thought about it, then stumbled a few feet away, straddled a large rock beside the trail and sat. He said, "You said in the van you knew who did it. I got scared. I figured you'd come after me sooner or later, so I tried to get you in the tunnel while I had the chance. That was self-defense, man. I never saw Toylee on your back till it was too late. It was self-defense. Same as Raymond. A guy's gonna get you, you get him first. Simple as that."

It took almost two hours to find the weapon in the tunnel, a .32 automatic. Luther looked at it when we got it into the light and said, "That's Laronda's old pistol. Shawn musta got ahold of it somehow."

"Funny how that happens," Kathy said.

By the time we got back to the vehicles, Toylee was asleep in the backseat of Dion's car. Shawn's two friends had high-tailed it toward the highway while we were retrieving the weapon.

On the drive back to Seattle, Balinda told us what started the shooting. Benjamin Aldrich had said to Shawn, "We're brothers, man. You and I. Don't you see it? We're brothers?"

I couldn't help wondering what position Shawn would take up in the family if and when he got out of prison. How do you sit around the table at Thanksgiving and reminisce about the time you shot Uncle Raymond and dragged his body into the bushes? It wasn't going to be an easy family to be in. But then it never had been.

We took Shawn downtown to Homicide/Assault, handed over the weapon, and waited while the paperwork was processed. Luther felt so bad about the whole thing that he went into the rest room and threw up. Balinda gave an amended statement. Although he hadn't come in with us, it was clear they were going to write up a warrant for Dion, as well as for Shawn's friends who'd been in the pursuing car the night of Aldrich's death.

Luther spoke to me in the corridor near the elevators.

"Thomas, this is the worst day of my life. It's worse than when Lyle died. At least we knew Lyle was sick. This came out of the blue." Luther looked at me. "His mother's not going to believe I let this happen."

"She's no innocent herself," I said. I didn't have any business critiquing his life or hers, but I couldn't stop myself. "She thought it was more important to shack up with that cop than to have her own son with her. She abandoned Shawn for a lover."

"What about me? I been chasin' pussy all these years instead of raising my kids. Family's the only thing there is, Thomas. I blew it."

CHAPTER 49

Two weeks later Luther, Laronda, Kathy, and I all stopped by Catfish Café after work and had dinner together. Raymond's funeral was long gone, and we talked about that for a while. Most of the rest of our conversation revolved around catching up on all the members of the Sands family.

Pookie was still having a hard time with the loss of a son and a grandson in the space of ten days, and Laronda was afraid she wouldn't pull out of it.

Laronda was up for a promotion at work and felt pretty certain she was going to get it.

Shawn Brown was being held in the juvenile detention center at Twelfth and Alder, ironically the same facility Raymond had spent time in as a youth. The city prosecutor hadn't yet decided to charge Shawn as an adult, but Kathy had the feeling they would. He had committed two murders and so far showed more hubris than contrition. Luther and I were certain the gun we'd found in the tunnel would prove to be the weapon that fired the bullets taken out of both Benjamin Aldrich and Raymond Sands.

Dion was still in jail, but since he'd tried to stop Shawn, it looked as if he would be released eventually, charges dropped.

Balinda had signed up to take classes at Seattle Community College and was working in a supermarket.

I'd driven to Tacoma for one last visit with Mary Aldrich. Her husband, George, was in the room holding her hand as I told the story. I didn't know what sort of relationship they'd drifted into after all the revelations, or whether they'd even spoken about the revelations, and I probably wasn't going to find out because she would be dead before I could come back for another visit. She thanked me profusely for finding her son's killer and seemed genuinely relieved that it had been cleared up while she could still appreciate it.

The story we'd heard about a white man in a Mercedes near the Sands house the night Raymond was murdered turned out to be true. Police tracked down a friend of a neighbor who owned a Mercedes and who verified that he had stopped a black man on the street to ask for directions to his friend's house; the two had been in the Marines together.

Having taken off when the trouble at the end of the tunnel erupted, Shawn's two friends had been picked up late Sunday evening trying to hitchhike from Issaquah to Seattle and were released to their mothers.

Luther looked across the small table at me, clear-eyed and calm now that all the dust had settled, took Laronda's hand under the table and said, "We got kind of an announcement." He looked at Laronda, who looked happy about whatever it was he was going to say. "We're going to get married."

"Oh, congratulations," Kathy said. "That's wonderful."

"Congratulations," I said. Laronda smiled and patted her hair and sat a trifle closer to Luther.

"It's something I shoulda done a long time ago," Luther said. "Maybe I finally got all growed up." He grinned.

Maybe it was gauche on my part, but I asked what they were going to do about the living arrangements. My supposition was that Laronda and the kids would move into his house. It would be a tight fit, but he had a nice little place over by Gai's Bakery.

He said, "I'll be stayin' over with Laronda and Pookie and them. I was gonna sell my place, but I decided to hang on to it for a while, see how we all feel when things have settled down."

After Luther and Laronda left, Kathy looked across the table at me and said, "I hope it works out for them."

"They've been together a long time. Sort of together, anyway. I don't think it's a good sign, him keeping his house."

"So this thing really got solved by accident, right?"

"By persistence. Shawn knew we weren't going to give up, and the pressure that put on him made him crack. The police use that kind of pressure all the time."

"But it didn't have anything to do with the family history."

"Only insofar as Ben and Balinda being brought together as a result of their history and Shawn and Dion misinterpreting why they were together."

"I can't believe Shawn was going to shoot you in that tunnel like it was nothing. Kids without consciences. Where do they come from? Can't you help thinking that if Luther had married Shawn's mother and they had a loving relationship, Shawn would have turned out differently?"

"I have thought that. But then what about Laronda and her kids? And the mothers of his other children."

"Why does he have all those women? Do you think it makes him happy?"

"He has them because they're there. There are more available black women than black men in this country. He's like a kid in a candy store. He can't stop eating even if he knows he's going to get a stomachache. In fact, he's used that analogy himself."

"What would you do if you had women throwing themselves at you all the time?"

"I do have that."

"Be serious. I mean besides the oh-so-willing Sonya, who,

by the way, has decided to stay on in our basement for the summer."

"That's the bad news. The good news is she's found a boyfriend—and it isn't me. If I had my pick of women, though? Like I was a rock star?"

"Yes."

"I'd take you."

"No, you wouldn't. You'd take whatever came along. You'd break down in two seconds."

"Only you. I mean it."

"No wonder I love you so much." Kathy smiled. "It's too bad Luther and Laronda don't feel this way about each other. Have you ever asked Luther why he never married Laronda before?"

"He was afraid to ask her. He figured she would have messed with his head and after she was done with that she would have said no. He didn't want to give her the power. Those kids were all the glue she needed to keep him close. If she was having his kids, he must love her. If all those women love him, he must be lovable. It's a battle that's been going on between them for a couple of decades."

"Thomas, do you think Shawn would have shot Balinda if she'd told the police?"

"He seemed pretty eager to shoot me."

"He did, didn't he?"

Kathy leaned across the table and kissed me gently over my left eye. I'd had a pretty good black eye from running into the tunnel wall Sunday, and there were plenty of jokes at my expense around the office. I didn't mind.

"You got any more riddles?" Kathy asked. "I'll make a bet with you. You give me one I can't solve, I'll be your sex slave."

"And vice versa."

"Right. So you got a puzzle?"

"Okay. You have a deal. Let's see. You have eight bricks. Seven of them weigh the same. One weighs a tiny bit more. You have a balance scale. You can use it twice to weigh the bricks against each other. How do you figure out which is the heavier brick using the scale only two times?"

"Are you sure this is the puzzle you want to give me?"

"Yeah. You heard it?"

"No, but it's pretty easy." Kathy stood and said, "Come on. Let's get home. I think you're going to make the perfect sex slave. Who knows? You might even enjoy it yourself."

"Wait a minute. What's the answer?"

"Well, you place two bricks to the side. You weigh the remaining six, three on each half of the scale. If one side is heavier, then you only have the three bricks on that side of the scale to contend with. You weigh two of them. If they're equal, the third brick is the heavier. If they're not, you have your answer right there on the scale. If the six bricks all weigh the same, you put those down and weigh the two you originally placed to the side. Voilà. You've only used the scale twice. By the way. Do you still have those black silk boxer shorts I gave you for Christmas?"

"You're kidding, right?"

"No jokes here. Come on. We're going home."

Kathy laughed and took my hand as she led me through the front door of Catfish Café, looking at me in a manner that indicated this was going to be a glorious night. And it was. Only after I lost a second bet and then a third did I discover that she'd found my puzzle book and read it cover to cover.

ABOUT THE AUTHOR

EARL EMERSON is a lieutenant in the Seattle Fire Department. He is the Shamus Award–winning author of the Thomas Black detective series, which includes *The Rainy City, Poverty Bay, Nervous Laughter, Fat Tuesday, Deviant Behavior, Yellow Dog Party, The Portland Laugher, The Vanishing Smile, The Million-Dollar Tattoo,* and *Deception Pass.*

Earl Emerson lives in North Bend, Washington.